Advance Praise for
Lolita at Leonard's of Great Neck

"If only we had this book when we had our clandestine meetings in the Ladies Room during Sabbath services at the Great Neck Synagogue."

–JACKIE HOFFMAN, Broadway, TV and film actress; author and performer of solo shows

"Shira Dicker's delightful short stories are filled with poignancy, nostalgia, and heartbreak. Rich as the desserts on a Viennese table, this collection engages with transgression, sexuality, and selfhood through a sassy Jewish feminist lens."

–AMY GOTTLIEB, author of *The Beautiful Possible*

"Dicker's narrative voice is fresh, smart, and sassy; her female characters self-aware, sexy, and transgressive (in a good way); each story artlessly evocative of a rebellious Jewish feminist sensibility in the act of giving birth to itself."

–LETTY COTTIN POGREBIN, a founding editor of *Ms. Magazine*, author of twelve books, including *Shanda: A Memoir of Shame and Secrecy*

"*Lolita at Leonard's of Great Neck* is a vibrant, sharp collection of short stories that manages to be audacious, moving, and entertaining all at once. Shira Dicker is a force all her own."

–TOVA MIRVIS, bestselling author of *The Ladies Auxiliary, Visible City, The Outside World* and *The Book of Separation*

"Shira Dicker's story collection goes down easily like Lolita's Whiskey Sours. All the more pleasure for the reader—Dicker's writing is delicious, wild, freeing, hilarious, and tragic."

—JANE MUSHABAC, author of *His Hundred Years, A Tale*

LOLITA
AT LEONARD'S OF GREAT NECK
and OTHER STORIES from the BEFORE TIMES

SHIRA DICKER

WICKED SON

A WICKED SON BOOK
An Imprint of Post Hill Press
ISBN: 979-8-88845-232-5
ISBN (eBook): 979-8-88845-233-2

Lolita at Leonard's of Great Neck and Other Stories from the Before Times
© 2024 by Shira Dicker
All Rights Reserved

Cover illustration by Harry Anesta
Cover typography by Jim Villaflores

Post Hill Press
New York • Nashville
wickedsonbooks.com
posthillpress.com

Published in the United States of America
1 2 3 4 5 6 7 8 9 10

To Ari, with whom I spent several sultry Shabbat afternoons in Central Park reading aloud from my favorite childhood book during that long-ago summer of 1983.

"Dear Harriet, I have been thinking about you and I have decided that if you are ever going to be a writer it is time you get cracking. You are eleven years old and haven't written a thing but notes. Make a story out of some of those notes and send it to me."

—Ole Golly's letter to Harriet from
Harriet the Spy by Louise Fitzhugh

AUTHOR'S NOTE

PERSONAL AUTONOMY AND SELF-ACTUALIZATION HAVE been dominant themes in my life. While these are perhaps universal quests, they have particular resonance for women like me who are the daughters of the first wave of feminism, born in the Sixties, coming of age in the Seventies in the epicenter of the universe: New York City.

Add to the zeitgeist of that time the complications of being Jewish, curious, and female and the ground is richly seeded for conflict. The characters in this collection all struggle in their quest for authenticity. Anna in "Persephone's Palace" is locked in an existential battle with her parents, her goody-two-shoes cousin Mandy, and the cultural norms of a shtetl-like Jewish community in Queens in the late 1970s. Claire in "The Museum of Eroticism" is a pretty young woman who passively floats through life, astonished to find that she attracted the powerful, egomaniacal Brian Wasserman. Childish and naive, she colludes in her own objectification. Her great awakening takes place in a tacky sex museum in Paris on her honeymoon.

Sarah of "Two Writers" is having an extramarital affair with a self-absorbed famous writer, though she aggrandizes it with elevated ideals. She is married to a pediatrician in Manhattan's Upper West Side who recently became a regular guest on *Good Morning America.* Affluent and privileged, she has allowed her own career as a writer to stall while she ping-pongs between two well-known men. Rachel of "The Jerusalem Lover" is the wife of a renowned Columbia professor who flees her long and happy marriage when her husband becomes a conspiracy theorist and outspoken anti-Zionist.

Perhaps the most taboo topic raised by these stories—underage sexuality—is found in "Lolita at Leonard's of Great Neck." Therein, spirited thirteen-year-old Rebecca finds herself alone at a bar mitzvah with the object of her desires, Mr. Miller, her math teacher. This story, set in 1974, plants a series of actions and decisions that bring Rebecca and Mr. Miller together in a way that is both risqué and innocent.

My stories turn a female gaze on girls and women. Many deal with Jewish identity and what it meant to be an American Jewish girl and woman in a particular time and place. My characters are bound by, or rebelling against, external expectations and social roles. It is never simple.

And speaking of things never being simple, last year, around this time, I had the pleasure of babysitting my small grandchildren in their cozy home in a town on the banks of the Hudson River. As we were snuggling down to watch Disney's iconic cartoon film *Dumbo*—a treat to distract Neil and Arlo from the fact that their parents had gone out for the evening—I was surprised but pleased to note that this movie now features a disclaimer that warns viewers that the film contained racist stereotypes that "were wrong then and are wrong now." As I briefly worried that one of the films most beloved by my own kids would be hopelessly mangled, I read on. "Rather than remove this content, we want to acknowledge its harmful impact, learn from it, and spark conversation to create a more inclusive future together," stated the disclaimer. Whew.

I thought of that well-worded trigger warning and Disney's delicate decision as I edited the five novella-length stories that comprise *Lolita at Leonard's of Great Neck...and Other Stories from the Before Times.*

Not because they contain racist stereotypes, but they do contain language that was commonly used until quite recently as well as sexual situations which we now understand to be problematic. The language is, frankly, unkind. I would never use it today and would be upset if I heard my grandkids using it.

Similarly, I would be beside myself at the prospect of my grade-school granddaughter sexually experimenting, worst of all with an adult male, or a teen girl going to visit a European businessman in his Manhattan hotel room.

However, it is the domain and very definition of art to explore that which is true if uncomfortable.

Like Disney, I chose to keep the original language and complex situations intact in these stories for reasons of authenticity. As I want to preserve the way a group of kids from Long Island, New York, would have spoken in the 1970s, I also want to pay homage to the reality of schoolgirl crushes, emerging sexuality, and the thorny nature of human desire.

Finally, a word about art and the disturbing, often dystopian nature of life in these times. We need our writers, our filmmakers, our painters, our dancers, our playwrights, our musicians, our sculptors, our architects, and our actors to tackle that which is true, if uncomfortable. We need them to comment upon and curate our reality, provide us with modern Midrash, and show us the way toward transcendence. We cannot return to that golden era of life in America that existed postwar and pre-pandemic. The only way forward lies ahead through unfamiliar terrain.

Shira Dicker
July 17, 2023
New York City

LOLITA AT LEONARD'S
OF GREAT NECK

MR. MILLER LOOKED REALLY CUTE at Jesse's bar mitzvah with his overgrown David Cassidy hairdo and light blue tux, shaking Jesse's father's hand and smilingly handing him a cream-colored envelope. Mr. Miller looked a million times better than any other teacher at the party, including Miss Glick, the gymnastics teacher, who suntanned her entire back for about a month because she was wearing a halter dress and had her hair streaked the week before. Mr. Miller even looked better than Mr. Walters, who is really a teenager named Robbie who helps Jesse with his homework because his mother is too busy doing Transcendental Meditation and is normally the cutest guy I know.

The party had already been going on for about an hour when Mr. Miller arrived, which meant that he was catching the end of the smorgasbord, which was really, really, *really* amazing, with different stations of food from all over the world.

I mean, Mr. Miller really looked great, even better than Mr. Allen, whose real last name is Abramowitz and whose daughter Cindy is the biggest bitch in the entire school and who is famous for looking like Paul Newman, except tall and with brown hair. Mr. Miller looked the best of all the people in the room, including the teenagers, who all looked retarded or high.

After he left Jesse's parents, Mr. Miller looked around the room and then walked—kind of slid, actually—over to the bar, ordered, and stood there sipping his drink, one elbow leaning on the counter, looking very cool, just like the Marlboro Man.

That was my cue.

"Hi, Mr. Miller," I said, walking up to him and leaning opposite him in exactly the same way. "Do you happen to have a cigarette?"

Mr. Miller looked at me, a long look that began with my face and swept down over my dress. "Rebecca!" he said, laughing. "You look so different dressed up! I hardly recognized you." He paused and pondered me. "Do you really smoke?" he asked.

I shrugged. "Sometimes," I said in a way that I hoped was mysterious. Let him wonder what secrets I might harbor, what a sophisticated and complex person I must be to crave cigarettes at such a young age. "I just get into the mood to smoke at parties because cigarettes go *so well* with drinks," I said in my best, world-weary Lauren Bacall voice.

Mr. Miller raised one eyebrow, which made my heart break into a gallop. "Drinks," he repeated. "What are you drinking?"

"Whiskey Sours," I said proudly, presenting my empty glass. I had been in the process of avidly sucking then chewing the maraschino cherry I fished out of the bottom of my glass when I first saw Mr. Miller and now the drink was seeping slowly into my limbs. It caused a falling-backward feeling, which I really liked. I imagined myself standing with Mr. Miller in my parents' room, falling backward with him onto their bed.

"Whiskey Sours," he repeated. Was he a tape recorder or something? "Want me to order you another one?"

I guess he didn't notice that I had just become as loose-limbed as Gumby. "Sure," I said. Mr. Miller turned toward the bartender, a short, bald guy with thick glasses, and placed his order. I smiled. This was pretty cool...he didn't have a problem with thirteen-year-old girls drinking.

When the drink arrived, I stirred it around with the plastic thingy and then took a long sip. It was good—really strong and really sweet. I looked at Mr. Miller. He was staring at me.

"What are you drinking?" I asked.

"A Screwdriver," he reported. He took a sip. Most of it was gone.

"So, what's in it besides orange juice?"

"Vodka."

"Can I taste it?"

"Sure." He handed me his glass. I took a sip and grimaced. Yuck. He laughed.

"Not your kind of drink, I suppose."

I wiped my mouth and quickly gulped some Whiskey Sour to obliterate the sharp taste of the Screwdriver.

"It gives me shivers," I said. "Not in a good way."

Mr. Miller looked around the room. "So, what usually happens at these bar mitzvahs?"

I shrugged. "Depends. Jesse already had his Torah-reading thing yesterday at shul," I corrected myself, "I mean, *synagogue*, so this is a party. Usually there is a smorgasbord. Then, someone starts flashing the lights on and off and you go out of this room into a hallway with tables that have place cards telling you what table you are sitting at. Then, you sit down and there is a *meal* meal, with waiters and stuff. The orchestra plays music between courses. It usually begins with a big hora or some Jewish dancing thing, then Israeli dancing, then slow dancing, then rock. Sometimes they play rock when people are coming into the room. It depends on the kids' parents. And there are always speeches between the courses."

I searched for Jesse's parents. They were interesting...unlike most of the Queens kids' parents. I heard they had bought a house in Great Neck and they were planning on moving there by next fall, which meant he'd go to public school, a place called Great Neck North, which sounded thrillingly big and modern. I was being sent to a horrible Jewish girls' school in Queens, of course, where almost everyone was pathetic, poor, pimply, retarded, fat, sweaty, smelly, or a lesbian.

Anyway, judging from what I knew of Jesse's parents, I guessed that the party was going to be less about Jewish stuff and more about fun stuff. I already heard that his mother ordered carnival carts filled with candy to come out during the Viennese Table. I hope you know what a Viennese Table is because, next to the smorgasbord, it is the best part of a bar mitzvah. It is an ancient custom or something from Vienna, where they like to give you lots of choices for dessert. Essentially, it is like dying and going to dessert heaven.

Just on cue, the lights started flashing on and off and ladies in black vests began politely telling people to move out of the room. At the flashing of the lights, there was a sudden beeline for the bar, as if no one would be able to get a drink again during the party or maybe for the rest of their lives. Mr. Miller quickly turned backward and ordered another Screwdriver, stiff. The bartender expertly tilted a vodka bottle with a silver spout into the cup, which was filled halfway with orange juice and ice.

I don't know if it was psychological or anything, but just at that moment, I felt a kick under my skin and all the colors looked really sharp and bright and had the feeling I was watching myself from outside of my body. Sarah and Amy, my two best friends, were coming toward us from the smorgasbord. Sarah already had a smoosh of spaghetti sauce on her pink satin dress. Amy was tottering in heels that were too high for her. Sarah had braces and really frizzy hair and she was the smartest kid in the class. Right now, she was not what you would call pretty, but her mother was beautiful, and she would be, too.

Amy's claim to fame was that she had big boobs. She was skinny and blond because her mother wasn't really Jewish, and she had a big nose because her father was. Aside from the boobs, she literally got all her parents' worst traits. Her lips were rubbery (father), her skin was too pale (mother), she was prone to rashes (mother), and she had a million allergies (father). She also wore glasses (father). The thing about Amy was that she was hysterically funny. She was planning to be a comedian when she grew up. Boys were always making perverted comments to her because of her boobs and the male teachers just stared. It was impossible not to notice.

"Hi, Mr. Miller," they said together, then broke out giggling. Oy.

"Hello, girls," Mr. Miller said. "You both look very nice."

"Thank you," they said together, then giggled again. I rolled my eyes. The three of us were best friends since fifth grade, but sometimes I wanted to kill Amy and Sarah.

"Uh, I'm going to go and find my place card for the meal," said Mr. Miller, moving away. He waved. "G'bye."

"See you," I said, taking a huge gulp of the remains of my Whiskey Sour. I watched Mr. Miller walk up to Mrs. Howell, the science teacher, who greeted him with a hug. They walked out of the room together.

"So," said Amy, flicking her hair. "When's the wedding? Did you decide on the children's names?"

"Cute," I said, placing my empty glass down on the bar. There was a rustle of fabric and a heady blend of shampoos, perfumes, leather, and cigarette smoke as grown-ups swept past us. Most of the kids had run out first to find their cards and get the best seats at their tables. Now, everyone left in the room was heading out the door into the hallway.

"Let's go," I said as we turned to walk out of the room.

Jesse's mom had arranged for all of the kids in Jesse's class to sit at the dais, which was a really long table with party favors on it. Because we were late, Sarah, Amy, and I couldn't get seats next to each other. I was stuck between Josh Entenmann, whose family was related to the cake people and Carol Weisberg, the quietest girl in the class. Amy was sitting next to Jackie Berger, who was nice but really fat, and Rachel Levi, who was Persian and really, really rich but for some reason no one liked her. Maybe it was because she wore expensive but really weird clothes that were probably from Persia or someplace like that. Sarah was sandwiched between Jesse's little brother Marty and Howie Wolfson, last year's star basketball player.

"Hi," I said, pulling out my chair to put my sweater on top of it. "In case anyone asks, someone is sitting here."

"Okay," said Josh, who was eating breadsticks. I was dying to go to the bathroom, probably from the Whiskey Sours. My legs felt wobbly and the music sounded really loud. We were right next to the band, which had five people, with a singer who was wearing a shiny gold jumpsuit. They were singing "Yesterday." Some old couples were slow-dancing and a group of boys from my class were standing next to the stage, singing into their forks. I was going against a current of people trying to get into the room and I had to say "excuse me" about fifty times. If I didn't make it to the bathroom in the next five minutes, I was going to be in trouble.

The bathroom was the most lit-up, mirrory room I had ever seen in my life. There were little stools with cushions in front of individual vanities and baskets with stuff like sanitary napkins, bobby pins, hairspray, hand lotion, and tissues. There was a black lady wearing a maid's outfit sitting by the door, looking kind of depressed. She had a bowl of money in front of her. I felt bad that I didn't have any money on me but maybe if I didn't use any of the stuff from the baskets, I didn't need to tip her.

Lenore and Lisa, the two most popular girls in my class, were stationed in front of the mirrors when I came out of the stall, putting on layers of lip gloss. Both looked like teen prostitutes in their really short dresses, shiny stockings, really high heels, and gobs of light blue eyeshadow. Because they were there, I made a huge show of washing my hands with soap. Normally, I just try not to pee on my hands.

I walked out of the stall section of the bathroom, patting my hands dry on my hips (I didn't take a towel so it wouldn't be an insult not to tip the black lady). I walked over to another mirror to arrange my hair and dress. By unwritten agreement, I was a social inferior to Lenore and Lisa and was not to speak until spoken to.

Relieved of the responsibility to make small talk, I turned my attention to my mirrored image. My hair was short and black and perpetually looked like someone had just given me a vigorous shampoo. Though technically straight, the ends of my hair flew out at angles and it was only after five nights of sleeping on it without washing that my hair lay flat against my head.

In many ways I was a thirteen-year-old tomboy, but I loved velvet and satin. I had been begging my mother for a pair of high heels for a year now but the closest I got was the shoes I was wearing tonight—babyish patent-leather Mary Janes with a one-and-a-half-inch heel. Ugh.

I loved climbing trees and riding my bike but on top of my dresser, I collected gift-size bottles of perfumes with such exotic names as Givenchy, Chanel #5, Joy, Jean Nate, Norrell, Shalimar, and My Sin. I shaved my legs and underarms and that line of fuzz from my bellybutton to my you-know-what. And I was insanely in love with Mr. Miller.

Mr. Miller was on my brain at all hours, but especially after hours. I had the most unbelievable fantasies about him. I knew all about sex from having read *The Happy Hooker* by Xaviera Hollander, who is Jewish, believe it or not, *Esquire* magazine, *Playboy*, and *The Godfather*.

With the help of these resources, I had an endless supply of locales and plots to play around with.

I was pretty convinced that there was a strong conspiracy going on between my body and my brain because the more I thought about Mr. Miller, the more my boobs grew, and the more my boobs grew, the more I wanted to act out the Sonny and Lucy wedding scene from *The Godfather* with Mr. Miller. Though I was completely flat at the end of seventh grade, I had started to grow boobs over the summer and now they were coming in fast and furious. In a few months, I had gone from no bra to a 32AAA Teencharm to a 34A Maidenform and now, at Jesse's bar mitzvah, I was pushing out of the 34A!

I made my mother buy me a fiberfill bra during our last visit to Alexander's because I was in a constant state of nippilitis or Noticeable Nipple Syndrome. My relatives all yented and vented about how nicely I was "developing," which made me feel like a Polaroid picture or bacteria in a petri dish or something. And my weird uncle Heshy, who never married, had taken to looking hungrily at me like I was a roast beef sandwich or something.

Standing in the multi-mirrored bathroom of Leonard's at Jesse's bar mitzvah, my new boobs pressed against the front of my dress, creating a teenage shape in the black velvet. When I wore this dress at the beginning of the year, it hung straight down and hit the bottom of my knees. Now, it rested about two inches above my kneecaps.

"Nice anklets," snickered Lenore, indicating my frilled white cotton socks. I rolled my eyes while I finished putting on a coat of Bonne Bell lip gloss, Teen Scene Pink. "They look really innocent, perfect for a teacher's pet."

God, how annoying. Even at a bar mitzvah, there was no escape from these morons. "Shut up," I said, turning to her with my hands on my hips. "Not flunking half my classes like some people I know doesn't make me a teacher's pet." My confrontation stance made my velvet black dress ride several inches up my bare thighs. I saw myself reflected from several angles and must say that I was impressed by the ferocity in my face.

Lenore looked surprised. This was the first time I had actually responded to one of her insults. I was more than a bit surprised at myself and then realized that it was probably because I was sort of drunk. Don't they say that alcohol loosens your tongue?

"Shut up," mimicked Lisa in an ugly voice. Uh-oh...it was time to leave. I smoothed my dress out and headed for the door, but Lenore blocked my way. She stood right in my face and I smelled Dubble Bubble on her breath. The fear I normally would have felt was muted by the two Whiskey Sours.

"Little white socks for a little prude," Lenore taunted.

"I'd rather be a prude than a whore," I said, looking evenly at them. "Get outta the way."

"Larry told me that you wouldn't even let him get to first base during Seven Minutes in Heaven at Rona's house. You've probably never even kissed a boy," Lisa taunted. Ugh. This was so stupid. Larry is the grossest boy in the class; he has the most revolting, bumpy red acne all over his face and permanently greasy hair, but for some reason he's popular. It was true that I refused to kiss him at that party but that had nothing to do with being a prude. I kissed two boys at camp last summer.

"I kissed two boys at camp last summer," I announced. "Move!"

Lenore stood still, Lisa at her side.

"French kiss or plain?"

It had been a plain lip-against-lip kiss. "None of your beeswax!" I snapped.

"If you're not a prude, I dare you to French kiss someone tonight. The make-out room is the coat closet." Lenore folded her arms.

"Yeah, yeah…I might ever go to a make-out room to watch you two go to third with half the class," I said. The two of them were complete tramps. I heard that Lisa jerked off Larry in the back of the bus on our way to the Museum of Natural History last month. I was really sick of this conversation and the smell of Lenore's bubble gum breath. "Would you please let me out of the bathroom?"

At that minute the door opened and Mrs. Landsman came in. She was Jesse's aunt and her daughter was in fifth grade. I smiled gratefully at her. "Mazel tov!" I sang out, stretching forward to shake her hand.

Mrs. Landsman looked surprised but took my hand and said, "Thank you, dear."

Smiling broadly, still gripping her hand, I stepped around Lenore and Lisa and bolted out of the bathroom toward the dais.

A new mood had taken hold of the party room when I returned and zillions of people were dancing to "Satisfaction." Sarah saw me and pulled me into her orbit, which included Amy, Miss Dahan—the abnormally energetic nineteen-year-old Israeli gym teacher—and Moishe Shmuel, Jesse's ten-year-old Hasidic cousin from Boro Park, whose parents seem to have abandoned him at the bar mitzvah and fled because it was too irreligious.

The bass chords felt like they were vibrating right through my rib cage. Amy was dancing like she was possessed and Sarah looked completely goofy. I saw her lips moving and realized she was trying to keep to the rhythm by counting and doing every step evenly in both directions. This made me laugh out loud; it was just like Sarah to strive for symmetry and perfection, even while dancing at a bar mitzvah. I had been taking dancing lessons since I was five so I had to say that

I felt okay on the dance floor and just tried not to do anything really show-offy.

"Satisfaction" blended right into "Jumpin' Jack Flash," which made the fork-singing boys turn into really pathetic, Jewish teen imitations of Mick Jagger, playing air guitars and having spaz attacks. Amy, Sarah, and I had choreographed our own dance to "Jumpin' Jack Flash" at Aaron Mandelbaum's bar mitzvah. I'll admit it—we thought our dance was amazing. I'm sure that Lenore and company were watching us and laughing their heads off—they were way too cool to dance, of course—but I seriously did not care. School was out next week and I would never see their retarded faces again.

If Lenore was watching us, she wasn't the only one. Four songs later I stumbled to the bar to get a seltzer because I was going to drop dead from thirst and who should I meet there but Mr. Miller! Had he been camped out there, drinking Screwdrivers for the past half hour? God, I hoped not. This might mean that he is Irish and not Jewish, though couldn't he be Jewish *and* Irish?

"Nice dancing," he commented as I leaned against the bar, breathing heavily and sweating like a pathological liar or a pervert.

"Thanks," I gasped. "Seltzer, please."

"No more Whiskey Sours?" he asked teasingly.

"Not just yet." The glass was plunked in front of me and I grabbed it, guzzling it down. Where were Amy and Sarah? Oh yeah, they said they had to pee. They always seem to get the urge together.

"You got quite a workout there," said Mr. Miller. "Do you always dance so vigorously?"

"Can I have another seltzer?" I asked the bartender, plunking my glass back down on the bar. I turned to Mr. Miller. He didn't seem drunk or anything. "Yeah. That's my claim to fame," I told him, not untruthfully. Everyone tells me I dance like a maniac.

"You'll keep in really good shape if you dance like that all the time," he said. Keeping in shape was not something on my mind but I took his word for it. Meanwhile, my hair was sticking to my forehead and neck and I felt like my cheeks were crimson. I was dying to get some air. Mr. Miller read my mind.

"You look like you could use some air," he said. "Want to go outside?"

"Yes!" I said happily. Grabbing my replenished seltzer, I led my math teacher out of the room.

Jesse's party was on the third floor of Leonard's, so we jumped into the elevator to go downstairs, thereby avoiding the incredibly annoying winding staircase, which makes you feel dizzy as you walk down. A group of little boys from another bar mitzvah or wedding were crowded into the back and you could tell that they had been hanging out in the elevators for like the past hour, just going up and down, as if it were an amusement park ride or something.

Meanwhile, these kids had been fooling around with the buttons so the elevator didn't stop at the lobby but went straight down to the basement and before either Mr. Miller or I could reach around the kids, who were chattering like chimpanzees, we shot straight up, kind of like the elevator in *Charlie and the Glass Elevator*.

"Great," I muttered as we passed the third floor and headed upward. Mr. Miller's hand suddenly shot over the heads of the boys and pressed 4. The elevator jerked to a stop. "Come on," he said, grabbing my arm and pulling me out of the elevator. "Let's take another elevator down, otherwise we'll be in here all night!"

I stumbled over the boys into a darkened floor. Mr. Miller and I looked at each other and laughed, for no particular reason. I think it was just the relief of getting out of that insane elevator.

The fourth floor of Leonard's had offices, all of which were closed, except for one, which was opened a crack, creating a long triangle of light across the floor. "Wow, the business floor of Leonard's!" I whispered. "Come," I beckoned to Mr. Miller, tip-toeing toward the light. The office door was marked "Caterer," and I craned my neck toward the opening to see who was inside. Nobody. We were alone on the floor.

"Let's go downstairs," said Mr. Miller in a low voice. "Nobody's here."

"Wait," I said, holding out my hand as if stopping traffic. I wanted to explore a bit. This was kind of cool.

Continuing to tip-toe, I passed doors marked "Bookkeeping," "Executive Director," "Marketing," "Administrative Director," and "Housekeeping." The floor was really clean and shiny and there was a smell of fathers—cigarettes, ink, and leather. There was a water cooler, silver and shiny, in a small alcove, and a basket affixed to the wall marked "US Mail." A bit farther down there was another door, marked "Roof Access."

"Hey, look!" I whispered loudly to Mr. Miller, beckoning broadly with my arm. "You can get up to the roof from here!!"

Mr. Miller was standing near the elevator bank, waiting for me. "Rebecca," he whispered back, also loudly. "I don't think we should be here. Let's go downstairs."

"C'mere!" I insisted. "Look! The roof! Let's just check it out and then we'll go downstairs." Mr. Miller walked over to me and examined the door. He shook his head.

"It's not a good idea. Those doors are usually alarmed." I pushed against the door and it creaked open. "Rebecca!" No alarm sounded, but Mr. Miller looked, well, pretty alarmed himself.

A rush of crisp, cool spring air washed over me. "Ahhhh," I said, leaning back against the open door.

Mr. Miller looked so panicked that I burst into laughter. Leaning forward to grab his arm, I pulled him over the threshold with me onto the roof. He looked dubiously at me and then started to laugh as well.

We stood cracking up together for about a minute. It's neat to find out that grown-ups can have a sense of adventure, too.

"Wait, wait..." he said, still in a loud whisper. "We need to find something to keep the door open, or we can get locked out."

He was so smart...that never occurred to me! "What should we use?" I asked, looking around. I had nothing on me and using my patent leather shoes was not a good idea.

Mr. Miller patted himself down. "I can't put my wallet there," he said, sounding apologetic. I never expected him to. His white leather dress shoes also looked like they could get ruined. Hmmm. I was thinking hard, looking around.

"Look! What's that?" I saw what looked like a booklet on the ground, just a few feet past where I stood, propping open the door. Mr. Miller walked over to it and picked it up. "*The Wedding of Barbara and Joseph*," he read. "*November 18, 1972.*" He turned the booklet over and opened it, squinting at the pages. "This looks like Hebrew. Is it a prayerbook?" He handed it to me. I knew what it was even before I touched it.

"This is a *bencher*," I explained. "It has *birkat hamazon* in it. That's a prayer you say when you finish eating. You get one at bar mitzvahs and weddings. We'll probably get one today before we leave. Hey, are you Jewish?" Mr. Miller's religion was the subject of much debate between Amy, Sarah, and me. We had first assumed that he was, then we thought that he wasn't, because he knew nothing at all about being Jewish, then Amy said that of course, he's Jewish...just look at those soulful brown Jewish eyes, and now the Irish possibility entered the equation, though Mr. Miller hardly seemed drunk, come to think of it.

"What do you think?" he asked, smiling.

I shook my head. "I don't know."

"I was born Jewish, but my parents are atheists, so I don't know anything about Judaism or any other religion for that matter. I never had a bar mitzvah. I guess that math is kind of my religion," he said, shrugging.

"Wow," I said, trying to imagine not understanding what it meant to be Jewish. I was so Jewish that there was not a day that I didn't think about it, about God, about praying, about Israel, about doing mitzvahs, which are good deeds, and talking to God when I said *Shema* every night before I go to sleep. Knowing this interesting tidbit of information about Mr. Miller made me more curious.

"So, how old are you?"

"Rebecca!" he admonished me, laughing. "That's none of your business! I'm your teacher!"

"For only one more week," I reminded him. "Come on…I won't tell anyone!" Yeah, right…I was taking notes in my head, barely able to wait until I could run downstairs and tell Amy and Sarah about this conversation.

"Okay. I'm twenty-four," he said. I looked at Mr. Miller with squinted eyes. He looked like a young grown-up, for sure, not really a teenager. I was trying to see what he might have looked like as a kid. "Is there anything else you'd like to know about my life, Rebecca?" He looked at me with a crooked smile on his face, not mad or anything, kind of teasing, really.

I blushed. "Sorry…I know I'm really nosy. It's just that you're probably our most normal teacher and I was curious about your life."

He smiled back. "It's all right. I sometimes wonder about your lives."

I made a face. "Ugh, what's to wonder about? Little Neck is really boring and ugly and Great Neck is beautiful but horrible because of all the rich people."

Mr. Miller nodded thoughtfully, as if I had said something deep. I suddenly remembered that I was leaning against the door and we needed to find something to prop it open with. *The bencher!* Wait…

wasn't that kind of disrespectful? Yeah, we couldn't really do that. As if reading my mind for the second time, Mr. Miller said, "You know, I'm probably not going to need this jacket for the rest of the evening. Why don't I just fold it inside out and put it between the door?"

"You're sure?" The floor looked really dirty on the roof.

Mr. Miller shrugged. "It's really fine." Bending his shoulders, he took his light blue tuxedo jacket off, pulling on the sleeves. His white shirt was thin and I could see his muscles and nipples beneath. His chest was smooth, I could see, with light brown hair peeking out the top of the shirt. I felt a rush of heat move up my stomach.

I know I sound like a nympho or something but watching Mr. Miller write on the blackboard, explain algebraic formulations, and solve problems made me really hot. And I couldn't believe that I was getting to have a private, grown-up conversation with him on the roof of Leonard's. It kind of reminded me of the opening scene of a porn movie.

Mr. Miller carefully set his inside-out jacket down between the door and threshold, then straightened up and walked toward me. I think my face betrayed the way I was feeling because he looked at me quizzically. I quickly turned away and ran up the steps toward the actual roof.

The roof of Leonard's was really ugly, just black tar and antennae and stuff, but the view was really cool. I could see all the way down Northern Boulevard and it reminded me a bit of being in New York City at night, with everything lit up. The air was fresh and cool and there was a muted, *swoosh* sound to the traffic below. I walked along the perimeter of the roof, looking out in all directions.

"Neat," Mr. Miller agreed, standing with his hands on his hips and turning around. He extended his arms out at either side and windmilled them. When he saw me watching him, he stopped abruptly and laughed.

At that moment, I wished the wind would blow the roof door closed and Mr. Miller and I would be stuck on the roof of Leonard's for like a week or something. Lenore had called me a prude. How wrong she was! A prude is someone who never thinks about sex and I think about sex all the time...just not with gross eighth-grade boys. Also, jerking off boys in the back of the bus or in the bathroom and letting them stick their grubby fingers into you doesn't make you sophisticated—it just means you're the biggest slut in the universe. While it was true that I had never French-kissed anyone, it didn't mean that I wouldn't if the right person came along.

"Mr. Miller," I said. "Can I ask you a personal question?"

He lifted his eyebrows. "It depends," he said.

"How old were you when you French-kissed a girl for the first time?"

"Rebecca!" Mr. Miller looked completely shocked. He stared at me and I felt like I had just been caught cheating or something. Omigod, I totally blew it. I am *such* an idiot.

"Oh my God, I'm so, so sorry." I stumbled over my words. "That was a completely retarded question. Mr. Miller, I'm so sorry." All the warm feelings of a minute ago were gone and I felt like I was going to cry. *Oh no, let me not cry in front of Mr. Miller.* I bit my lip down and looked hard at my shoes.

Suddenly I heard Mr. Miller laughing. Tentatively I looked up. He didn't look mad at all, just completely puzzled. "Why do you want to know?" he asked.

I was so relieved that Mr. Miller wasn't mad at me that my words came out in a rush. "Because some of the girls in my class have been French-kissing boys since seventh grade and I've never done that, and

I've been called a prude even though I have done regular kissing and I don't think it makes you a prude not to make out with boys just for the sake of making out with them. Lenore dared me to French-kiss someone tonight in the make-out room, which is the coat closet, but I think you have to really like somebody in order to French-kiss them and get so close to them, so I wondered how old you were and what your opinion was on this matter."

God, that sounded retarded, especially the part at the end, what his "opinion was on this matter." I sounded like I was reading a script or trying out for the part of a doctor on a soap opera. Meanwhile, I looked at Mr. Miller expectantly. He looked at me directly and said, "Eighteen."

"*Eighteen?!*"

"You heard me. I was eighteen the first time I French-kissed a girl," he said with folded arms. Eighteen. Wow, I hope I don't have to wait that long. Eighteen! That is really late.

"That's so old!" I blurted out. God, my mouth had a mind of its own!

Mr. Miller shrugged. "Not really," he said. "I didn't really think of kissing girls much before the first time I did it. I was too busy." Wow. This really proved that Mr. Miller was part of another generation. Everyone today is trying to go to first base by the time they're twelve and second base by the time they're fourteen and third base by the time they're sixteen and finally lose their virginity before they graduate from high school. It's like a dirty word to be called a virgin if you are eighteen or older, Amy told me. Her older sister Barb is in college and she should know.

Mr. Miller broke my reverie. "You know, Rebecca, you're going to hear a lot of things about what makes you normal, or the right age to do different things and you really just have to decide for yourself what is right and what is normal and what you want to do." My heart sank. Blah, blah, blah…how disappointingly predictable and boring. Mr. Miller sounded just like a regular grown-up, giving obvious advice on life.

"Yeah," I said because I didn't know what to say. I started thinking about going back down to the party. Sarah and Amy would wonder where I was. And they were probably serving the first course, which I heard was going to be eggplant Parmigiana at the kids' table. Next to Chinese food, that's, like, my favorite food in the entire world, even if they make the kosher version here, just with hamburger meat and a parve cheese sauce on top.

"So, what do you want to do?"

"Hmmm?" I looked over at Mr. Miller. "What?"

He put his hands on his hips. "What I said is, you should ignore what other people are telling you and decide what it is that you want to do. For instance, I know that you don't want to go to the make-out room, but is there anyone you'd like to French kiss tonight?" He looked at me expectantly, as if he were waiting for me to come up with the solution for a math problem he had just written on the board.

My eyes widened and my heart nearly stopped beating. The heat returned to my stomach but didn't stop there. I gulped—he knew how I felt! I was completely transparent! Omigod, how embarrassing!

Yet something else was brewing inside me, drowning the embarrassment. It was a swirl of the most unbelievable excitement—like when you're on a roller coaster and your cart is poised on the top of the first major hill and you know that the drop is going to feel like dying and flying all at once and part of you wants to get off, but you know that there is no way out.

Licking my lips, I nodded and my legs felt trembly. Mr. Miller smiled and walked toward me. *Omigod.* He put his hands gently on my shoulders and drew me close to him. I felt like I was going to pass out. His lips brushed mine and I brushed mine against his. He pulled back, looked into my eyes, smiled, and pulled me toward him again. I was trembling all over. His hands moved down my arms and his lips pushed against mine again. I closed my eyes and stopped looking over his shoulder at the Great Neck sky. I felt his heart beating and I inhaled his scent, which was good. I felt like I could breathe him in all night, possibly forever. I lifted my tentative, terrified hands and put them on his arms. His muscles were strong beneath my hands and I got all mushy inside. I moaned—I couldn't help it—and pushed myself against him. I wanted to tell him that I loved him. I know that's insane, but I really did.

After our lips were softly pushing against each other, I felt Mr. Miller open his mouth and I got excited/scared. My heart was thumping. I loosened my lips and Mr. Miller kissed me deeply, so deeply that I felt it in the core of my stomach. His hands moved over my back and down to my bottom. I felt his grown-up body pressing into mine and a verse from the Torah popped into my head, the one from *Beresheet*, Genesis, where it talks about Adam and Eve becoming one. I never really understood this passage—it made me think of two-headed aliens or Pushme-Pullyous—but now I got a glimmering of how it was possible. I started making noises and kissed him back and to call this a French kiss would be to deny this kiss its galactic force. This was not a French kiss or an American kiss or even an earthly kiss. This kiss was beyond time and space, above time, literally out of this world. No one has ever kissed me as deeply since, and I have never kissed anyone else with such passion, force, and excitement.

After an eternity of kissing and holding onto each other, Mr. Miller stopped. His eyes were dreamy and his hair messy around his face. I would have given up my life for him at that moment. He gave me a kiss on my lips, just a lip kiss, and smiled. "You are no longer a prude," he said. I nodded, supremely happy. "Let's go," he said, taking my hand.

Mr. Miller and I took the elevator down one level and I made a bee-line for the girl's room. I needed to compose myself before I met Amy and Sarah because everything—good, bad, or otherwise—shows on my face. Facing the mirror, I saw a young girl with very messy hair and very flushed cheeks and very shiny eyes and a great big smile.

Naturally, Sarah and Amy demanded to know where I had been for half an hour, missing the entire soup course—it was a choice of mush-room barley or matzo ball soup and the mushroom barley looked just like cooked vomit—and I don't know how to explain this, but my pre-vious plan to tell my friends everything just evaporated and with the ease of a pathological liar, I casually told them that I had gone outside to get some fresh air with a whole bunch of people, that's all. Amy, the more insightful of the two, peered closely into my face and asked me if something else had happened. Without a shred of difficulty, I shrugged and shook my head.

"You're sure?" Amy pressed, skepticism knitting her brow.

"Yeah," I said, reaching for a glass of water. The waitresses and waiters were clearing the soup bowls away and the smell of eggplant Parmigiana hovered in the air. As I was replacing my water glass, the band struck up "I Feel the Earth Move" and Sarah, Amy, and I shrieked hysterically, running onto the dance floor. Next to "Jumpin' Jack Flash," this was our favorite dancing song and we had made the most incredible choreography, especially during the piano solo. Unlike "Jumpin' Jack Flash," whose words are incomprehensible, we knew all the lyrics and sang along as we danced.

In the middle of dancing, it occurred to me that not even ten min-utes earlier I was having the best moment of my life, being kissed by Mr. Miller on the roof of Leonard's and now I was dancing madly with

Sarah and Amy and hundreds of people at Jesse's bar mitzvah, and no one had a clue of what had happened to me while I was missing from the party. Amy might have had her suspicions but they eventually faded in the face of my repeated denials and the question was never raised again.

I had been transcendently happy kissing Mr. Miller and I was happy now, shaking it up on the dance floor, in fact, it seemed to me in those days that aside from people like Lenore and Lisa—who were just stupid sluts after all, not Charles Manson or anything—the world was good and filled with benevolent people and if I just did my school work and basically listened to my parents, everything would be okay.

Three decades have passed since that June evening and I can still taste Mr. Miller's kiss, still inhale his fragrance, still feel the heat of his young body pressed against my even younger one. There was an urgency and sweetness in our desire and my older self smilingly reflects back upon that rooftop rendezvous, grateful to my math teacher for both fulfilling my fantasy and knowing where to draw the line.

I'm glad that I got to be a kid before the world got horrible. There was no one telling me to look at Mr. Miller as a criminal or recast myself into the role of victim. He was my first, true love. Our secret kiss is etched indelibly upon my body and soul; its power and passion have proven impossible to duplicate. That balmy June evening occupies an exalted position in my treasure chest of memories. It is the place that I return to in my thoughts and somnambulant dreams decades later, trying to find sweet solace in a world gone mad.

PERSEPHONE'S PALACE

THE DESSERTS AT PERSEPHONE'S PALACE are works of art, arranged perfectly on a revolving, mirrored glass carousel, positioned to capture your attention at the precise moment you enter the diner and hold it throughout your stay.

There are lush triangular slices of chocolate layer cake, of course—frothy half-inchfulls of icing between each slab of velvety cake and thick frosting culminating in a heavenward flourish. There are pristine and plump pieces of strawberry shortcake, the albino version of the chocolate layer cake with the charming addition of strawberry slices nestled throughout the whipped cream frosting and garnishing the cake on top.

There are creamy, carnal cheesecake wedges in a variety of flavors—plain, marble, cherry, and pineapple. For the comfort-seekers, there are cups of custard, chocolate pudding, and rice pudding and a compelling creation consisting of cubes of brightly colored Jell-O. For the cosmopolitan thrill-seekers, there are cannolis, Napoleons, and éclairs. And for the children—and child in us all—there are large, flat chocolate chip cookies.

Here's the truth about the dessert carousel at Persephone's Palace: the offerings look delicious yet they are dreadful—ersatz and overly sweet, lacking even a modicum of integrity. The Italian pastries are imported from Arthur Avenue in the Bronx, so they are fairly reliable, I guess, though I've never sampled them because it is rumored that they are made with lard and are therefore considered *treyf*, unkosher, forbidden for consumption by Jews according to the dietary laws set down in the Torah.

On this Monday morning in late August 1978, Persephone's Palace is enjoying a brisk business. The door is in perpetual swing mode with diners coming in and out at a steady clip. A lively buzz fills the air as dozens of conversations blend and swirl, punctuated by frequent laughter and the percussion of silverware scraping porcelain plates. The décor is faux Greek, with brightly colored murals and plaster columns. The atmosphere is kinetic, chaotic, reminiscent of a party.

There are schoolteachers, secretaries, salesmen, and students; there are businessmen, burly all-night truck drivers, housewives, retirees, and travelers coming from or going to Manhattan, New Jersey, Connecticut, Kennedy, La Guardia, Long Island, and other places. Middle-aged women in oversized t-shirts decorated with kittens, horses, bunnies, or gardening tools are settled happily into booths, talking intimately over enormous platters of food. Their male counterparts, wearing windbreakers and golf caps, gather in groups of two or three or more, trading jokes, talking sports, shooting the breeze.

There are the old Jewish couples, the old Italian couples, the old Greek couples…all eating with supreme concentration, grateful for the gift of quiet companionship. To lend a little spice, there are one or two mistress types dining with men in tacky suits. To impart an air of glamorous cool, there is a smattering of counter-cultural characters, looking like Mick Jagger, like Joey Ramone, like Ozzy Osbourne, like Alice Cooper, like Kiss, like Jesus Christ.

The waitress appears by our table, impatient and cracking gum, pissed off to have two teenage girls as customers. "What'll it be, ladies?" she says, looking around, as if she couldn't be bothered to speak directly to us. Her pad is open and she clutches a pen, poised to write. Dotty—

her name is actually *Dotty*, according to her name tag—is a sobering sight, especially so early in the morning.

For starters, she has terrible teeth, a disappointed mouth, a thin ski-slope nose and long, stringy bleached hair. Secondly, Dotty is as skinny as a heroin addict. Her black and white outfit hangs loosely on her form, a strap falling off one bony shoulder. She looks about forty but might also, scarily, be close to our age.

Mandy looks at her menu carefully. She is a firm believer in break-fast—"the most important meal of the day." I've had about seven ciga-rettes and three cups of coffee for my most important meal, an act that has succeeded in completely killing my appetite. Still, I can always be seduced into ordering the Persephone's Palace vanilla malted, one of the house specialties.

"Ummmm," says Mandy, flipping a page. I can tell she has hardly begun to make up her mind. So many breakfast options, so little time. If she were really intent on keeping kosher, Mandy's options would be dramatically reduced to about four items on the menu—bagel and cream cheese, bagel and tuna, bagel and egg salad, or a fruit plate.

However, because of our parents' loopy conviction that the Persephone's Palace omelets are somehow kosher (which negates the fact that they are cooked on the same griddle as the sausage and bacon and therefore contain the *treyf*est of all *treyf* ingredients—pig), Mandy is painstakingly making her way through the list of fried egg offerings on the menu.

In my opinion, our collective parents, who often seem to share one brain, are completely hypocritical for declaring griddle-fried foods kosher while shunning cannolis or cheeseburgers. They get hysteri-cal imagining lard in pastry or the revolting combination of milk and meat but conveniently deny that they are consuming pig grease along with their scrambled eggs and lox. This illogical approach to keeping kosher is based partly on denial and partly on economics. You see, the tiramisu (about one-by-three inches) is $2.99 a slice, the cannolis (tiny really, like half a cigar each) are a dollar apiece, but the Persephone's Palace oversized omelet platter is a great deal—three eggs with your choice of up to four fillings, toast, potatoes, lettuce, and tomato for only $3.99. Where else can you find such a bargain?

"I'll take a vanilla malted," I say, eager to distance myself from my parents' hypocrisy and minimize Dotty's aggravation at the same time. Poor Dotty! I bet she has five kids and lives in a trailer in a parking lot in Ozone Park or someplace dismal like that. Maybe she lives with her toothless mother who doesn't read and watches soap operas all day and wears stained housecoats and smacks the grandkids around. Maybe her husband is an auto mechanic.

I study her as she waits for Mandy's order. Yeah, I could see her coming home at night—bone tired, of course (she already looks bone tired and it's only 9:30 in the morning)—to a scrawny guy wearing oil-stained overalls, pockmarks all over his face. He's sitting next to the toothless mother on the crummy couch, eating a TV dinner on his lap and chewing really loudly. The kids have been beaten into submission and cower in the background. Dotty drops a bag of groceries by the refrigerator and goes to kiss her kids. She falls asleep in their room without eating. This happens every night.

Back at Persephone's Palace on Queens Boulevard on the Monday that Mandy and I are meeting for breakfast, Dotty shifts her weight from one hip to the other. Her second strap falls down. She has no boobs to speak of. Come to think of it, she doesn't look like she has a husband. Dotty is nobody's wife.

"Okay...vanilla malted," sighs Dotty, jotting it down on her pad. She peers at Mandy with barely concealed impatience. "D'yuh know whatchu want?"

Mandy smooths her menu down and points to the Number Five in the omelet section. "I'll have the Spanish Omelet," she says, sitting up in her seat and wiggling a bit.

"White, wheat, or raisin," Dotty recites, writing.

"Do you have rye?"

"Nah."

"Um, wheat, please....oh...is that whole wheat?" Mandy is studying to be a nutritionist. She looks at our waitress with bright eyes, encouraging her to report that, miraculously enough, this mecca of fake food actually stocks whole wheat bread, preferably from an organic farm in Vermont.

Dotty has no idea what Mandy is talking about. "They give you two slices," she offers by way of complete non sequitur. Mandy quickly concedes defeat. "Wheat is fine," she says.

"Home fries or mash?"

"Home fries."

"Coffee for youse ladies?"

Mandy grimaces and I shake my head. One more cup and I'll be awake for the next century. Tucking her pad into her skinny waist, Dotty saunters off to the kitchen.

"So..." Mandy begins, tucking her dark hair behind her ears. Her eyes look owlish behind her wire-rimmed glasses. Mandy is my cousin, eleven months older. She is the great hope of our extended family, the academic superstar, the positive role model, the community leader, the modest, self-motivated overachiever. I am the family fuck-up.

"When did you get back from California?"

It's been two interminable weeks living in my parents' house, facing their quiet (and occasionally explosive) fury. They are furious at me because I ran away from my job at Camp Sabra in Simi Valley and spent five weeks bumming around California with my Israeli boyfriend, Barak. Actually, they don't know about Barak. He is a secret I've managed to keep from my family.

Trust me. There is no way I could tell my parents about Barak and live to see another day.

It is the last week in August and school begins in ten days. School as in City College East, about ten minutes by car from my home in Forest Hills, where all the nice Jewish girls from the neighborhood go. City College East, according to my parents' decree, despite the pleas of my high school academic advisor and the principal of the school himself.

City College East, which Mandy loves, where all of her friends go, where she runs the Jewish Student Union and eats at the Kosher Caf. Which she understands is the best college that her parents can afford and never makes them feel bad for failing to send her away to a school that requires a competitive admissions process and provides dormitories for its students.

Though Mandy knows all about my disgraced summer, her role this morning is to draw me out and get me to unburden to her, expressing the shame, guilt, and regret I must feel. She will listen selflessly, offer her shoulder to cry on, and deliver firm but loving advice.

"Two weeks," I reply. "Just think, about thirteen days ago, I was sleeping out at Newport Beach."

The minute the words leave my mouth I realize that this is not the sort of information that Mandy wants to hear. Though she is nineteen, Mandy sides with the enemy—in this case, our parents. She does not think that I just had the most amazing summer of my life traveling to San Francisco, Berkeley, and Southern California. She is aghast that I would run away from my job at Camp Sabra and spend five weeks being a complete bum.

She cannot understand why I hated being a counselor for ten-year-old illiterate brats, the children of Hollywood producers and screenwriters and plastic surgeons. She is amazed that I returned home with a second pierce in my left ear but hasn't seen the best addition to my body—a small rose tattooed to the inside of my right hip.

I had it done in San Francisco, in the Castro district. It cost twenty-five dollars and hurt like hell.

Mandy clears her throat and looks uncomfortable. She worked at Camp Friendship as the assistant to the camp nurse. Her boyfriend, Stu, came up with her and was a basketball coach. They've been going out for two years, since high school. Stu goes to Hofstra. He is handsome in a completely uninteresting way like Ben Casey the TV doctor. His hair is light brown and wavy and combed in a neat side part; his posture is straight; he is tall, neither thin nor fat, without an ounce of muscle. In other words, he is completely *parve*. I am fairly certain that if I offered him a blow job, not only would he turn me down but there is a good chance that he might also tell my parents.

Stu is hailed as the Messiah within my extended family, especially by my mother. He is her ideal man. "Maybe when you go to Camp Sabra, you'll meet a guy like Stu," she said hopefully as I was packing my duffle bag before leaving New York. I had just finished burying a box of tampons into which I had secreted a pack of condoms. I still hadn't gone all the way, but that was one of my goals for the summer.

My mother fell silent following her pronouncement, during which time I know she had a full-fledged fantasy that began with a shy conversation between a rehabilitated version of me (i.e., herself at age 18) and Stu's pod-person and ended with marriage, preferably by the end of my sophomore year of college. Why not? It happened to her.

My parents and I have such completely different ideas about everything relating to me that it is hard to believe that we come from the same planet or live in the same era. Before the age of Stu, my mother had a brief love affair with Doug Applebaum—no, not an actual affair, but an obsession with him as my ideal mate.

Doug Applebaum, who lives on Yellowstone Boulevard in a one-bedroom apartment with his parents and twin ten-year-old brothers, looks like someone's middle-aged, hen-pecked husband at the age of twenty. He wears his pants about five inches above his navel. He has an annoying "I know everything" voice. Whenever he talks to me, I can barely squelch the urge to hit him. But he is pre-med and runs the Jewish Student Action for Israel club at City College East and his mother and mine know each other from Philadelphia so my mother keeps trying to push us together.

Once, after I rejected him to his face several times, I caught my mother apologizing to his mother, explaining that I was shy and just needed time. "*Shy?*" I yelled the minute she got off the phone. "I am the least shy person I know! How about breaking the news that Dougie is the biggest loser in the world? How about saying that I'd rather go out with Marty Feldman?" I had just seen *Young Frankenstein.*

It was scary to think that parents could be so out of it! Honestly, who should know you better than the people who raised you from birth? Maybe my parents were misled about my true nature because I, their only child, had been a relatively easy and agreeable little girl. Perhaps they felt they were victims of a bait-and-switch scam. According to them, I had been a perfect child but since I turned nine I had become "a handful," "challenging," "impossible," and various other words connoting extreme hardship to them. Lately, my father's favorite name for me was "Little Miss Independence," pronounced sneeringly. As if it was a bad thing!

"So, did you meet anyone special at camp?" Mandy leans forward hopefully, smiling encouragingly. *Everyone knows you're a fuck-up, but we girls can still talk about boys.*

I toy with the prospect of telling my cousin about my "special" relationship at camp. What on earth has happened to Mandy? She never used to be so Pollyannaish; in fact, I distinctly remember shoplifting little pink lacy underpants from Alexander's with her when we were twelve and thirteen. When our parents would go out together to a movie or something, we would go to each other's homes and spend hours making phony phone calls! Three Passovers ago, we even ordered ten pepperoni pizzas to our rabbi's house on a Seder night! When exactly did she turn into the Stepford Teen?

While Mandy was practicing being perfect, I was planning my escape from Camp Sabra with my boyfriend Barak who comes from Tel Aviv and was a paratrooper in the Israeli army and worked as a dishwasher and had a car. He had a car because he was planning to go cross-country for three months after he finished working at camp. I just convinced him that he was finished after three weeks.

So, while Mandy and Stu were leading campfire sing-a-longs with guitars and tambourines, Barak and I were smoking hash near the pool or splitting 'ludes in the middle of the ball field. While they were naughtily "necking" on a bench at 9:30 p.m., we were in Barak's bedroom until 4:00 a.m., not having *sex* sex, but doing pretty much everything else. Oh, and plotting our escape from camp.

Though my instinct is to withhold all the above information, I weaken and offer Mandy the following tidbit, which I know will be immediately relayed to my parents. "I had an Israeli boyfriend in camp."

"An Israeli!" Mandy claps her hands and looks genuinely delighted. She is envisioning Moshe Dayan, David Ben-Gurion, possibly even Moses, as played by Charlton Heston. Mandy smiles indulgently at me, all the while stripping me mentally of my overalls and black leotard, subduing my wild hair into braids, removing the offending feather earring, fitting me into simple cotton shorts and sandals; in short, transforming me into a wholesome and idealistic field laborer, toiling in the orange grove of a kibbutz while humming Zionistic folk melodies, working side by side with my macho yet religious Israeli husband, who is outfitted with a *kippah* and rifle.

"What's his name?" Mandy is leaning forward, all girlish anticipation. I feel like Sandy from *Grease*. I can barely refrain from rolling my eyes. *Tell me more, tell me more.*

"Barak," I report, regretting having opened my mouth at all.

"Baruch?" she repeats hopefully. She is friendly with a boy named Baruch, whose father owns a big diamond concession on 47th Street. He is rich and religious and drives a BMW to City College East from his home in Woodmere, Long Island.

"No.... Barak. It means bolt of lightning," I say, asking myself why, oh why, did I feel moved to share any of my personal life with Mandy Blandy? I shift gears, try to get less personal. "The original biblical Barak was an officer in the army of the prophetess Deborah." Now I sound like one of the boring rabbis at Camp Sabra.

She frowns thoughtfully. "Is he, *Barak*, going off to the army now?"

"He's already been. After the army Israelis usually take a trip around the world. That's what he's doing."

"So, he'll go to graduate school when he returns to Israel?"

"No," I correct her with the falsely patient inflection of a mother being driven out of her mind by her retarded child. "Israelis go to the army *before* they go to college. He is going to college now."

"How old is he?"

"Twenty-one."

"College at twenty-one!" she exclaims, sounding scandalized. For someone reputed to be so smart, Mandy has a shocking lack of knowledge of the world. No one she knows goes to college at such an advanced age...except the working class kids at City College East who have jobs at places like Woolworth's, Korvettes, Waldbaum's, Shell, Sunoco, Carvel, or Baskin-Robbins or the housewives who have been dumped by their husbands and need to support their kids on something more than minimum wage or the old people who are auditing classes just for the hell of it.

I see a blur of black and white coming toward us. Dotty has arrived with our food. Balancing her tray with impressive grace, she gives Mandy her platter of eggs and plunks my vanilla malted right under my nose, adding a tall striped straw. Faced with my malted, I temporarily forgive Mandy for being so irritatingly stupid.

"Enjoy, ladies," Dotty says, walking to her next customer.

I may have told Mandy about the existence of Barak, but what I withhold from her is the story of my escape from Camp Sabra. It took a great deal of planning but I got started on the second day of camp.

The way I engineered it is that Barak and I drove off at two-thirty in the morning on Tisha B'Av. In case you've never heard of it, Tisha B'Av is a day of mourning for the Jewish people in commemoration of the destruction of the First and Second Temples and a bunch of other Jewish calamities. It is a somber fast day and on the eve of Tisha B'Av—which means the ninth day of the Hebrew month of Av—the *Book of Lamentations* is read in a very dramatic fashion, sitting on the floor of a darkened room, usually by candlelight.

The *Book of Lamentations* tells the tragic story of the destruction of Jerusalem in the year 70. For Tisha B'Av night at Camp Sabra, the camp director and rabbi devised a very moving program, which nearly made me change my mind about running away. The camp *makhela* (choir) performed a program of traditional dirges, the *rakdanim* (dancers) performed an impressive modern dance called *Diaspora* and each bunk got to be an actual Jewish community that had sprung up in the—guess what?—Diaspora. The camp education director made photocopies of material on each community so we could teach our kids who they were supposed to be and they would learn some of the history. My girls were to represent Salonika, Greece.

I had dutifully read the printout and learned that Salonika (Thessaloniki) played an important part in Jewish history. Though I explained to my girls that the Saloniki Jews considered themselves Spanish because most had originally been expelled from Spain and Portugal, these bubble-brains nevertheless insisted on wearing togas (bedsheets) and wreaths in their hair because that was just *really Greek.* Then they drew Cleopatra-like lines around their eyes because it was so *ancient.*

There were so many things wrong with this that I hardly know where to begin. First of all, the togas looked completely retarded, second of all, Greek Jews had their own (very dignified) dress and third of all the eyeliner looked moronic…not to mention Egyptian.

The girls—Chloe, Tiffany, Bethany, Amber, Angelina, Nathalie, Jade, Jasmine, Kirsten, Candy, and Faygie Devora—however, were tickled pink and came to evening services for Tisha B'Av primping and simpering and whispering and giggling, wearing lipstick and fresh nail polish (which you could smell from a mile away)—in other words, incredibly inappropriate. They didn't get even one one-thousandth of the message of Tisha B'Av. It was really depressing. I felt completely embarrassed by them and somehow responsible even though their stupidity was beyond my control. I truly could not see being their babysitter for the next five weeks.

It was probably disrespectful, but Barak and I chose Tisha B'Av as our time to escape because we knew that it was the one night that counselors would actually be sleeping in their beds and not sneaking out to have sex with each other in the woods. In addition to not eating and not wearing leather shoes (a sign of luxury in the old days), or doing anything celebratory, you were definitely not supposed to have sex on Tisha B'Av and we pledged that we would also refrain, not that we were having *sex*-sex, but because fooling around is also forbidden. Besides, we would have no time since we would be busy running away from camp.

Running away from a Jewish summer camp takes precision planning. At two in the morning, I got out of bed and silently lifted the stacks of clothes from my bedside cubby into the duffle bag beneath my bed. I rolled up my sleeping bag and stuffed my pillow into the duffle. Tip-toeing to the bathroom, I peed and brushed my hair and teeth, then I took the note I had written earlier and placed it on my bed. The note was addressed to my junior counselor, Sunshine. That is her actual name, as written on her birth certificate. Sunshine's last name was Klutznick and her nickname was Klutzy. She had an IQ of about 2.

Here's how stupid Klutzy was—she had never heard of Martin Luther King, Jr. "Is he, like, a young king, you know, like a *junior* king, you know, like when someone is born and the wise men in the kingdom say, 'This boy will be king someday'?" she asked when one of the camp teachers did a program on civil rights. Even my campers thought she was a retard.

My note to Klutzy (written in extra-big block letters) read: "Dear Klutzy…I had to leave camp suddenly. I will not be able to come back. Please say goodbye to the girls. Anna."

By the way, my real name is Hannah, but I dropped the H's in ninth grade. My parents named me after the biblical Hannah, the mother of the prophet Samuel. Hannah is a fine name, but it kept making me think of a lamb. Maybe there is a lamb in the Samuel story. After my bat mitzvah, Hannah started feeling all wrong, like a pair of pants that shrunk in the wash. Anna fits me so much better. Hannah is a *kallah maidel*, a girl whose sole aim in life is to get married. Anna is bound for adventure.

Even though I was starved for adventure, I will not pretend that what I did was even remotely justifiable, leaving a bunk full of little girls in the middle of the night, giving no advance notice to the camp administration, not contacting my parents for half a week. I know that it was terrible but at the time it made sense and it tasted like justice. Creeping out of my bunk, I imagined myself as the Jewish version of Holly Golightly. It took all I had not to scribble a lipstick farewell on the bathroom mirror.

Let me skip over the really hideous part—the reaction of the camp director and my parents that following day…which I found out only when I returned back home. Suffice it to say that I was a wanted woman…the top billing on two hit lists. However, by having only one phone conversation with my parents until I got back to New York, I managed to avoid learning the horrible truth for five weeks.

Because there was no way I could raise the issue of leaving camp with my parents and live to tell the story, I had written them a letter and mailed it on the day before my great escape. I didn't want to take a chance that the mail would arrive with supernatural speed and they would find out about my plan beforehand. In the letter (which took something like a million drafts to get right), I explained that I was leaving camp because I hated it and never wanted to be there in the first place. I told them that they forced me into this summer plan just as they forced me to go to City College East and that I would return to New York on August 15, as I had planned. Until then, I would be spending my time traveling with "friends."

I also left a note for the camp director, Mike Waldman, asking him to please call my parents in order to reassure them that I was not being kidnapped. In my note, I apologized for my middle-of-the-night departure but said that I thought I was a terrible counselor and didn't belong in his camp, or any summer camp, for that matter. Before we walked out of the front gate, I taped this note to Mike's office door.

Barak had already placed all his belongings in the trunk of the car, which he had parked earlier that evening about twenty yards outside of the entrance to the camp. According to our plan, we met at the *chadar ochel*—the dining hall. Udi, Barak's friend from Israel, was on *sh'mira* (night watch) that night and he was the only one who knew about our plan. Udi had worked in army intelligence and was an amazing liar.

I tossed my stuff in the backseat of Barak's Peugeot, slammed the door, and climbed into the front. Barak got in on the driver's side, sliding his long denim-clad right leg toward me, fitting himself behind the wheel and closing his door. He was long and lanky and adorable; he smelled of cigarettes and hormones. I was completely in love.

Cocooned from the outside world, we both lit cigarettes (totally permitted on Tisha B'Av) and laughed. Barak turned the ignition key, which sounded thunderously loud in the middle of the Simi Valley night, making my adrenaline surge, waking me up entirely. We then drove out into the night, free, giddily and gloriously out of communication, miles and miles away from the nightmarish confrontation that I knew would be awaiting me upon my return to New York five weeks later.

Seated next to Mandy at Persephone's Palace, the elation I experienced running away from camp completely eludes me now. I am back and I am trapped. Instead of the carefree girl skinny-dipping on Laguna Beach, sleeping under the stars in Golden Gate Park and skipping barefoot through Santa Cruz, I now feel like the subject of a documentary film on teen delinquency.

I know that Mandy would feel better about things if I were even slightly repentant—or embarrassed—about the way I spent my summer. If I were only stewing in guilt, she might be able to extend a comforting hand and lead me back on the road to wellness.

My lack of remorse in general makes things difficult between my parents and me, as well. I've tried to feel bad about what I did over the summer, yet the only remorse I feel is for myself—the victim of parents who cannot let go.

I often ask myself how, in an era rampant with examples of irresponsible adult behavior, did I get stuck with a mother and father who possess over-developed senses of parental responsibility? Why doesn't my mother go off and have an affair with her hairstylist or start a consciousness-raising group? Why doesn't my dad join est or the Moonies? While grown women discover their clitorises for the first time and suburban dads sneak off to orgies, my parents remain completely impervious to the zeitgeist. Why don't they get divorced, develop a drug habit, or just plain neglect me?

How I wish they would embark upon a quest of self-discovery and forget they have a daughter, like Alice Goldstein's parents who left her and her three little sisters with their grandparents and ran off to follow the Maharishi! "Poor girls!" my mother said on the night I shared the news at the dinner table, shaking her head, while I drooled with envy for Alice and her sisters. As if to reassure me of their undying love (and the impossibility of their leaving me in a similar way), my father rose from his seat and pressed me to his chest in an emotional bear hug that lasted about three minutes, while my mother dabbed at her moist eyes with a hankie.

I've analyzed the situation endlessly and concluded that the problem with my parents is that they have the worst possible trait of Jewish parents—over-protectiveness—without the best trait, chiefly, that famous desire for your children to succeed wildly. Perhaps owing to some kind of mutation, my parents are sadly missing that gene that gives you the urge to brag to other parents, "My daughter got into Haw-vawd!" or, "My daughter, a sophomore at Yale, recently told me blah blah blah...."

The mere fact that I aspire to something grander than City College East is a slap in their collective face. What makes it especially difficult for me is that my parents seem to have forged a pact with a group of other Jewish parents in Queens who also insist upon keeping their kids at home, so it's me against the world. And too many of these other kids are lambs, like Mandy, which makes me seem like a lion intent upon tearing my parents' hearts out.

Mandy has tucked into her omelet, eating with obvious appetite, wiping her mouth diligently between chews. She meticulously buttered only one slice of toast. For some reason, she considers it a religious prohibition to have more than one slice of bread per meal. After my initial joy at seeing my vanilla malted, I find myself slipping into a miserable reverie about my life and the start of the school year and am therefore unable to take even take one sip.

"Have you had any of your malted?" Mandy asks, though she knows I haven't. I sigh deeply and take a sip. Ahhhh, it really is heaven. The cold, sweet/salty, thick vanilla creaminess consumes my consciousness. For one blissful moment, everything in my life is okay. As I am taking a second sip, I notice two businessmen slip into the booth next to us. They are young and trim and wearing stylish suits. They both have really good haircuts. The one facing me catches my eye just as I am inhaling my malted. He watches me intently and I reflexively pull away from my straw, embarrassed to be seen having ice cream, especially at this time of day. I move my glass away toward the middle of the table.

"Anna?"

"Yeah?" I look at Mandy. She is halfway through her omelet platter and radiates well-fed serenity.

"I asked if there was something the matter with your malted." Mandy really is concerned; that's the touching part. I shake my head and say, "Nah…it's just really sweet for this time of day." Mandy looks vindicated. She moves her platter toward me. "I'm almost full," she says, completely unconvincingly, settling back into her seat and puffing her stomach out. "Please take some."

I shake my head and then shoot a look to my left. The young businessman is still watching me. When our eyes meet, he smiles and gives me a little wave.

Dealing with horny businessmen is something that all girls from New York—even Queens—learn to cope with at an early age. Since I started riding the subways, guys in suits would rub up against me and, as an added attraction, press their erections into my butt or hip in the process. It was gross, but most girls I knew put up with it. The way to deal with horny businessmen is to completely ignore them. I pledge that I will not move my eyes away from Mandy. What were we talking about? Nothing really—aside from me, my depressing life, and my delinquent summer. Okay, search for another topic of conversation, or at least come up with a question….

"So, do you know what courses you will be taking this semester?" I sound like a desperate television morning show host interviewing a really boring guest.

Mandy smiles. She loves to talk about her courses at City College East, where she is already applying for her master's degree in nutrition. She begins to answer me and I am sorry but I cannot keep my mind on her answer. Instead, I find myself thinking about the businessman to my left who looks distinctly different from the subway perverts I usually encounter. For starters, he is young…maybe twenty-seven or twenty-nine or something. Secondly, I have to admit that he is cute.

"So I decided that I should also take some computer science classes because everyone keeps talking about computers as a great career and it could be something to fall back on if nutrition doesn't work out, or maybe I could use computers in my nutrition work and Stu is really great at computers and can help me..." Mandy is really warming to her subject.

I sit opposite my cousin, brows raised in false interest, hands twisting in my lap. I nod my head constantly, like one of those weird toy dogs on the dashboards of cars. I probably look completely demented, but this is the only thing I can do to keep myself from looking to my left to see if the businessman is still checking me out.

*Don't look, don't look, don't look...*I hold out for about three minutes, during which time I don't think that Mandy stopped talking long enough to breathe, and then I cannot help it...I look. The businessman is having a close conversation with his friend, heads bent toward the inside of the table. I quickly turn away, relieved and disappointed at the same time.

"Which brings me to nineteen credits, which is kind of a lot, but not really, because I really want to graduate a semester early and my parents are getting me a used car so I don't have to waste time and get to school by bus...."

Oh Lord, what is she talking about? Is she like this with Stu? How does he put up with her? Like an angel, Dotty magically appears just as Mandy is about to launch into her plans for the City College East September Shabbaton.

"Are youse done?"

"Yes," I say, sliding my malted toward her. God, that thing probably had, like, five thousand calories! I'm glad I came to my senses—I could have gained ten pounds in one sitting!

Mandy breaks from her chatter and considers her food. "I think I'll take a few more minutes," she says apologetically. I realize that I am dying for the bathroom and excuse myself, sliding out of the booth.

The bathroom at Persephone's Palace is located at the bottom of a treacherous flight of stairs. I swear they should make you sign a life insurance policy before you go to pee. The bathroom itself is poorly lit and filthy with a nauseating pee-cigarette-air freshener scent. Unfortunately, I am wearing overalls and a sleeveless leotard, so this makes my stay longer than I would have liked. After I unhook my shoulder straps and drop them down, making sure they don't fall into the toilet, I unsnap the sides of the overalls and slide down my black leotard...all the while making sure that the bottoms or straps do not touch the sticky floor. What a production.

The sink is so scuzzy that I am afraid to wash my hands, so I merely swat them against my thighs a few hundred times. Believe me, my pee is a thousand times cleaner than whatever is lingering on that faucet. I gaze in the mirror and proudly note that I look like a beach bum—a Jewish beach bum, of course—my tanned face surrounded by a mass of wild curls, my feather earrings competing with my hair. Around my neck I am wearing a Mexican pendant on a black leather strap. My father gave me a look of supreme disgust when he saw me this morning. One thing is sure: I do not look like anyone else in the entire borough of Queens today.

I lean into the bathroom door with my hip and almost die of fright when I discover Dotty on the other side. I yelp slightly and jump. Dotty smiles, actually smiles, and says, "Sorry. I didn't mean to scare you."

"It's all right," I assure her, though my heart is about to burst out of my chest. Did she follow me downstairs? I am about to launch into a massive paranoid panic attack when I find myself considering how dramatically different Dotty looks a: up close and b: smiling. I realize that she is not my age but probably not much older either. I also see that there is a glint of something—mischief? irony? curiosity?—in her eyes that I didn't see before.

"Hey, youse about to start college again?" she asks. Maybe she overheard our conversation, but more likely, we look like the kind of girls who go to college.

"Yeah," I say.

"Youse go to CCE?" she asks, lighting a cigarette. I nod. She takes a deep drag and turns to her right, letting the smoke plume out toward the men's room.

"I started CCE but hadda drop out," she reports, her eyes narrowed behind the smoke.

"Really?" I say, genuinely surprised. "When were you there?" Dotty takes another drag and says on the exhale, "Oh, seventy-four, seventy-five...somethin' like that."

"So why did you have to drop out?" This is probably really rude, but I am curious.

"My old man died and my old lady is blind, so I hadda take care of her. I still take care of her."

There goes the image of the soap opera addict in the trailer. Dotty's mother is sightless, not toothless. That is really sad. I don't even know what to say. "You're lucky that you can go to college. Me, I work two jobs to make ends meet. I'm here every day until three, then I watch some neighborhood kids in my house after school. It helps with the nursing bills for my mother." She says it "muthuh."

"I'm a sophomore," I say, because I don't know what else to say. Dotty nods sagely, takes another drag. I really want to tell her to stop smoking because she seems kind of unhealthy.

"I dropped out followin' my first year," she says. "I'm tryin' to figure out how to take a night class or somethin', you know, work toward my degree slowly. The thing is, it takes me two hours from my place, which is in Sunnyside. We're lucky, you know, to have CCE here." She says it "hee-uh." "It's the jewel of City University," she says, something my parents say all the time, but coming from her, it sounds reverential, unattainable.

"So...where'd you get that tan, college girl? Jones Beach?" Dotty smiles at me, arms folded across her chest.

"California," I say, feeling embarrassed suddenly. "Newport Beach, Santa Barbara, Big Sur, all up and down the coast." Dotty gives me an impressed look, shaking her head, really laying it on.

"You go to Hollywood?"

I nod. She nods too, looking suddenly like the girlfriend of a rock star. "That's cool," she says. "You're lucky."

The "lucky" reverberates in me and I suddenly feel like I have to get out of this conversation. "My cousin..." I gesture lamely up the rickety stairs. "Yeah," she says. "And I gotta go." She indicates the bathroom with her head.

"Nice talking to you," I say, like the nice Jewish girl that I am.

"Hey, be good," says Dotty, crushing her cigarette on the aluminum bathroom door, before pushing it in.

As I walk toward our booth, I can see Mandy reviewing the bill with a pen. Also, I see the young businessman reviewing me with his eyes. I meet his gaze for one startled second but then I become horribly self-conscious and look away abruptly.

Focusing idiotically on the mural of Crete on the wall to my extreme right, I position myself to slide into my seat when suddenly he is on his feet, extending a business card to me.

"Joachim Hermann," he says in softly accented English, pronouncing his name *Yo*-a-khim. It sounds beautifully exotic the way he says it. I straighten up, look at his card and see that his name is printed beneath a logo for Deutsche Bank. I have no idea what Deutsche Bank is. Is it a bank in Holland? Does he want to do business with me? I don't have much money of my own.

Staring at the card to avoid looking at him, I am aware of Mandy putting her pen down and springing into action. "Can I help you?" she says in a suspicious big-cousin voice. Her vigilance gets on my nerves so thoroughly that I find the courage to look Joachim Hermann in the face.

Joachim Hermann is not just cute; he is insanely attractive. His eyes are brown, flecked with gold and they bore into me. He smiles and extends his hand. "I'm very delighted to meet you," he says, far less business-like.

I take his hand and shake it slowly. "I'm Anna," I say.

"She's eighteen years old," barks Mandy from her seat. Oy. I look at Mandy. She is giving me the look of doom, something she learned from both our mothers. It is a look I really hate. Seeing it on Mandy's face makes me defiant. "Where are you from?" I ask.

"West Berlin," Joachim Hermann says. "I'm in New York on business with my bank."

"She's Jewish!" chirps Mandy triumphantly, pulling out her secret weapon, the number one reason why Joachim Hermann—a German— has no right to talk to me.

He turns his head to her and looks startled. I start to giggle. "Please ignore her," I say under my breath.

"I'm staying at the Hilton, on Sixth Avenue," he says, also quietly. "The room number is on the back of the card. I'm visiting for one week. I would like to get to know you."

"What's that?" cries Mandy, having jumped up and practically positioned herself between the two of us. "Listen, I'm really sorry but my cousin and I have got to get home *right away.*" And with these words, Mandy literally begins pulling me away by grabbing onto my arm.

"Mandy!" I shake her hand off. Will I never be free of my family? I compose myself. "I don't want to be rude. Let me talk to Mr. Hermann for a minute while you pay and then we'll go right home." I give her a "gimme a break" look. Though unwilling to surrender her guardianship of me, she concedes. "I'll meet you by the register in one minute," she says sternly, turning with exaggerated haughtiness.

"Are you really eighteen?" he asks as she walks away. I nod.

"I'm also really Jewish," I say.

"That makes no difference," he says stiffly. "Are you in school?"

"Yes. College," I reply, praying that he doesn't ask where.

He doesn't. Instead, he looks deeply into my eyes and says, "You are very beautiful, also very clever. Your skin has nerves very close to the surface. You are very responsive."

I might be responsive, but I have no idea how to respond to Joachim Hermann's words. I just stare back at him, blood rushing to my cheeks. He smiles and I suddenly feel horribly disloyal to Barak, to Mandy, to my family and possibly the entire Jewish people. His fingers graze mine and he says, "I'd like to see you. Alone. Please call me."

"Anna!" Mandy is in a snit, yelling from the register.

"Okay," I say, mesmerized, then add, "Maybe," then finally, "I don't know," before throwing over my shoulder, "Goodbye," as I skip-run toward my cousin.

The ride back to my parents' home is torture. Mandy completely snaps out of her Stepford mode and becomes school principal Mandy. I am in trouble, that's for sure. Mandy lectures me the entire ride back about talking to strangers, but not just any strangers—German strangers. What if this guy's father was a Nazi officer? What if he himself is a Nazi?

"When strange men start talking to you, just ignore them," she instructs me. "That's what I do." As if Mandy gets picked up by men on a daily basis! As if men flock to her, drawn by her animal sexuality. Mandy is the original Ivory Snow girl; in fact, she often smells, boringly, of Ivory soap. What had Joachim Hermann told me? That I was responsive. That my nerves are close to the surface. And that I was not just beautiful but very beautiful. Oh, and clever. My dazzled sensibilities nearly succeed in drowning out Mandy's tirade.

"These men just want one thing, and you know what it is! Men are much stronger than women, you know! All they need to do is get you alone and they can rape you. Or even kill you! How would you feel if you lost your virginity by being raped and killed and not on your wedding night?"

How to shut Mandy up? "Look," I say in complete exasperation. "You're too late...I already lost my virginity. I had sex with my boyfriend over the summer."

"What?!" Mandy literally screams and the car suddenly swerves off of Queens Boulevard and into a lamppost. The impact throws both of us forward toward the dashboard. We are wearing seatbelts, but mine is slack and I am thrown violently against the glove compartment fast enough to have the wind knocked out of me. *Oh yeah*, I find myself thinking. *Aunt Audrey always said this seat belt was defective.*

There is a moment of utter silence and then Mandy begins crying. Why is she crying? I wonder irritably through the haze of shocked pain. We were traveling east on the service road, so the car hit on my side. Steam is rising from the hood, which looks damaged. The front tire of the car jumped up on the curb, so the car is tilted slightly. People are coming out of shops to either gawk or help us. I can barely find my breath, but then I inhale deeply and discover that everything appears to be in working order…except for the feeling that I was just kicked in the ribs by a donkey.

I unbuckle my useless belt and open the door, stepping gingerly out onto the sidewalk. I take small, mincing steps, grimacing from pain. I know exactly where we are—about a quarter mile from my parents' house. Shoppers fill the sidewalk at this time of day, going into the world-famous kosher bakery—renowned for its cheese danish, the popular yet mediocre kosher Chinese takeout place, and the discount pharmacy. I am horrified by the thought that we could have hit someone. I walk slowly around the car to make sure that no one is caught beneath a tire.

"I call the police, okay?" A middle-aged man with a thick Hungarian accent is talking to me. He wears an apron around his middle and a white paper hat. I recognize him from the bakery. His shirtsleeves are rolled up. I see blue numbers on his left arm. His eyes track mine. "I call, okay?" he asks gently, waiting for my assent before heading back into the bakery.

"Is your friend hurt?" asks another man—young, American, with dark hair, wearing a white lab coat and a yarmulke pinned to his head. He wears a plaque—he is a pharmacist. If he is outside on the sidewalk with me, who is inside filling prescriptions? We walk toward Mandy's side of the car. She is crying uncontrollably.

The pharmacist—Dr. Zissner, according to his plaque—knocks on the window. Mandy looks up. The doctor-like lab coat seems to startle her into sudden composure. As suddenly as she began crying, she stops, blowing her nose into the hankie she keeps in her purse, removing her glasses, patting the wetness around her eyes. She rolls down her window. "Yes, doctor?" she says expectantly, ever the cooperative patient.

"The police should be here any minute. Are you hurt?" Dr. Zissner asks, leaning in on her window. I stand behind him.

Mandy considers his question for a moment. "No," she says. "I don't think I'm hurt. We were wearing seatbelts." I stare at her in amazement. Did she not see me fly into the dashboard?

"Good," Dr. Zissner says. "Do you want me to call anyone for you? If you like, you can use the phone in the pharmacy and make the call yourself."

Mandy pauses, thinking. She looks worried. "Is the car really wrecked?" she asks anxiously. "It's my mother's."

Dr. Zissner walks around the car. He looks carefully at my side. The steam is still rising from underneath the hood. He shrugs. "I don't really know much about cars," he concedes. "The police will come. The car will probably need to be towed."

"Oh…" says Mandy, dissolving into pitiful wails. I know what she is thinking. That it is her mother's car, that her mother depends on it to get to work, that she is going to kill Mandy.

"Come inside and call your mother," Dr. Zissner says again, softly, taking Mandy by the elbow. She follows him, weeping into her hands. Though I should probably call my parents as well, I sit down on the curb instead and smoke a cigarette, something I never do in broad daylight in my own neighborhood.

I'm wondering if something happened to me in the crash because my brain is acting weird all of a sudden, refusing to allow thoughts to finish. My rib cage feels incredibly sore and my knees hurt as well, having jammed underneath the dashboard upon impact. Every time I try to analyze what just happened, my mind goes off on a tangent and I end up thinking whether I should cut my hair or how to sneak a pet hamster into my bedroom or something equally unimportant and irrelevant.

I've seen cars whiz by with the driver and passenger yelling at each other and they manage to stay on the road. Who drives a car into a lamppost when they hear something that surprises them? You have to have better control as a driver! You'd totally flunk your road test if you did something like this! Would Mandy have done the same thing if she turned on the radio and heard, for instance, that Israel was just attacked by another country, like during the Yom Kippur War? (Not that Mandy would have been driving on Yom Kippur, but still.)

Mandy's mother, Aunt Audrey, is a difficult woman and I worry about how she will react to the smashing of her car. She works part-time and today is one of her "off" days. I know that Mandy had to negotiate the car and that my parents probably were part of the decision, making the case that Mandy would try to talk some sense into their wayward daughter.

I had planned to finish my cigarette before going inside to check on Mandy's mental state, but Mandy comes outside while I am in the middle of taking a drag. Her eyes are red-rimmed and puffy behind her lenses and her normally neat hair looks mussed, like a picture drawn out of lines. The sight of me—delinquent runaway slut cousin—engaging in yet another bad activity registers in the slight lifting of her eyebrows, the compressing of her lips.

I pat the piece of curb to my right. "Have a seat," I say. Mandy smooths her ironed Lee jeans to her bottom and sits down, rather prissily, next to me.

"So..." I prompt.

"My dad is coming to pick me up. He called his mechanic, who will send a tow truck. We called off the police," she says. Her voice sounds hollow.

"Is he mad?" I ask.

Mandy does not answer immediately. I turn to her. She is looking at me with a completely new look. It is something that combines pity and hatred. "At me?" she asks, with a spooky edge of remove. "Why would he be mad at me?"

"I don't know…just for smashing up the car, I guess. You know how parents can be." I should call my own parents, but why, really? I didn't smash their car. They're at work right now and will find out later, anyhow. Still, perhaps I'll call in a little bit. Maybe after I walk home.

Mandy is silent. I stub out my cigarette with my sandaled foot; it seemed too obvious to do it the minute she came outside. Suddenly, I feel unbearably hot in my overalls.

"Anna," says Mandy. "Isn't there something you need to say to me?" She is still speaking in *that* voice.

"What do you mean?" I ask, leaning back on the curb and fanning myself with a flyer from the pharmacy.

Mandy looks at me in exaggerated disbelief. "I can't believe you!" she says.

This really pisses me off. "Why?" I ask.

She is looking at me now as if I am a mass murderer. "Can't you even say that you are sorry? You just made me drive off the road and wreck my mother's car and you can't even apologize?"

The ridiculousness of Mandy blaming me for her crash nearly causes me to laugh. "May I point out that *you* wrecked your mother's car? *You* drove it into the lamppost. How could this accident possibly be *my* fault?" If my cousin was Pollyanna an hour ago, now she has metamorphosed into a stern—if completely illogical—litigator.

"You do this all the time," Mandy says. "You are the most irresponsible person I know."

Now it is my turn to be angry. "Excuse me," I say to my cousin. "*You* drove. *You* are at fault. *You* are the responsible party here. Why is this suddenly *my* responsibility?"

Mandy stares at me, shaking her head. "I cannot *believe* what I'm hearing! You are *such* a liar!"

"Liar!" I shout. "What am I lying about? You smashed up your mother's car because I told you the truth! I told you something you didn't want to hear, but it was the truth! And you were so shocked that you smashed the car. That is *not my fault!*"

My words, screamed loud and clear, linger in the air. Pedestrians are avoiding us and I see the Hungarian baker looking out the window at us in concern. I feel trashy and uneducated, having a fight in public.

"See, you can't even control yourself here, in your own neighborhood," she says, with a smirk of superiority. I really want to smack my cousin. What on earth happened to turn her into this smug little shit? There is nothing to be gained by sticking around and waiting for my uncle to arrive. This is very depressing. Everyone in my family hates me.

"If it makes you feel better to blame me for your own stupid driving, then go ahead," I say, standing up and stretching. I wince; my ribs really hurt. Not that my injury has even registered in Mandy's mind.

My cousin sits on the curb, shoulders hunched, clutching her balled hankie. Her owlish eyes are watery behind her glasses. Suddenly, I get a flash-forward of her life. She will be engaged to Stu by the end of the year and married before she graduates from City College East. They will move into a tiny apartment near the train station in Kew Gardens. Stu will go into his father's linoleum business and ride the train to Astoria every day with his lunch, prepared by Mandy, nestled inside an insulated nylon bag.

In a show of super-efficiency, she will make all of Stu's lunches on Sunday evening so that by Friday, the Pathmark brand whole wheat bread of his sandwich will have completely dissolved due to the oil from the Pathmark brand tuna fish mixed, nauseatingly, with Miracle

Whip dressing—a family tradition. In an act of secret rebellion, Stu will toss out his lunch every Friday and buy a Greek salad, savoring every bite.

Mandy will get her master's degree in nutrition and share an office on Austin Street or Continental Avenue with an accountant and a social worker. They will have two mediocre children. She and Stu will stop having sex about five years into their marriage. He will have a brief and pathetic affair with his father's fifty-three-year-old secretary, which he will tearfully confess to. The secretary will be the only woman in his life who ever gave him a blow job and he will remember this for the rest of his life. Mandy will magnanimously forgive him for this indiscretion yet use it against him in subtle and not-so-subtle ways until he dies. Their children will go to City College East. Their grandchildren will go to City College East. They will never leave the borough of Queens.

I know that I'm only stuck in Queens until I figure out how to escape. "I'm sorry that my life is such an ongoing shock to you," I tell my cousin, confirming myself as completely lacking in remorse. "I'm sorry that you're so sheltered that the idea of me having S-E-X with my boyfriend made you drive off the road. I hope that you and Stu have lots of fun being virgins until your wedding night. I'm going home."

And with these words, I pick myself up and walk to my parents' home, crossing Queens Boulevard, barely mindful of the cars whizzing past me.

I return to a blessedly empty house, peel off my overalls, and jump in the shower. When I emerge, I am surprised to see that I have spent about half an hour just standing beneath the water, replaying the reels of the accident, turning this way and that, trying to ease the intensifying soreness of my chest. The shock of the initial impact interfaces with the closing scene—Mandy's spiteful accusation. My mind edits out the intervening, insignificant scenes.

There is no doubt that Mandy has already blubberingly told her parents the story of the accident, sobbing as she related how Anna the fuck-up almost got her killed. I have lived in my family for eighteen years and know that this version of the story will become the official rendition. Probably at this very moment, my aunt Audrey is calling my mother to break the news. Aunt Audrey, the passive-aggressive control freak, will have a moment of noble soul-searching as she ponders exactly how to tell my mom about the accident without breaking her heart because her only daughter is a complete whore.

I should be worried about a fall-out from my parents, but I am so weary of starring in *The Messed-Up Life of Anna A.* that I find myself incredibly calm. Putting on shorts, a t-shirt, and sneakers, I walk to Jewel Avenue and catch the bus to City College East.

Now that I am back, I remember just what I hate about City College East—it feels like an extension of high school except that all the losers, delinquents, and Special Ed kids are suddenly popular. The truly cool students—the Europeans and starving artists, for instance—are too cool or busy to actually hang out on campus. I spend most of the day registering for my courses with about one-half of the population of the entire Third World and a posse of abnormally gregarious Jewish kids who all had "amazing" summers working as counselors at Jewish summer camps and are now diligently filling out course cards and swapping tales about professors.

One thing must be said in CCE's favor: it has a good film studies faculty and I am planning to major in this field. So far, my registration card looks a bit unbalanced: I want to take A History of the Horror Film, Film and Political Theory, The Cinema of Truffaut, Moviemaking 101, and Woody Allen: Social Critic. Just as I am wondering if I should substitute Moviemaking 101 with The Artistry of Chaplin, I am approached by Shosh Engle-something, the daughter of one of my parents' friends from the Queens Orthodox Synagogue.

"Hi, Anna," Shosh says, balancing about a billion books on her hip. Not only has Shosh registered for her courses, but she has already purchased her books. Bravo, Shosh. "Here," she says, taking a postcard out of her pocket and handing it to me. There is a cheesy picture of the Western Wall in Jerusalem on one side, superimposed with smiling faces of boys and girls. The postcard is promoting a singles party/information night for study programs at the Hebrew University in Jerusalem and it takes place tonight in the city.

Here's the thing about Israel: within my community, it is the only acceptable alternative to going to CCE, or Brooklyn or City College or Yeshiva University in Manhattan. Granted, most parents will allow their kids to take only one year abroad at Bar Ilan or Hebrew University (somehow deluding themselves that there is no drug use, sex, or dating of non-Jews on these programs) but every now and then you hear of someone daringly going off to study for their entire undergraduate degree in Israel, coming home only during the summer.

Mistakenly, such kids are regarded as possessing extreme Zionistic fervor and the entire community applauds when they set off for the Holy Land (even as their parents secretly try to figure out where they went wrong). There is even a special word for the act of immigrating to Israel; it is *aliyah*, which literally means "going up" because moving to Israel is regarded as moving closer to God.

Not to knock the motives of everybody who makes *aliyah*, but the truth is that in many of these cases, Israel presents the only possible escape hatch for kids desperate to get away from their parents. Ironically, American campuses with dormitories are all somehow deemed *treyf*...but a campus located six thousand miles away is perfectly kosher.

Believe me, the prospect of running away to Israel has occurred to me about a hundred million times, especially since Barak became my boyfriend. On the night we parted, he told me that if I came to Israel, I could live with his family and go to Hebrew U or any other school I wanted. His parents would be completely cool with this idea, he said; I could even sleep in his room.

I was incredibly touched, but I swear I wanted to suggest that his parents have their DNA checked because they sure didn't sound like any Jewish parents I knew.

While Barak's suggestion was practical, the problem with going to Israel is that I really wanted the *American* campus experience. I wanted to feel like a full-fledged member of my own generation; I didn't want to be a stranger in a strange land. (Even if I was taught that Israel *was* my land because God gave it to Abraham for his children for all time.) Let's be real: Israel is the Middle East, which is cool, but it's not where I was born. To quote David Bowie, I was a young American.

What I *really* wanted was to go to college in Manhattan or Boston or Ann Arbor or Providence or Hanover or Madison or New Paltz or any of these other tantalizing places that had bars and restaurants and used bookstores and head shops and little boutiques selling Indian skirts and incense and gauzy shirts and crocheted bags and stuff like that.

I wanted my freedom, yes, but on my own turf.

"This party is going to be *amazing*," says Shosh, enthusiastic as a Mouseketeer. "It's to let people know about college programs for American kids at Hebrew University. They have tons of scholarships for smart students. You can even get your degree there if you want! It's a five-dollar admission and half the money goes to Israel."

Shosh's eyes are shining as if she's a Moonie. After what I've been through today, I don't have the heart to blow her off. Also, I wonder if the time has come to reconsider the Israel escape option.

"Thanks," I say, taking the postcard. I see that the party begins at 8:00 p.m. in someone's apartment on Central Park South. "I'll try to come."

"Great!" enthuses Shosh. She's so joyous that I wonder if I accidentally told her that she had just won a million dollars. This girl is just one of the scores of pathologically upbeat Jewish kids who valiantly attempt to get me involved in religious life on campus. Their perpetual high spirits really get on my nerves.

"I need to get cute girls to come," she says, stepping closer, lowering her voice and the degree of hype. "You know how these things are. You get a lot of chubby yeshiva girls." She places a hand briefly on my arm and looks meaningfully into my eyes. "It would be nice if you could come."

Whoa...was that a come-on? Is Shosh Engle-something, daughter of my parents' friends a secret lesbo? I nod and pull away from her. "Great," I say with a frozen smile, continuing to nod my head. "Maybe I'll see you." I slip the postcard into my bag, wave and take off like a bullet.

When I get home, it is already after six o'clock. Something very weird is happening with time today; it is moving at warp speed, slipping through my fingers. Also, I am having trouble lifting my arms on either side; any upward movement hurts like hell. Both my parents' cars are in the driveway, which is not surprising, since they eat dinner every single night at 6:30 sharp. I shout a "hi" into the den, where I know my parents are watching the evening news on Channel 4 and run hurriedly upstairs. I know that a major cataclysm is waiting to happen. Perhaps if I leave the house fast enough I can avoid it for at least another day.

I check my phone messages. There is a message from Talia, one of my best friends, just back from her summer at Camp Kadima in Canada. She wants to get together. She has amazing news. And did I hear about the Hebrew U party tonight in the city? Let's go!

What's with this party? Shosh must have canvassed the entire borough of Queens, roping in everyone under the age of fifty. I cannot wait to speak to Talia. She has no idea what has happened to me since we didn't speak all summer and her parents are not friendly enough with mine to find out. Like me, Talia is at City College East, but her parents have not expressly forbidden her from applying to other schools. She went simply because all the girls in her neighborhood went and she was too lazy to fill out any other applications.

I rush into the bathroom and jump into the shower, brushing my teeth in the stall to save time. Once finished, I shake out my hair, spraying myself recklessly with my waning supply of Chanel #5—last year's Chanukah present from Aunt Esther. I feel wildly indulgent yet frantic, like I am eating caviar with an ice cream scoop, like a contestant in a real-life episode of *Beat the Clock*, racing to save my life.

Running into my room, I attempt to call Talia back while putting on my underpants and then hang up the phone when my legs become entangled in the telephone cord. I have to stop once or twice, overwhelmed by stabs of pain in my sides. Tip-toeing to the closet, I grab a red cotton sundress, pull it over my head, tie the straps over my shoulders, shake my hair once again, and grab the phone, calling Talia.

After screeching our heads off for about five minutes in the sheer joy of reconnecting after two months, we arrange to meet at the subway station at 71st Street and Continental Avenue in half an hour and take the train into the city for dinner, followed by the Hebrew U party. That is, if I can get out of the house alive.

Now to escape.

I take a deep breath and run down the stairs gingerly, on the balls of my feet, with my bag. *Ow, ow, ow, ow, ow…*I think on every bounce. "I'm meeting Talia and we're going to a party in the city. I'll be home late," I yell in the direction of the den where my parents are hunkered down for battle. They are eager for a showdown, I know. Naturally, I want to get the hell out of the house as soon as possible. But as I dash to the front door, my father steps out of the shadows of the living room like Norman Bates and grabs me by my wrist.

"Where do you think are you going?" he says between clenched teeth.

For the second time that day, I almost die of fright. My father drags me into the den like a prisoner of war. My mother is sitting in the rocking chair, face red and mottled from crying. My father lets go of his iron grip on my wrist and stands next to her, his hand on her shoulder for comfort. They are the deranged Jewish version of *American Gothic.*

The nightmare begins. No, Audrey didn't have the pleasure of telling my parents the headline of the day; she bestowed that honor upon Mandy. I could just see the little Goody Two-shoes bravely holding back her tears while she told my parents that I spent the summer having sex with my boyfriend. She was so sorry to tell them this news; she was deeply aggrieved, like a doctor giving a diagnosis of cancer to concerned family members.

In this demented game of telephone, *Anna is not a virgin* turned into *Anna is a whore,* at least in their minds. My mother cannot stop crying. The tragedy of this situation eludes me. "So you didn't just run away from camp. Now we learn that you spent the summer sleeping with your boyfriend," my father spits his words.

"I didn't spend the summer sleeping with my boyfriend. We did it just once," I say, arms folded across my chest, holding my ground. It occurs to me that this conversation belongs to 1958, not 1978. My parents and all their cronies—who now include Mandy—are stuck in a time warp. Honestly, don't they know that kids in public school start having sex when they are thirteen? It is only because they are in such a close-minded and sheltered community that their expectations are so out of step with the times!

"You little tramp!" My father strides toward me, slapping me full across the face. He has never laid a hand on me in my entire life. I feel the stinging impact of his palm, literally feel flames of fire where his fingers were. My life seems to end at this moment, collapsing in on itself. His face is so impassioned that it is dark. He looks like a monster in a Japanese horror film.

You little tramp. I am without words. My father hit me. My father called me a tramp. I hold back my tears, meeting his eyes defiantly. I see a scary stew of emotions—rage, frustration, love.

And then...horror and regret.

"Anna," he says in a whisper, reaching out his hand to me. But I move backward, away from him, shaking my head, refusing his contrition. Why can't my parents just let go of me and allow me to have my own life! Why are they stalking me like spies, like bloodhounds, like Sons of Sam?

A howl rips out of my throat. It is the sound of the abyss, of the ocean at night, of a woman giving birth. I turn and run out of the den. "Anna!" I hear my father call. I grab my bag by the steps and gallop out the front door. "Anna!" I think my father is coming after me. Gulping down my pain, I run down the block, nearly the entire way to the subway, half a mile away. When I meet Talia, my tears have been dried by the wind.

What a sight I must have presented, the mad marathon runner in a red sundress sprinting toward the subway! My knees, banged up during the accident, are aching, but I breathe the pain away. My lungs are killing me. I look around, expecting to see my father coming after me in his Cadillac. I grab Talia and we run into the subway station together.

On the subway platform Talia gently traces the now-pinkish outline of my father's hand on my face. I feel lightheaded and numb. Something happened to me with that slap; I am not the same person as I had been earlier in the day. I am removed from my own body, observing myself as if through the lens of a camera. I am the director or cinematographer of a movie starring myself. And I realize that I have the power to completely rewrite the story of my life.

Talia and I ride the F train to the N train to the promised land of Manhattan. What a relief to leave Queens! At the Bloomingdale's station, we get out, stepping over the famous beggar who is always camped out there reading the *Daily News* and munching on red licorice and head toward our favorite restaurant in the entire city—Green Fields—where Talia had a waitressing job last year. Because of her job, Talia got to come into the city every day. She met interesting people, both waiters and patrons. It opened up her world. She tried to get me a job there as well, but my mother forbade it.

Over dinner, Talia hesitantly tells me her good news: she is going to Barnard in the fall. Her English professor from freshman year had encouraged her to apply and her mother hand-delivered the application on the day it was due. The acceptance letter came only two days earlier; someone must have deferred her admission at the last minute. At any other time, I would have been paralyzed with envy but find I am completely and unequivocally delighted for my friend. She will dorm on West 116th Street in a suite with five other girls. To celebrate the occasion we order a bottle of wine.

"Do we really have to go to this party?" The wine is long gone and we are leaning back in our seats, smoking. Neither of us really wants to go to the Hebrew U party, but it is our alibi for being in the city. The question on the table now is how long we plan to stay.

"Half an hour," I propose.

Talia takes a deep drag, thinking. Exhaling, she nods. "Yeah, half an hour sounds right," she agrees.

Leaving the restaurant, we link arms and walk along Lexington Avenue to 57th Street. In the waning light of the day, the cars look bejeweled, the fabric of women's dresses shimmer and the pavement itself glitters. Even though there is a smell in the air of too many cars and too many people, even though there is not even the faintest hint of a breeze, I feel intoxicated with freedom.

Eventually, we reach Central Park South and stand outside the party building, smoking. Sincere yeshiva kids file past us in twos, groups, and solo. Shosh was right; there are lots of chubby girls, decked out mostly in long jean skirts and Lacoste shirts, the fad of the moment. Periodically, some cool kids show up, wearing the teen uniform of jeans and rock concert t-shirt. There is also a smattering of kids who are most definitely not Jewish but nevertheless interested in Israel.

It always amazes me when non-Jews are interested in Jewish stuff. I mean, I'm into Judaism and think it's great and beautiful and eternal and all that but if I'd have been born Christian, there is no way I'd be interested in this weird religion where it is a sin to eat at McDonald's or drive on Saturday and every hundred years or so people decide that you are the cause of all the world's problems and try to kill you.

After a group of boys with longish hair goes inside the building, we stub out our cigarettes and join the party, which is held in the drop-dead gorgeous apartment of some lady who is an art collector. After wandering around taking inventory of the Picassos, the Magrittes, and the Chagalls, not to mention the Alice Neel portraits, the Andy

Warhol lithographs, the Ben Shahn posters, the Calder mobile, and the three Henry Moore sculptures, we feel ready to dive in.

The party is actually an information fair with music and food. Its sole purpose, it seems, is to get young Jewish people to make *aliyah*. There are helpful adults with Hebrew University badges who ply us with brochures and applications, representatives from El Al, the Israeli consulate, immigration, and even moving companies. I take one of everything.

As planned, we leave the party around the thirty-minute mark, making sure that Shosh not only sees us but *kvells* over us as if we are her grandchildren. Leaving, we walk together until Sixth Avenue and then part ways after an emotional hug. Time seems to slow down for the first time all day and I have a monumental awareness of impending change. The soreness in my chest has spread to my shoulders and jaw. I blow air out through my mouth in short puffs.

Talia heads toward the Upper West Side to spend the night with Steve, her boyfriend from Canada who is attending the joint program at Columbia and the Jewish Theological Seminary. Her parents think she will be sleeping over at my house. For the first time in my life, I haven't given my parents a fake alibi and I realize that there is a great relief in not having to lie.

I actually have no idea where I am heading—or spending the night. How can I go home tonight, or ever again? The sun is setting and the New York night stretches before me—romantic in twilight and rich with innumerable possibilities.

I begin walking down Sixth Avenue, considering my options. Perhaps I'll head down to the Village, I think, and walk around, buy some earrings on 8th Street, maybe even a pair of shoes. Perhaps I'll catch a film. I have about $120 on me from my first and only camp paycheck—I can do anything I want…maybe even stay overnight in a hotel! I pass by elegantly attired couples coming in and out of the Hilton, returning from dinner or heading out to a concert, a show, or a club. There are a million destinations in this town and all hold limitless promise.

I am down on 50th Street when I stop cold in my tracks. The Hilton. Joachim Hermann. Hermann Hilton, I think. Mandy's Nazi. He looked deeply into my eyes. He said I was beautiful and clever. He gave me his card; he told me he wanted to see me. I fumble inside my bag, pushing aside Israel information, loose change, papers, receipts, tampons, lip gloss, subway tokens, my driver's license, and sand from Newport Beach. One of the advantages of never cleaning out my bag is that everything is there when I need it. I see the card. *Joachim Hermann, Deutsche Bank.* I turn it over. *Room 1207, the Hilton Hotel.* The seven is crossed, European-style.

I stand completely immobile on the corner of 50th Street for about five minutes. Would he be in at this hour? Shouldn't I call? I was raised to call before dropping in on anyone. I see a phone booth on the corner and stride toward it. I pick up the receiver. "The Hilton hotel in New York," I say.

"Just a moment," the operator says in a nasal operator voice. I wait a fraction of a second before slamming the receiver down.

No, I can't go. This is insane. I might be adventurous but going to visit a businessman in his hotel is a recipe for disaster, I know. I've seen tons of made-for-TV movies where nice girls get lured to their deaths this way. Okay, maybe it usually takes place in a motel in Nebraska or something, but the idea is the same.

I decide to walk over to the Ziegfeld and catch the next showing of *The Deer Hunter.* If it doesn't start for another hour or so, I'll just hang out at Coliseum Books or watch the musicians in front of Columbus Circle.

Don't ask me how it happens, but within moments I find myself standing inside the lobby of the Hilton. It is as lively as an airport. People are talking and laughing, smoking and holding drinks in their hands. Seated in deep plush chairs or clustered standing in groups, they exude *life*—electric and vital. Observing from the sidelines, I am hungry, jealous, emboldened. I want exactly what they are having.

I walk to the elevator bank and stand with a group of young men. They appear to be my age and are dressed in near-identical uniforms of navy blazers and light-colored pants. One of them, a redhead, looks hard at me and I look away. They are WASPs—from their fair hair down to their white bucks. Next to them I feel like Pocahontas or Maria from *West Side Story*.

The elevator arrives and the boys cram in with me. I'm not worried that they will harass me; they are too well-bred to heckle girls. I press twelve and a hand reaches over me, pressing fourteen. I notice that there is no floor thirteen. No one is talking and the silence feels like a passenger we are all trying to ignore. With a small ding, the elevator reaches the twelfth floor and I prepare to leave. "Nice perfume," says a voice from the back of the elevator. They probably think I am a Spanish whore. *You little tramp!* I walk out of the elevator, head held high.

"Chanel No. 5," the boy adds. "It smells really good on you."

I turn to look at him. He is Nordic blond. His friends are all looking at me expectantly, especially the redhead. These guys probably go to Princeton or Yale. If I were a student there, they would be in my classes or living in my dorm. If I were a student there, we would study together and have epic conversations about the meaning of life. Maybe I could even be persuaded to wear headbands and pleated skirts. I would be their equal, not their inferior.

"Thanks," I say to them en masse. The doors start to close.

"Hey, can I be your boyfriend?" one of them yells as the elevator closes, rising toward the fourteenth floor.

I study the numbers on the wall, searching for the location of room 1207. Hotel guest floors are so confusing! They should have people stationed, like theatre ushers, to point visitors in the right direction. Then again, such an usher would point me straight downstairs. Let's see. To the right are room numbers 1200–1236. To the left are 1238–1272. I start walking to my right. *You little tramp!* Blood starts pounding in my ears. 1211...1210... 1209...1208...1207.

I stand in front of room 1207 and feel like a call girl. *You little tramp!* I raise my hand to knock and am suddenly possessed by the fear that I might have food in my teeth from dinner. That would never do! I race down the hall to the elevator bank where there is a large mirror. I grimace and locate a tiny poppy seed between my two front teeth. Aha!

I march resolutely back toward Joachim Hermann's room. This is completely crazy. I should go to a movie, or even return to that Israel recruitment party. I raise my hand to knock, at first tentatively and then more strongly. Five knocks in all. They reverberate down the hall and make me want to shout, "Open up! It's the FBI!"

The door opens. Joachim Hermann is wearing a white robe tied around the middle. I can tell he has just come out of the shower; his hair is wet, his skin looks incredibly clean, and he smells like expensive shampoo. He is surprised, possibly amazed, to see me. His lip quivers a bit. His eyes glide over me and I feel suddenly scared, but not scared enough to leave. He looks intently at me, serious, unsmiling.

"The little Jewish girl from the diner," he says, standing still for a moment. "But you changed from your hippie clothes into a summer dress. May I say that it is quite becoming?"

"Thank you," I say, wondering briefly if I should comment on his bathrobe. "Are you busy?" I ask.

He frowns. "Busy? No, no, please do come in," he says, extending his arm and ushering me into his room. His hand is on my bare shoulder; it is warm, no, not merely warm, it is scalding hot, branding my skin. Joachim Hermann closes the door and leans against it. I am facing him, standing close to his mirrored closet. His arms are folded against his chest. Now he smiles at me. "So you came to me. You are curious."

I really don't know what to say. Am I curious? Perhaps. *Traumatized* might be a better word. Curiosity presupposes a question or a quest of some sort and I have no agenda. I am just reacting to the events of the day. Or responding. He said earlier that I was responsive. Very responsive.

The way that the robe hangs on Joachim Hermann's body, I can see that he is naked underneath. *I am alone in a hotel room with a naked man,* I say to myself. I am completely impressed at my own sense of daring. Alone with a naked German businessman at the Hilton hotel!

Yet just as I am congratulating myself on my adventurousness, I begin to tremble ever so slightly. It begins in my knees and runs through me like a current of electricity. *You little tramp!* My ribs feel brittle, as if they are made of shattered glass. It hurts to breathe. I hug myself around the shoulders to stop my shaking.

"You are scared," he says gently. "Don't be scared. I will not hurt you." He locks the door behind him.

"Look…" I begin to say, but he walks toward me, taking my hand and leading me into his room, which I now see is more like a little apartment. I think it is called a suite.

"Please sit down," he says, gesturing to a sofa. "Please feel at home."

Joachim Hermann's hotel suite at the Hilton is so unlike my own home that I can barely sustain the images of both in my mind at the same time. For starters, there are no paintings of the Old City of Jerusalem in Joachim Hermann's hotel suite, no portraits of rabbis blowing shofars, no baby grand piano stacked with reams of classical sheet music—Mozart and Mussorgsky, Rimsky-Korsakov and Rachmaninoff and Chopin, no ornately-framed black and white photographs of austere grandparents and humiliating family portraits, no stacks of bat mitzvah and wedding albums on the coffee table, no bookcases sagging under the weight of *Maimonides*, the *Encyclopedia Judaica*, the *Talmud*, the *Great Works of Western Civilization*, innumerable collections of fiction and poetry and well-worn *chumashim* and *siddurim*, no mezuzahs on the doorposts.

No weeping mother, sitting silently in a rocking chair, mourning the loss of her daughter's virginity. And no furious father slapping me, calling me a tramp.

I try to settle in on the beige suede sofa of this thrillingly unfamiliar suite, looking out the window. Jazz music is playing softly in the background. Was it on all the time or did he sneakily just turn it on to add atmosphere?

"Can I get you anything to drink?" asks Joachim Hermann, standing next to a bar, complete with a sink and refrigerator. A clock on the wall reports that it is eight-thirty. I am still trembling. This is not running away from camp or sleeping with Barak on Newport Beach. This is something completely different.

My German banker friend is politely awaiting my order. Yes, it would be incredibly sophisticated to have a drink with Joachim Hermann in his hotel suite. I am still fairly buzzed from my dinner wine, but I feel it beginning to wane. I am curious. What do adults drink at this hour?

"Brandy?" I remember that brandy is something people drink in the evening, from some movie or another. Or is it sherry? "A glass of sherry is fine as well," I add.

Joachim Hermann opens a cabinet. There is both brandy and sherry inside. It occurs to me that both are women's names. Turning his back, my host reaches into a cabinet and takes out two crystal wine goblets. The reaching movement allows me to see the muscularity of his shoulders, his calves, his buttocks. This must be a European thing. No guys I know are that muscular. Even the star basketball players at school, even Barak, who went through the Israeli Army, doesn't have such well-defined muscles.

Joachim Hermann presents me with two bottles. He tilts his head inquisitively. "Brandy? Sherry?"

"Umm, sherry," I decide, for no particular reason. He uncorks the bottle and pours sherry into two glasses. The sound of the liquid pouring makes me think of sex. Naturally. Everything taking place in this suite is about sex.

"So, little Anna, how does it happen that you end up in my hotel room?" Joachim Hermann lifts his goblet to me. *L'chaim*, I think. I raise my goblet to him and take a sip. Fire. Thick, sweet, dark fire. It goes down burning and tastes like really strong kiddush wine. Wow. I drain my glass; it stops my shaking and takes the edge off the burning pain in my chest. Joachim Hermann lifts an eyebrow and refreshes my drink instantly.

How did I end up in his hotel room indeed? The journey from this morning to the present moment is impossible to relate, especially to a stranger. I touch my still-tender cheek. "Well...I was walking around the city and remembered I had your card," I say.

"And is there no other place you should be right now? No mommy or daddy waiting for you?" He smiles but I see that the question is a serious one. I guess the German banker doesn't want to have a run-in with hysterical Jewish parents.

"Nope," I reply. "They think I'm at a party."

"There is no lover waiting for you? No little boyfriend?" At this, I hesitate. Sensing my hesitation, Joachim Hermann nods, almost imperceptively. "I see. There is a little boyfriend. This will be one of the many secrets you keep from him."

I am astonished. *Quick*, I think, *deflect the conversation away from myself.*

"So...what is your job at the bank?" I ask, imagining him as a teller at Chemical Bank, standing behind a thick glass window. In my mind's eye, all the signage of the bank appears in scary, Weimar-era Bavarian-style lettering, with a few swastikas thrown in for ambiance.

While Joachim Hermann tells me about his job, the devastating scenes of the day replay themselves in my mind, over and over, an endless loop: the car crash and the showdown with my father. My focus hop-scotches from one frame to the next. I watch with horrified fascination.

"So, during the conference in Frankfurt, we decided to diversify and I'm in New York to set up this new division!"

Following this proclamation, Joachim Hermann pats my thigh for emphasis. I nod, not certain what I'm agreeing with. He might have just said that Jews control the international banking industry, for all I know. After making his point, Joachim Hermann leans back, looking philosophical. His hand, however, remains on my thigh.

Joachim Hermann's hand on my thigh becomes the elephant in the room. We continue to talk as if I don't notice it is there, as if it is indeed not there at all. We discuss movies and music and even books. And then his hand begins to move up my leg, caressing, pushing my cotton sundress with it. I look at the expanse of naked thigh Joachim Hermann has exposed. *You little tramp!* My California tan has not faded in the least. Naked but for his alabaster hand, my leg is golden brown, like the leg of Pocahontas. This golden-brown leg seems to belong not to me, but to someone else entirely. A naked, tanned leg like this in a hotel room with an amorous German businessman must surely be the leg of some exotic sophisticate, not a Jewish girl from Queens, New York.

Joachim Hermann leans over, lifts my masses of curly brown hair, and kisses my neck. Now *that* is something that teenage boys or very young men do not do. Kiss necks, I mean. It feels tickly and irritating and nice all at once. While Joachim Hermann kisses my neck, he moves his hand ever higher till he is right near the band of my underpants and his body is leaning urgently into mine. The sherry has moved through me like a brushfire. I feel it in my fingers and toes, in my brain.

It dimly registers that I am wearing my Thursday underpants and it is only Monday. The word *Thursday* is embroidered in hot pink thread on my underpants just below my right hip; you can see the top petals of my rose tattoo peeking out over the top. I know how you say Monday in German—*Montag*—because I once had a piano teacher with this name, Mr. Montag. "Call me Mr. Monday," he used to say with a weirdo smile. Mr. Montag smelled like erasers and had bright white fingernails, like a dead person. Will Joachim Hermann find my Thursday underpants weird? Maybe he won't notice.

"Have you had dinner?" I ask inanely.

"Mmmmhmm," he murmurs between kisses, his breath hot, his tongue tracing circles on my skin. "Mmmhm, yes. I've had a very nice dinner...and you are my very, very nice dessert."

I remain completely still, head leaning on the back of the couch, eyes shut, barely breathing at all. I have no idea what I am thinking or even what I want. Though still trembling slightly, I am beyond fear. I have a feeling of unreality. I guess that Joachim Hermann is correct; that the truest thing to be said is that I'm curious.

Joachim Hermann gently turns my face toward him with his other hand, the one that is not skirting the edge of my underpants. I open my eyes. His cheeks are flushed and his lips are rosy-red and his eyes are more gold-flecked than ever. His gaze is, well, penetrating. I am suddenly very aware that he is really an adult and I am not. He looks deeply, inquisitively at me, "Anna, you are sad?" He looks concerned. I start to shake my head but then find myself nodding. Tears spring to my eyes. "Oh," he says softly, kindly, caressing my bruised cheek. "Shh, shh. Don't be sad."

And with these words, Joachim Hermann kisses me on the mouth. The kiss is so violent and so hungry that I can hardly focus on recip- rocating; the only thing left for me is to allow myself to be devoured. I lie helpless against the couch, feeling robbed of all resistance, allowing this strange man to suck and bite at my mouth and at the same time, sneak his hand inside my Thursday underwear. His fingers rove and roam and explore and suddenly the top of my sundress is pulled down and I am naked to the waist.

Joachim Hermann lifts back to look at me, his dessert. "Lovely," he whispers in a hoarse voice. "Exactly as I imagined." I shiver. He kisses my breasts gently, his tongue a feather. Now all is lost. I close my eyes and sigh deeply, a flow of heat radiating from my core. He was right about what he said earlier—I am responsive, very responsive.

I am also very injured, I realize, as a dull pain radiates down my arms. Joachim Hermann is touching me exactly the right way in exactly the right place, though, making the pain recede. I hear a sound in the room and realize it is my own voice. I am so swept along on a current of sensation and so intoxicated that I don't even have the pres- ence of mind to feel embarrassed when I come, gasping and yelping, for what seems like ten minutes.

As I fall back down to earth, Joachim Hermann hugs me close to him, kissing my forehead. I feel like an obedient child instead of the tramp that I obviously am. "That was good. That was very good," he assesses, pronouncing good the German way—*goot.* I open my eyes and everything looks different to me, no longer alien.

Just as I am contemplating this fact, Joachim Hermann leaps in front of me like Superman, and with a quick yank of his terry belt, his robe falls open. And then I shriek, turning abruptly away from him.

Not at the sight of his nakedness—I am not my cousin, after all—but because Joachim Hermann is not circumcised.

The shriek leaves my lips B-movie–style—with my hand pressed against my mouth, eyebrows lifted in horror. Joachim Hermann looks completely mortified and quickly closes his robe, tying it shut.

My orgasm-dulled, inebriated, injured brain slips into gear. If sex with a German Christian older man is bad, then sex with an *uncircumcised* German Christian older man is far worse. Oh God...can I really allow that thing inside of me? It's so weird, like an oversized finger or a miniature elephant's trunk! I realize how nice-looking Jewish penises are, the only kind I have seen so far. Uncircumcised men are called something in the Torah...what is it? *Arel,* I think. As far as I can tell, *arel* is hardly a complimentary term.

Now that the shock is beginning to fade, I feel horrified to think that I have insulted Joachim Hermann on the basis of his penis. That doesn't present Jews in a very positive light, I know; it kind of feeds on that Jewish superiority thing. I'd hate for him to form a bad opinion of Jewish people just because of me. What if he goes back to Germany and tells other Germans this story and they start to hate Jews and begin the Holocaust all over again?

Joachim Hermann has slumped down next to me, breathing deeply. "Anna," he says, voice full of woe. I bow my head, feeling deeply ashamed. I don't even know what to say. I feel like a complete idiot, a little girl, really. I have had sex only once in my life. What is this bogus attempt at adulthood on my part?

But what is this? Joachim Hermann has taken my hand and is stroking it. What's more, he is apologizing to me! "I am sorry," he says in the most sincere voice I have ever heard. "I did not behave like a gentleman. I lost control… I am just so aroused! You are a young girl who needs to be made love to, slowly. I see that my behavior was shocking to you. Anna, please forgive me!"

I look at him in amazement, unable to believe my ears. He feels that *he* offended *me?* Well…okay. I am so used to being the accused, so used to being guilty. It's nice to be on the receiving end of an apology for a change.

I study Joachim Hermann. He is the very picture of remorse, that quality I so seem to lack. He looks really distressed and that is too bad, because he is really attractive, especially with his hair all mussed. I have just been handed an opportunity to rip up the script and leave the set, yet this drama has not reached its denouement.

"Come," I say, taking his hand and pulling him to his feet. "Come to bed," I say, leading him to the queen-sized playground in the other room of his suite. Holding hands, we walk together toward the bed and I feel like a Barbie and Ken bride and groom or like the little plastic dolls on the top of a wedding cake. Like a *kallah maidel* with her *chassan*.

Or like a lamb—Hannah the lamb—being led to slaughter.

We reach the bed. He turns down the bedclothes while I turn down the lights. Trying not to wince, I lift my dress over my head and step out of my underpants, imprinted with the wrong day of the week. At the side of the bed, Joachim Hermann stands still, watching me. He is an adult, and I am just playing at being grown up. His eyes sweep over my naked body, pausing at the rose tattoo. I come up close to him and pull open his robe. He watches my face intently, his chest rising and falling. I reach inside his robe. He closes his eyes. I push the robe from his shoulders and kiss him roughly on the mouth, as he had first kissed me. He has a beautiful body—ivory-hued, smooth, as sculpted as a Greek god.

We fall onto his bed in a tangle of limbs and lust. His hands are all over me and we feed hungrily on each other's mouths. I am quite literally breathless now and inhale only in gasps. Yet I push against him with my hips, my breasts, my shattered rib cage, my shoulders. I throw my legs over him and rock him from side to side. He rolls me over until I'm on my back and then pins my hands down to the bed. He is breathing heavily, sweat forming on his upper lip. His eyes—all fiery gold—are the eyes of a lion, a wolf, a predator.

Joachim Hermann thrusts into me more forcefully than I imagined possible. It sends shocks up my spine and I cry out. It feels like rape, yet it also feels like redemption.

I listen; he is saying things, words I do not understand. There is an ocean in my ears, the sound inside a shell, the echo of an abyss. I am breaking; my bones are cracking like walnut shells. He is yelling now, in German, holding me down, hurting me, yet I do not feel scared.

His movements become frantic—he grips my shoulders, his face turns fierce, he shouts. He looks like he's going to turn into a werewolf or kill me or die himself and then he comes, howling, for what seems like an eternity.

In the quiet clarity that follows this crisis, I float out of my body, out of the Hilton hotel and sail westward, returning to Newport Beach to the bygone summer. I see myself walking with Barak on our last night together. We are exhausted. Barak rolls out his sleeping bag and we collapse gratefully onto it. The air is sweet/salty and warm. The beach is secluded and the sky is practically moonless. When we begin kissing, I realize that this night will indeed be different from all the other nights we have shared over the past eight weeks.

What happened on the beach with Barak is not in the same universe as what just took place with Joachim Hermann. Being with Barak was sweet and safe and somehow *milchig*-pure, though it rid me of my virginity, which is an inherently *fleishig* act. Being with Joachim Hermann, on the other hand, is the very essence of *treyf*—forbidden, dangerous, delicious. My parents were right to keep their *kallah maidel* under lock and key.

Lying pinned beneath my German lover in his room on the twelfth floor of the Hilton hotel, I recall how I felt when Dotty called me lucky outside the ladies' room of Persephone's Palace thousands of years ago this morning—chastened yet also desperate to explain myself. Though she had me pegged as a child of privilege, what she failed to see was that I was internally injured, a wild girl tearing at her invisible restraints, dying to be free. To my parents' great sorrow, I would never become the obedient, fearful, uncurious child they wished me to be.

Nor anything else.

The weight of Joachim Hermann's arm across my breasts now causes me to take rapid, shallow breaths. My lungs are on fire and my head is heavy. There is a ringing in my ears. It is hard—no, it is impossible—to breathe. The phrase *internal injuries* drifts idly through my mind and then I realize that these very words are being spoken out loud. Cold fingers touch me. The room has become as dark as a tomb. *Hey,* I try to say. I have a sensation of being carried and then I have no sensation at all.

Time collapses inward, becomes origami-like, unfolds, and forms a tunnel. Through this tunnel I am able to see the weeks of my life—more than nine hundred in all—and I pass through them as if they were subway cars. When I reach the final car, I emerge into the unbearable present reality of my parents' weeping as they bend, broken, over a very unresponsive version of myself. From my aerial perspective, I look beautiful, wrapped in a white bed sheet (taken, no doubt, from Joachim Hermann's bed), hair fanned out around my face, brown ballerina arms beseechingly open-palmed. The rose tattoo—forbidden by Jewish law—is discreetly hidden beneath the sheet. From my lofty point of view, I look like a sculpture, a still-life, a work of art perfectly arranged.

If you've never experienced it yourself, the most maddening aspect of being dead is that you cannot talk back...or talk at all. And that's what I really want to do right after I die on the operating table of Roosevelt Hospital, where I am taken after a horrified Joachim Hermann awakens to find me lying beneath him, unconscious and gray.

The doctor talks to my parents, explaining that I have died from internal injuries I had sustained earlier that day in the car accident. The young man in the waiting room is not responsible for my death; I should have sought medical treatment immediately after the crash. My father nods, taking in the doctor's words, and then breaks down on my mother's shoulder, weeping bitterly. My mother is ashen and silent; her tears have been spent. Their impossible, independent daughter is gone. The fighting is over.

My parents' grief makes it scarily real. I am dead. A rush of regret for everything I could have been overtakes me and I linger for an eternity in this moment, which unfolds to accommodate a sort of panic, reminiscent of that which I felt when I was little and my parents were going out for the night. But the moment passes and a torrent of love—powerful and pure—surges through me, filling me with lavender light and perfect peace.

Following the somber exit of the doctor who has failed to save my life, I hear the nurses in the operating room expressing sympathy not only for my parents but also for the visibly shaken young man who rode with me in the ambulance. I must admit that I am impressed by this news; I supposed that I was only a confection to him. I catch a brief glimpse of Joachim Hermann as they wheel my body past him in the hall and see that his gold-flecked eyes are beautiful, filled with tears. He is trembling as I had trembled in his room earlier that night when I was still alive. I feel sad for him, so far away from home with no one to comfort him.

Unless it's happened to you, you may not know that you are unable to linger in the world of the living after you have died. You are given a chance to visit your body, as if to confirm the truth to yourself, and then you must begin to move on.

The act of moving on is kind of weird and nice and scary and wonderful all at once. If you've ever doubted that heaven is located up above the sky, moving on will dispel all such thoughts. Heaven is most definitely above the earth and that is where God lives. As you move toward God, you begin to lose your ties to your earthly existence.

But God is all-merciful and I am granted an extra moment with my parents.

And so I hover over them, weaving a protective canopy, a *chuppah* of memories—the joy of my birth, the milestone of my first steps and words, the warmth of our weekly Shabbat dinners, the pride in my achievements, the dreams for the future. I see the fear that made them cling to me, refusing to let me go, as if they had a premonition of this moment. The fear is cold and amorphous and purplish-black; it dwelt between them like an unmoving mass, like the third party in their marriage. I banish it to the underworld and encircle them seven times with strength and forgiveness and the memory of my love before taking leave of this earthly realm.

When I move heavenward, I am as happy as a child who has finished her homework and is given permission to go outside to play. I turn cartwheels and handsprings in the air. I giggle. I am weightless and without pain. I am free.

As I flip and float and turn, I cast a glance downward and my last earthbound thought is that there is something of vital importance that I need to say.

But celestial voices are singing a psalm of praise—*sing unto God a new song! Sing unto God the whole of creation!*—and I am lost in the taste, the texture, the smell, and the sound of the magnificent music. It swirls around me, buoying me and massaging me. It tastes like a vanilla malted; it smells like the inside of a brand-new car. It is jewel-toned and pendulous and multi-dimensional. I weep with happiness and a sorrow whose source grows more distant by the moment.

The gateway to heaven locks after each new arrival; it is like one of those subway turnstiles that work only in one direction. Once you have left the world of the living, there is no going back.

And so, I am forever unable to inform my grieving parents and the somber doctor that the car crash earlier that day had been no accident. I have been murdered. What I suspected at the time, but now know for certain, is that my dear cousin Mandy—perfect daughter, *kallah maidel*, model member of my community, surrogate for God Himself—did not accidentally drive off the road upon hearing of the shocking loss of my virginity to my Israeli boyfriend. Instead, she deliberately plowed the car with the defective seatbelt into a lamppost in an enraged attempt to kill me, thereby meting out justice, restoring order to the universe and destroying those who dare to challenge the definition of what it meant to be a Jewish girl in Queens, New York, in the summer of 1978.

THE MUSEUM OF EROTICISM

THE RAIN HAD BEEN FALLING softly yet steadily on this, the penultimate day of their honeymoon in Paris. After a solid week of unseasonably chilly winds beneath a gunmetal sky, Claire felt personally affronted by the rain. It had arrived at just the moment when she, a new bride and an American visiting France for the first time, ought to have been rewarded with abundant sunshine for her perseverance and willingness to envision the glittering possibilities of Paris through the unremitting gray.

Honestly, it was hard not to feel duped and misled by the travel agent who *absolutely guaranteed* that Paris in August was *glorious* and *blessedly empty*. Yes, the city was largely emptied of its native inhabitants, but in their place were throngs of tourists, many of them rambunctious Australians or self-important American college students. Claire's own mother had urged Las Vegas on her, making a phooey face as she considered sharing sidewalk space with all those snooty Parisians (who were anti-Semitic, besides) and while in Vegas, couldn't Claire visit that hotel with the reproduction of the Eiffel Tower and have the best of both worlds?

Claire grimaced as she recalled how her mother's chatter had embarrassed her in front of Byron, whose own mother had hosted a salon in the Latin Quarter in the late fifties. At the time, in order to overcome the humiliation of the exchange, Claire retreated into a childhood habit, narrating the incident to herself as it unfolded: "As Mrs. Seltzer extolled the virtues of Las Vegas in front of Claire's fiancé, *New York Times* metro editor Byron Wasserman, her daughter, a junior reporter at the *Times*, cringed in shame, not only at her mother's lack of couth, not only because she mentioned Claire's Barnard degree for the umpteenth time, but because she seemed in danger of revealing a fact Claire had gone to great pains to conceal: that having recently attained her twenty-fifth birthday, Claire had never even been to Europe."

Nothing could rival the sheer joy Claire had experienced announcing to anyone who would listen that she planned to visit Europe this summer on her honeymoon with Byron Wasserman, that's correct, Byron Wasserman of the *Times*. In a tone of studied nonchalance Claire imparted information and answered questions…no, he had never been married before; actually, they would *not* be staying in a *hotel* but in a friend's *flat* along the Rive Gauche, you know, that's the West Bank, whoops, the *Left* Bank, I must have gotten that mixed up with Israel's West Bank, but you know, ha, ha, Paris's Left Bank is *not* disputed territory, though there *are* plenty of Palestinians living in Paris…

Thankfully, that exchange never took place, though Claire lived in fear that some faux pas or another would pass her lips while bragging about her impending trip to Paris. Paris! It was all she could think of, especially because her wedding was a brief, impersonal ceremony in a judge's chambers in Westport, Connecticut, where Byron had a summer home and where he shipped her Tiffany engagement ring to avoid paying tax.

Her mother had been crushed by the lack of a lavish wedding ceremony for her only child and Claire consoled her by promising (falsely) that they would have a wonderful party in a few months' time or maybe in about a year. Or two. It was just too busy now to think about a wedding and between the two of them, not to mention Claire's mother, there were hundreds of people to invite and there was no way to properly plan such an extravagant affair without inadvertently offending someone or leaving someone out or having a nervous breakdown.

Paris! The word itself was exquisite and evocative—the elegant P a lithe, leggy ballerina poised in first position; the lowercase A a heartbroken chanteuse plaintively pouring out her sorrow on the cobblestone streets of the Place de Tertre; the R a rakish young writer smoking Gauloises in a St. Germaine café; the diminutive I an innocent schoolchild in blue pinafore and wide-brimmed straw hat walking with her *maman* along the Seine; and the sinuous S something more elusive, an unseen presence winding and weaving its way through the city's streets and boulevards, a sensual thread linking the arrondissements together into one magnificent, glorious whole.

In the weeks leading up to her honeymoon, Claire had taken to gazing into the mirror at every opportunity, mouthing the word *Paris* to herself (or *Pa-ree*, as the mood struck her), cocking her head to the side to see whether she might be taken for a native once she arrived.

"*Sacre Bleu!*" she imagined Parisians saying to themselves when they overhead her conversing with Byron in English along the Champs Elysees. "She is so chic! So petite! So gamine! *Pardon, mademoiselle*," they would interrupt apologetically, bowing slightly, "but why do you sound like an *Amereekane* when you look like you were born right here in *Pa-ree?*"

Growing up in Great Neck, New York, Claire's claim to fame had been her prettiness. Adults remarked upon it all the time. The popular girls at school granted her a measure of respect because of it despite the fact that she was quiet and bookish and impervious to fashion. Boys acted goofy around her and male teachers often stared.

Though Claire knew that being pretty was an achievement, the word echoed with emptiness when it fell upon her ears. Pretty was a façade, a petit-four whose essence was sugar, fluff, and food glaze, a confection whose shelf-life was distressingly short. Pretty was two-dimensional, predictable, boring. Instead, Claire longed to be complex, to have a haunted look, to broadcast melancholy or mystery, to beguile and bewitch. Or simply to project the seductive sophistication of her secret cinematic crushes—Nastassia Kinski, Emmanuelle Beart, and Juliette Binoche—French girls all.

Locally, Claire harbored a fascination with Miss Bendavid, the brooding, rail-thin Moroccan cook employed by her friend Sasha's family, whom everyone pitied because she was mustachioed, flat-chested, and unmarried. With her alluring aura of silent suffering, formidable homeliness, and absent first name, Miss Bendavid seemed a character out of a novel, the owner of a heart broken beyond repair, a woman rendered wise through irreparable loss.

The melodrama of Miss Bendavid's (imagined) life aside, fair-skinned Claire experienced her prettiness as utterly bland and devoid of any depth in a town increasingly populated by Jews of Persian descent—dark-skinned, rich, voluptuous, and most fashionably attired. The gaggles of Persian girls promenading along Middleneck Road—majestic noses leading manes of hair the color of midnight—often filled Claire with a sense of despair. These girls were the direct descendants of Queen Esther. Claire's delicate beauty gave her an unmoored, ahistor-ical feeling and made her feel like a foreigner among her own people.

Besides, the repeated affirmation of Claire's prettiness by the adults in her life seemed to carry an implicit warning: You have been handed a gift, young lady. It contains everything you need. Do not ask for anything more.

And indeed, this gift had given her Byron.

"You are very pretty, you know."

It was the first time they were together and Claire was completely awestruck. She had been with handsome boys, with rich boys, with bad boys, with popular boys, with boys who were the sons of famous men but this was completely different. For starters, Byron was a man, an adult, fifteen full years her senior. Secondly, he was her editor; he was Byron *Wasserman*, for God's sake—brilliant, demanding and desirable, famous or infamous, depending on whom you asked, the author of hundreds of articles and three books (one of them a bestseller), an international legend.

Claire, by contrast, was someone with absolutely no status and few achievements, a reporter-trainee at the *Times*, half a step higher than janitor on the hierarchy of the paper. If you Googled Claire, you'd likely turn up her college clips, a short-lived blog she started her senior year at Barnard, a *Times* byline or two, and a YouTube video she posted with her friend Ella.

Most of the *Times* staff had no idea who she was or what she was doing in their newsroom.

Until Byron Wasserman took notice of her.

And now, by virtue of her prettiness, twenty-four-year-old Claire Seltzer from Great Neck, NY was lying in *his* bed.

Byron ran his palm down the side of her face, his eyes sweeping the length of her smooth, pale body; he was a connoisseur appraising a fine wine, a collector admiring a vintage automobile, a diamantaire looking at an exquisite stone through a loupe. He meant his words not as a compliment to Claire but to himself. His acknowledgement of her prettiness was a professional assessment, proof of his high standards, a secret password that granted him passage into an elite club.

Claire shivered under Byron's gaze. It was thrilling to be given such a high rating, yet unsettling at the same time. She felt like a prize mare. A dozen eager adolescent questions bubbled up inside of her, the most pressing one being—"Yes, but do you think I'm a good writer?"— yet she swallowed them all, heeding her mother's advice that men did not like to be challenged.

The words "thank you" (with eyes cast modestly downward) seemed…well, lame. Yet it was awkward not to respond at all. She stared intently at Byron.

His face in repose was beautiful and she told him so.

"I'm beautiful?" he laughed, the ends of his eyes crinkling up. "Beautiful is a word men are not accustomed to hearing in reference to themselves. That's very sweet of you. Thank you." He kissed her on the tip of her pretty nose.

Yet Claire spoke the truth. Byron's face *was* beautiful; it had depth and intelligence and character—the eyebrows arching, the mouth strong, the cheekbones high. Claire's mother confided that she found Byron as handsome as a movie star, which helped to explain why she often acted completely weird around him, intimidated, no doubt by his superior…well, everything.

If Claire allowed herself to ponder all of Byron's achievements she, too, would be in a permanent state of intimidation. Forget about the Princeton pedigree, the innumerable journalism prizes, distinctions and awards, the instant access to important producers and power brokers, and the movie-star good looks. Byron was Claire's personal celebrity, a boldface Prince Charming, her favorite writer since childhood.

Claire had grown up reading Byron's articles in the Metro section of the *New York Times*, learning about the city through Byron's eyes. When she was in ninth grade, she followed an entire series he wrote about a housing project on Amsterdam Avenue, cut out each article and glued it onto an oak tag for her Urban Studies project. When he was given a column in the Monday paper, she went to sleep on Sunday night looking forward to reading Byron's *City Snapshot* column the following morning. When his column increased to twice weekly, she fell asleep each Wednesday night trying to guess what he'd write about in the Thursday paper.

And now, practically five minutes into adulthood, Byron was hers. In a city teeming with supermodels and celebrities and gorgeous young reporters, Claire could not believe that Byron had chosen her. Pursued her in a manner that quite took her breath away. Was gallant and passionate and aggressive in an attractive, alpha-male way. And then fell under a spell that she had no idea she was capable of casting.

He was, quite unbelievably enough, smitten with her.

"I'm smitten with you," he said, lying motionless on his back, arm folded beneath his head, staring at the ceiling as if attempting to figure the whole thing out.

"I'm smitten with you," he said via his cellphone, striding across the newsroom floor on his way to chew out some unfortunate reporter on deadline.

"I'm smitten with you," he sighed, cupping her pretty breasts in his hands as she sat astride him on the Eames chair he had in his living room.

"I'm smitten with you," he said, handing her the Tiffany box containing the sapphire and diamond ring she now wore on her right hand, its original location (ring finger, left hand) now encircled by the thick gold band of Florentine gold that had been his mother's.

"I...am...smitten with you!" he gasped, exploding inside of her, millions of Byron juniors (or Claire juniorettes) rushing her womb, the Harvard of all wombs, chosen for its youth and prettiness and power to smite powerful men.

The minute Byron entered her life, everything changed. Her personal video screen went from grainy black and white to thrilling high definition. Modesty gave way to luxury. Practicality was supplanted by impulsivity. His was a world without end. Byron had been everywhere she could imagine. He had seen every major art exhibition in town and interviewed every famous person she could think of. He was erudite and informed. Listening to him speak ignited brushfires in her own mind. His ideas collided with hers, causing glorious explosions.

By marrying her, Byron had blasted open the boundaries of her small, safe world.

Before Byron, the only other man possessing the power to redeem her from the blandness of her childhood had been her father, an infectiously optimistic songwriter who made a living writing jingles for local businesses (*Nor-thern Bou-levard To-yo-ta! We drive the com-pe-ti-tion aw-aaaaayyy!*) while nurturing the dream that he would one day write Broadway musicals with Billy Joel.

Alas, Arthur Seltzer died of an undiagnosed heart ailment at the age of thirty, one day shy of his daughter's fifth birthday. Within a month of his demise, his widow Suzie, Claire's mother, had thrown out all of his jackets and pants, smelling of vanilla and cigarettes, his scribbled lyrics and pages of musical compositions, his leather desk set, his files and notes, his dreams, his immortality.

(Suzie had just recently attended a self-help support group for widows held at the Samuel Field Y in Little Neck and returned home charged with the task of "moving on." Within the piles of paper was an unopened, personal letter from Billy Joel, thanking Arthur for sharing his lyrics over the past few years, saying that he would pay for the privilege of using several lines in his forthcoming song, "This Is the Time," asking him to please fill out the enclosed form in order to receive royalties.)

Though one might have expected the early loss of her talented father to lend Claire's childhood a distinguishing character—a mantle of palpable sadness, the dignity of genteel poverty, the rebellious rage of early abandonment, the burden of unresolved grief, the nightmare of a mother turned neglectful by dint of her own emotional trauma—

the rule of unremarkability was enforced within the fatherless rooms of their Tudor-style apartment.

The childhood Claire's mother created for her daughter was neither tragic nor happy, neither privileged nor disadvantaged. Instead, Claire's formative years were utterly average and forgettable, safe by virtue of their sameness, pleasant owing to the amenities and manicured lawns of their high-tax-bracket town, predictable due to the lack of adventure, devoid of cultural or intellectual content, presided over by Claire's widowed young mother, a librarian bereft of even the slightest literary ambition.

It was the Great Neck Public Library—her mother's employer—that saved Claire. Better than any supermarket or mall on the planet, the library sold redemption.

It was a monument to the idea that the mind was its own place.

It was within the commodious rooms of the town's library that Claire nurtured her dreams of transcendence through the books she read while her mother worked the late shift for the considerable overtime pay. The Great Neck Public Library, with its well-stocked shelves, comfortable chairs, and child-friendly décor, was Claire's alma mater, her *maman*, the mothership that patiently waited at the end of every school day in order to whisk her away from the alien landscape of Long Island.

And now she was being whisked away to Paris!

Claire had a great deal invested in Paris. She was banking on the city to bring out her cheekbones, to give new depth to her gaze, to instill her with a sense of knowing. This trip would rid her, she hoped, of her Long Island pedigree, and create a chasm between her upbringing and the life she knew she was destined to lead. And then, together with Byron, the most marvelously sophisticated man she knew, she could transcend her conventional childhood, supplement the years of misguided education, and become her best and truest self.

Now, on the morning of her eighth day in Paris, having ruined her brand-new ballerina flats splashing through the abundant puddles along the Place de Clichy and having had a huge blowout with Byron the night before, Claire felt her fantasies washing away in a torrent of disgust and disappointment.

Instead of an umbrella, Claire opted for her battered yet beloved Barnard baseball cap that morning, beneath which she shoved her hair. Unwashed hair, that is, having woken up too late (according to Byron's schedule) to shower. Their fight from the previous night had been unresolved and Claire was uncertain whether or not they were still at war. It was the worst fight they had had yet. As they got dressed, she was quiet and watchful, deciding to take her cues from her husband.

But Byron's memory slate seemed to have been wiped clean or else he had benevolently forgiven her. Rushing out of their borrowed flat, he was neither contrite nor contentious, simply his regular impatient, demanding, annoyed-to-be-running-behind-schedule self.

Now, after an hour of trudging through Montmartre's downpour, Claire's cardigan had fused with her t-shirt, which had bonded with her bra. Her capri pants clung to her like a second skin. The expanse of the lower leg left exposed by the pants was chilled and damp.

The unique misery of this moment impressed itself upon Claire.

Striding an impatient body length ahead of her, Byron seemed utterly unperturbed by the wicked weather, his own shoes (Mephisto) aggravatingly unmarred by the rain, his posture unbowed, his glare authoritative. Even on foreign soil, Byron Wasserman looked every inch the editor whose job and life calling it was to oversee the metropolitan New York news desk for the world's most important newspaper.

For possibly the one-millionth time in ten days, Claire considered Byron's broad-shouldered back with unabashed awe. *Byron Wasserman.* First he was her editor, then her secret lover, and now her new husband.

It worked like a drug. The satisfaction of this remarkable achievement obliterated Claire's misery, causing even the painful memory of their previous evening's fight to evaporate.

"Claire!" Byron stopped suddenly, causing his new bride to practically collide with him. "This is getting tiresome. Let's find a café and wait until the rain stops."

Like a prisoner offered a break during a forced march, Claire embraced the idea cautiously. On the one hand, being liberated from the soggy streets of Montmartre was a good thing; on the other, she was still wired from the two cappuccinos she had had about an hour ago at the café outside of Sacre Coeur. Nor (despite her misery) did she actually want to stop propelling herself forward through Paris; there was just one more day left and too much she hadn't yet seen.

As a matter of fact, she had thought to suggest to Byron that they jump on the Metro at Pigalle and ride it down to the modern art museum at the Centre Georges Pompidou, a risky proposition in the face of Byron's refusal, only two days earlier, to see the collection because the building was such an "architectural abomination."

"Coffee?" she repeated as if Byron had said *Uranium.* His eyes narrowed. *Uh-oh,* she thought…*I'm doing it again.* Just yesterday Byron had pointed out to Claire that instead of answering questions directly, she often repeated them aloud, a habit which might lead the unsuspecting to conclude that she was mentally impaired when she was just, in fact, buying time to consider a proper answer. Byron understood this completely. The problem, he explained, was that others might not.

Claire forced herself into a declarative mode. "Actually, I'm not in the mood to sit down," she said, surprising herself for her mother had trained her to agree with anything her boyfriends or husband might say, which is why she often repeated questions in the first place. "I'll end up having another coffee, which I don't want, or having a brioche and then my appetite will be ruined for lunch. It *is* horrible outside. Let's take the Metro to…"

Something across the street had caught her attention.

"Musee de L'Erotisme," Claire read aloud. Amid the lurid billboards and screaming marquees of Paris's seediest neighborhood, the façade of the museum was decidedly modest. And while Claire could not even be cajoled to attend a revue at the famous Moulin Rouge, the prospect of visiting an erotica museum during daylight hours seemed suddenly quaint, inviting, irresistible.

"Let's go?" She turned to her husband, prepared to engage in a protracted negotiation. Really, after he had a hissy fit in Les Halles over the Museum of Modern Art, he had to demonstrate some flexibility. *Compromise,* her mother had advised her. "Marriage is all about compromise," she said, even if what she really meant was that Claire should capitulate completely to her husband and compromise her own beliefs and desires in the name of marital peace and harmony.

Cautiously, Claire looked up at her husband, all six feet and two inches of him. She was prepared to face the Wall of Byron, her private term for Byron's stubborn resistance to almost everything she suggested and was therefore completely unprepared for the look of amusement on his movie-star face.

"Okay," he assented, looking down at her with a lopsided grin. "Let's go," he said, looping his arm in hers and setting out across the Place de Clichy.

After an hour of trudging through the chilly rain, merely being indoors evoked a delicious feeling in Claire, akin to wrapping oneself in a towel straight out of the dryer. A rash of goose bumps broke out

all over her body as the warmth of the Musee de L'Erotisme insinu-
ated itself between Claire's skin and her wet clothes. A not-young, not-
thin woman squeezed into a French maid's uniform handed Byron and
Claire what looked like large white dinner napkins.

"*Merci*," Claire murmured, shaking out her damp hair from underneath her baseball cap and patting it dry with the cloth.

"Well!" proclaimed Byron, looking expectantly around himself.
He held the napkin folded over in his hands, looking like a restaurant
patron who had become separated from his dining party. He stood,
with Claire, at the entrance of the museum. Ahead of them, through
the narrow turnstile, lay the exhibit area. The space seemed smallish
and a bit under-lit. Ancient, or pseudo-ancient, statues bearing oversized phalluses lingered on shelves to their right. A small gift shop was
positioned to their left. A sign on the visitor's desk promised seven stories of erotic artifacts and history.

An aged Joan Jett look-alike took their admission fees and waved
them through the turnstile. Claire giggled as she tripped over her
waterlogged shoes. The museum was sparsely filled at that hour—a
couple of lecherous Eastern-European men feigning academic interest in the sexual artifacts, a group of college girls, evidently British,
laughing at the fact that they were together in a sex museum, and a tall,
attractive American couple, possibly newlyweds, peering intently at
the displays while holding hands.

Claire and Byron stood before a mirrored case that contained an
Oriental vase decorated with scenes from an orgy. Beyond the vase,
Claire caught her reflection. With her tousled hair and damp clothes
hanging limply on her slender frame, Claire seemed smaller and even
younger than her twenty-five years. She was also exceedingly pale,
with her round eyes peering out of her face in a manner suggestive of a
Save the Children magazine ad.

Standing beside her dressed in a silk summer tweed jacket, with his healthy head of (prematurely) salt-and-pepper hair offsetting his summer tan, Byron looked like her benefactor, the kindly foreign gentleman who was her sponsor and who had her pathetic snapshot on his large American refrigerator.

The voices were low and murmuring inside the museum and Claire found herself drawn away from the mirrored case toward the interior of the room, drifting on a current of well-being. With seven stories to meander through, she felt fairly reassured that she was safe from the Parisian rain for at least an hour. Besides, even if the collection turned out to be low-brow—or downright pornographic—Byron would not be totally bored because, let's face it, sex was sexy.

The back wall of the first floor held little statuettes and figurines of couples or groups of people engaged in sexual acts. Claire was amazed to find carved-wood depictions of ménage-a-trois, especially those depicting oral sex. This seemed rather advanced for primitive society. Wasn't oral sex illegal until the twentieth century? She turned to ask Byron, who was reading the placard in front of a tapestry depicting Leda and the Swan when her question was intercepted by the shrill ring of his BlackBerry.

"Wasserman here."

There it was, the voice of authority, the editor whom everyone wanted to please, the It Guy, the man whom she had married. Byron's richly nuanced voice filled the space and made the museum's patrons stop and listen.

Instantly, the lady in the French maid uniform appeared to pantomime to Byron that he must not speak on his mobile within the museum. Holding the BlackBerry to his ear, he pantomimed back that he understood perfectly and began walking toward the front of the museum, depositing himself outside of the gift shop. Catching Claire's eye, he held up his right hand, fingers spread apart. Five minutes. That was all he needed.

Claire, ever-compromising, nodded back. *No problem at all.*

Turning back to the erotic artifacts of antiquity from Africa, Asia, Mexico, and some civilization that no longer existed, Claire found herself standing side-by-side with the tall American couple. They were exceptionally fit and attractive, well-dressed, and beaming with health. The man was the tallest Asian male she had ever seen, the woman was blond and shared her fair coloring and turned-up nose. They appeared to be the same age—early thirties. She guessed that the man was a stockbroker or did something with finance; the women struck her as a kindergarten teacher. They probably came from a place like Detroit or Cleveland or perhaps Rochester, New York, where acting friendly was not passé.

The woman caught Claire's eye and smiled. Her teeth were perfectly white and straight. Her eyes were as warm as cocoa. Claire smiled back, perhaps too eagerly. She felt small and pathetic, like an abandoned child or puppy. Take me home, she felt like whimpering. I want to sit in your lap and have you read me bedtime stories.

"There's a hostage situation on the East Side at the Barnes & Noble on 86th Street."

Byron appeared suddenly at her side, speaking in urgent, low tones, nearly making her jump. "A security guard was shot. The gunman is in the children's section right now. It's a hot day. The place is packed with kids."

Byron was a study in contained energy. He held his BlackBerry in his right hand and a flyer from the museum in his left. Claire saw the handwriting on the flyer; Byron had used it to take notes during his phone call. She could hear the sound of his blood coursing through his strong veins, tasted his excitement, saw in his eyes the to-do list he was already composing, the set of orders he would be giving his deputy editor sitting in New York.

"Listen, we've got to get back to the flat right away." Where his laptop was. Byron was jangling Euros in his pocket. They would hail a cab along the Place de Clichy. Without traffic, the trip should take about fifteen minutes. Maybe ten. Byron's head was like a GPS, tracking the reporters his deputy had dispatched to cover the story. He needed to get back to his central command post right away.

The 86th Street Barnes & Noble. Claire knew that store. She envisioned wide-eyed tots sitting in the laps of terrified nannies and parents, cashiers crying, police vans parked along Lexington Avenue, cops talking urgently on walkie-talkies, customers fleeing the ground level of the store, camera crews setting up along 87th Street, television reporters giving terse updates to viewers, the eyes of the world trained on the Upper East Side of Manhattan.

On a sultry summer day, menace invades the inviolable kingdom of Clifford and Babar and Curious George and Madeline. Claire felt her chest constrict in empathy. Poor kids. Poor grown-ups.

Byron stared at Claire. She smelled his impatience. They should already be inside the cab. He should already be communicating through the blue/white screen of his laptop back at their borrowed flat along the Rive Gauche. But she was slow, slow as molasses, keeping him waiting, holding him up.

Outside. The rain. Claire shuddered. To head into that chilly downpour again... In an instant, Claire saw herself sprawled uselessly on the massive bed in the preposterously ornate master bedroom belonging to Byron's friend Lisette, a former lover, attempting (for the millionth time) to read Michel Houellebecq while her husband masterfully commanded the reporting of the New York hostage story from his Parisian post at Lisette's dining room table, his mighty voice booming throughout the flat, making her feel small and suburban and stupid and doomed for obscurity.

"Umm, I think I'd better stay here," she said, aiming for a tone of mature decisiveness instead of the childish trepidation she felt. Byron stared at her as if she were something he had never seen before and didn't particularly like. She attempted a brave smile. "You go ahead. Don't worry about..."

But he had already turned, a looming wave that suddenly reversed its course. One moment he was there and the next, gone.

Stupefied, Claire stood alone, her mouth slightly agape.

"On the eighth day of her honeymoon, Claire Seltzer sent her newlywed husband back to their borrowed Rive Gauche flat, opting to stay on at the Musee de' L'Erotisme by herself," Claire silently self-narrated, climbing the stairs to the museum's second floor. "Just moments earlier, their idyllic honeymoon in Paris was interrupted by an urgent call from Byron Wasserman's deputy editor at the *New York Times*—where Mr. Wasserman served as the paper's legendary Metro editor—detailing a hostage situation on Manhattan's Upper East Side. A newspaperman through and through, Mr. Wasserman decided to put their private trip on hold in order to oversee the coverage of the story from the other side of the Atlantic. Though it had been assumed that Ms. Seltzer would go with Mr. Wasserman in order to provide wifely support during his ordeal as long-distance editor, Ms. Seltzer stunned her husband by failing to follow him home."

I just sent my husband away, she thought. Claire marveled at her own moxie. Climbing the stairs, her knees felt wobbly with nervousness. She giggled, then stopped abruptly, looking around to make sure that no one had seen her, the loose-limbed, pretty American girl who was married to the well-known man whose editorial mastery was so indispensable that he had to be contacted in the midst of his honeymoon.

"Why are you taking so long?"

It was the previous night. Claire had her foot propped up on the edge of the sink in Lisette's apartment, fitting her diaphragm in place. In it popped...and then, just a quick wipe of the contraceptive jelly and she was ready to join her new husband in bed. "Just getting ready," Claire called over the rushing water of the sink. Rubbing her fingers together under the running water to get rid of the sticky salve, she hastily dried them on Lisette's Egyptian cotton towels and scurried out of the bathroom.

Byron was sitting up in bed, the bed sheet resting just below his navel. His skin still shone from his recent shower. His stomach was completely tight. The smell of Acqua di Gio, his cologne, filled the room, making her nose tickle. "What took you so long?" he demanded of his new wife, who approached the bed naked but for her diaphragm.

What do you think? Claire wanted to say. Instead, she repeated, "Getting ready," as she sat down at the foot of the bed.

Byron's brow darkened. "Getting ready to *not* have a baby?" he asked, sitting up slightly. His muscled shoulders appeared suddenly menacing in the low lights of Lisette's bedroom. Claire detected the hint of a sneer. She curved her body forward, drawing her knees to her chest. Her brow furrowed. Was this a trick question?

"Getting ready to *not* have a baby?" The counter-question just popped out. She couldn't control it. Her grip tightened around her knees.

Byron's eyes flashed lightning. Claire felt pierced by his rage yet utterly confused. He had showered and then she had showered. She put in her diaphragm because they were going to make love. This was their honeymoon. She wasn't sure what she had done wrong.

"Well?" he demanded, arms crossed against his pectorals. She found it hard to hold his gaze. He was angry. He was half-naked yet powerful while she was completely exposed, pale, and powerless.

How did that happen?

"Byron..." she tried, licking her lips. Byron was a dangerous dog and she was negotiating for her safe passage. "I don't know what you are upset about. What did I do wrong?"

Byron fixed her with a look of incredulity. It quite took Claire's breath away. "What did you do *wrong?*" he cried. "What did you do *wrong?*" He leaned in toward her and she resisted her impulse to lean backward, away from him. "What *didn't* you do wrong is more like it!"

"What?" she asked dumbly. This conversation was out of a nightmare. She didn't understand a word of it.

"'*What?*'" he mimicked. "Do you not understand the *first thing* about me?" He was nearly shouting. Claire's mouth fell open. What was going on? What terrible thing did she do to Byron that betrayed the fact that she didn't understand him?

Quick, she urged herself. What was the most important thing for Byron? Cleanliness! Did she leave dishes in the sink? Did she pee on the toilet seat? Did she fail to make the bed every day? What else? Punctuality! Was she late? Did she take too long in the shower? Did she make him wait too long in the lobby yesterday while she went to the bathroom? Artistic appreciation! Was he angry that she wanted to see the modern art collection? Did she do something disgusting? Did she talk in her sleep? Did she fart unawares? Did she order too much yesterday at dinner? Did she chew with her mouth open, talk with her mouth full, use the wrong fork?

What, what, *what* did she fail to do right for her new husband?

"Don't try to bullshit me, Claire. I know you put the diaphragm in," he said, leaning back against the pillows. Claire's heart sank. *That* was the issue? The small latex device folded inside *her* vagina was the reason for Byron's belligerence? A flame of indignation flared within her.

"So?" she said coolly, unfolding her legs, allowing them to stretch out before her on the bed. She hoped she flashed him while maneuvering her legs, giving him a glimpse of The Vagina that Harbored the Forbidden Diaphragm.

I know you put the diaphragm in. She couldn't believe it. Byron came of age in the era of *Our Bodies, Ourselves.* He told her the heartbreaking tale of how he took Lisette for an abortion in New York about ten years ago, how difficult it was for her the first time they made love after that, how she cried after she came and how he cried too when he came. Claire learned many things from this story, including the fact that Byron was pro-choice…and, by extension, pro-birth control. So, how could they even be having this conversation now? How could they be engaged in a power struggle over her body's reproductive capabilities on their *honeymoon?*

"We've talked about this, Claire," he said in a weary tone, the chastising parent to the repeatedly naughty little girl. "I *am* forty years old, you know. I don't want to wait forever to have children."

Claire stared at Byron. During their engagement he had spoken of his eagerness to have children. Despite her youth, Claire had felt a wave of compassion toward him. Forty *was* kind of old to start having children; she knew that most of his friends had kids in grade school and he would be in his fifties at the very earliest before their children were even that age.

Yes, she knew that Byron wanted to have children but she had no idea that their honeymoon in Paris was the designated date for conceiving their first child. How could Byron expect her, at twenty-five, at the start of her career, to devote herself to motherhood? He didn't have a child at her age! How could he be so completely self-centered?

"Byron…" she tried again. His face was impassive. "Don't you think I'm kind of *young* to have a kid? At my age, you didn't…"

"Shut up!" he shouted suddenly, getting out of bed. "Who the hell cares what I did when I was your age? I'm not your age! I'm forty years old! It's time for *me* to have a child!"

Time for him to have a child? The question ricocheted inside Claire's own head, sparing him the annoyance of being given voice. Something was wrong here.

Byron had thrown back the bed sheets, stalked out of the bedroom and could be heard stomping around Lisette's apartment. Claire could not believe it. Was *Byron Wasserman* throwing a tantrum? Was he really that spoiled? If he wanted a child so badly, why did he allow Lisette to destroy their baby?

And what the hell were they doing in Lisette's apartment anyway... on their honeymoon? It was a bit gauche for Byron to have his new wife sleep in his ex-lover's bed, *n'est pas?* What was wrong with a hotel?

And why couldn't they have a normal wedding, like most people, with a party and a nice big cake?

Claire got out of bed. She pulled on the shorts and tank top that she had carefully folded on the upholstered stool in Lisette's bathroom. She turned on the water and splashed her face a few times, then brushed her teeth so vigorously that her gums bled.

On the second floor of the Museum of Eroticism, there was a circular bank of video monitors with folding chairs. The British girls were huddled in front of one monitor, watching with rapt attention until suddenly, they all fell out with groans and exclamations and peals of laughter. Another monitor held the attention of the honeymooning (Claire was now sure they were because they never dropped hands) American couple, who watched politely—and without comment—the drama before them, which was a turn-of-the-century porn film featuring a maid, a butler, and the mistress of the house.

Claire stood watching the film over the shoulders of the seated couple. The mistress and maid (both unappealingly fat) were making out with comically exaggerated gestures, then suddenly, the maid's head swooped low and she began licking her mistress's exposed bosom.

It was awkward, to say the least, for Claire to stand alone, watching this retro version of *Girls Gone Wild*, but she also didn't want to up and leave suddenly because that would seem prudish. Committed to proving her sophistication, she stood, immobile, watching with increasing embarrassment as the maid's tongue worked lower and lower until she had her mistress's fat legs splayed wide apart.

Claire was in complete shock. She never imagined that lesbian pornography could have existed over a century ago! She wondered what Byron would have thought of this film. One of the things he was smitten with was her thinness. Despite the repulsive bodies of the two actresses, it was pretty well known that men loved to watch women make love. Might Byron have found this a turn-on? Amusing? Culturally fascinating?

When a man, dressed in butler clothes, intruded on the scene, Claire stole away. Glancing behind her, she was astonished to see the newlywed couple, as clean-cut as Christian youth, sitting straight-backed and perfectly composed, watching this *fin de siecle* skin flick just as innocently as one might view, say, *The Sound of Music*.

Having left the movies, Claire wasn't sure where to go. The walls of this floor were filled with graphic photographs and canvases from the twentieth century. Some were tasteful, like the photographs of Josephine Baker; others were obscure, like an impressionistic orgy scene; others were raw or Warholian, stylized, removed from eroticism or even beauty, containing sadomasochistic scenarios.

Claire walked up to the third floor. The air was increasingly warm. By now, her thin clothes were completely dry and her hair fell loosely around her face, no longer weighted by water. She sighed deeply, felt enveloped by physical well-being and comfort. It was blessedly quiet on the third floor and the buzz of empty space made her suddenly sleepy. She fought the urge to lie down on the floor and go to sleep.

"Daddy?"

It was a Saturday night in November and four-year-old Claire was sprawled on her stomach, drawing a picture on the living room floor of her grandparents' house in Little Neck. In the room next door, at the dining room table, Arthur Seltzer was deep in conversation with her grandparents. Their voices were low and muted. Serious. Mommy had just come out of the hospital and was resting at home. The baby in her tummy went away. Everyone was sad.

With a pink crayon, Claire drew three large circle faces—her grandma, her grandpa, and her daddy. With a black crayon, she added eyes, noses, ears, and hair. With a red crayon, she drew large frowns. She imagined showing this picture to her teacher at school. "Because the baby went away, the grown-ups were very sad," she would explain.

Since her mother came home from the hospital on Thursday, Claire had been with her father the entire time. On Friday, he took her into his office in New York City and she played quietly with her Polly Pocket dolls, drew pictures, and watched *Cinderella* in a big room with a TV set and a video machine. Her dad's secretary, Amy, was really nice to her and got her pizza for lunch with a bag of M&M's.

On Saturday, which they called Shabbos, Claire went to synagogue with her daddy and lots of people came up to them, making her feel kind of famous. Everyone seemed to be sad. The president of their synagogue, Mr. Weiss, who was also the candy man, gave her an extra lollipop.

Then, at night, after Shabbos was over, her daddy took her to visit Grandma Mimi and Grandpa Sam and that's where they were now.

Claire was especially excited to see Uncle Theo, who was home from college because it was vacation. Uncle Theo was a lot younger than her daddy; she forgot how much, but it was a lot, maybe ten years. Uncle Theo was an artist. His room was on the top of the house, in the attic. He was up there right now, listening to music.

Clutching her completed picture in hand, Claire set off to show her artwork to Uncle Theo.

Claire climbed the stairs to the second floor, where Grandma and Grandpa's bedroom was and where Daddy's bedroom had been when he was little. Then she climbed the stairs to the third-floor attic that did not have carpeting on them, like the other stairs did. There was loud music in Uncle Theo's room and he was lying on his bed, under his blanket, with his eyes closed. There were pictures he had made all over his wall. Most of them were of naked ladies.

Claire stood in the doorway of Uncle Theo's room, holding her picture in her hand. She wanted to show it to him, but it looked like he was sleeping, though it also looked like he was scratching himself under the blanket. Claire wondered how he could sleep with such loud music. Then, his face started changing, like he was having a bad dream or something was hurting him. He was making a sound like he banged his knee. His head moved from side to side, then his mouth opened up really wide. Claire's heart beat quickly. Maybe he had heard her! Maybe she was waking Uncle Theo up!

As quiet as a mouse, Claire turned and tiptoed out of the room. Then she went hopping like a bunny rabbit down the attic steps to find her daddy, who had promised to take her out for Carvel for a vanilla cone with chocolate sprinkles.

The third floor was dedicated to genitalia. There were penises everywhere: ridiculous penises, obscene penises, weapon-like penises, and vulvas, too: inventive vulvas, tunnel vulvas, cartoon vulvas, terrifying vulvas. Claire could not imagine walking through this display of private parts with Byron. She wondered how long it took the museum staff to become completely immune to the shock value of these artifacts.

A montage on the wall along the staircase leading from the third to the fourth floor featured, among other things, stills from the film *Fritz the Cat*. Claire stared at the pictures, her mouth falling open. So this was *Fritz the Cat*. Last winter, about a month after they started sleeping together, she and Byron had gone to a cocktail party at the Reuters building to celebrate the publication of Anna Lewisohn's new collection of essays on kitsch culture. Even by a conservative estimate, Claire was at least ten years younger than everyone in attendance.

The subject of the conversation was Anna's chapter on kitsch porn and someone mentioned *Fritz the Cat*.

"*Fritz the Cat*!" Don Walters had exclaimed, groaning loudly and covering his face with his hands. He was the straight-as-an-arrow *Science Times* editor. "I got kicked out of Camp Raquette Lake because of *Fritz the Cat*!"

"What exactly would Fritz have to do with you getting kicked out of camp?" It was the trademark honey drawl of Lucy MacNeil, an acid-penned Metro columnist for the *New York Post* whose tall, mannish frame was topped with an impressive bouffant of Lucille Ball–like hair.

Don was laughing without sound at the memory of his *Fritz the Cat* misadventure, wiping tears from his eyes. His shoulders shook and he held up his hand, requesting a moment to compose himself. Watching the normally sober science editor dissolve in helpless hilarity, his colleagues could not help but laugh themselves. Even Claire found herself giggling, her drink splashing slightly onto Byron's right shoe in the process, causing him to shake his foot violently and move several inches away from her.

"Okay," Don said, clearing his throat. "I was the director of the basketball program that summer—I think I was twenty-two—and my friend Mitch, the head of the kitchen, found out that *Fritz the Cat* was playing in town, a midnight showing at one of the small art houses. The problem was me and Mitch and Ted, the tennis director, were supposed to be on night watch duty that night, because half the senior staff was away at an inter-camp competition, including the camp director. So, we bribed a couple of junior counselors and off we went. We figured that, worse comes to worse, we'll do the shift from, say, 3:00 a.m. to the morning. And no one would ever know! The only problem was the camp director was sitting two rows in back of us!"

Everyone exploded with laughter.

"What kinda camp director goes to porn movies?" demanded Marilyn Mirsky, an editor on the culture desk of the *Times*. "I sure as hell wouldn't want my grandkids going to that camp!" She was a fierce, no-nonsense woman with a salt-and-pepper bob and not an ounce of body fat. She turned suddenly toward Claire. "Hey, you probably weren't even born when *Fritz the Cat* came out!" The statement sounded like an accusation and Claire felt guilty as charged.

All eyes were upon her. Until this conversation, Claire had never heard of *Fritz the Cat*. Standing in an intimate circle with the media elite, she was about to be exposed as a poseur, or worse, a hanger-on. Obviously, a vital piece of American culture had passed her by. Obviously, she was the only person at this cocktail party who was so completely out of the loop.

Youth is power. Beauty is power.

It was a line from a poster Claire had made for a women's studies retreat when she was a first-year student at Barnard, a poster intending to mock the messages manufactured by the mass media, a project so shallow that she couldn't believe anyone might take it seriously. Yet two hundred young women (or womyn) did. She had displayed it in the conference room at the retreat center in Harriman, New York, and then danced barefoot with her sisters to African drums beaten by privileged black girls in protest of the shallow values of contemporary culture.

In a flash, the words from her former life appeared in boldface in her mind's eye: Youth is power. Beauty is power.

Marilyn's thin nose quivered as she awaited Claire's response. Up close, Claire could see that her mouth was puckered with vertical wrinkles. Remnants of her morning application of eyeliner gathered in the inner corners of her wary, watery editor's eyes, which were incarcerated behind wire-rimmed glasses. Claire decided to believe in the message she had scrawled on a poster board a lifetime ago. She would not be intimidated. She was not a philistine because she had no idea what *Fritz the Cat* was.

She, twenty-four-year-old Claire Seltzer from Great Neck, graduate of Barnard, junior reporter on the Metro desk of the *New York Times*, was powerful because she was young and beautiful.

Not to mention, the secret lover of Byron Wasserman.

"I was born in 1980," she replied.

Ed Wicks, the barrel-waisted editor of the sports section of the *Daily News* let out a whistle. He gazed at Claire hungrily, as if she were a bean burrito. "To be able to utter the words, 'I was born in 1980.'" He sighed.

"Face it," Byron told Marilyn. "You were squeezing out your youngest kid in 1980."

Marilyn stared at Byron, addressing him directly. "Claire is *twenty-four*?" As if she wasn't there.

"Almost twenty-five," piped up Claire, whose birthday was coming up in December. She flushed deeply, feeling approximately twelve years old, a little girl in her shiny Mary Janes and party dress, allowed to stay up to meet her parents' friends at their New Year's party.

"Shocking, isn't it?" Byron grinned boyishly, disarmingly, triumphantly, tilting his vodka and tonic back, emptying the glass.

The comic book panels for *Fritz the Cat* were displayed behind panes of glass at the Museum of Eroticism—Garfield's smutty older brother, a slovenly cat sitting on a couch with a female cat, leering lasciviously at her, his paw down her blouse. Big deal, thought Claire, breezing past the cartoons.

"On her honeymoon to Paris, Claire Seltzer finally learned the true meaning of *Fritz the Cat*," Claire narrated silently to herself, one year later, passing the comic book–style panels along the wall of the staircase, descending higher in the Museum of Eroticism, eager to discover what other revelations lay in store for her.

She picked up his scent before she saw him.

He had a good smell, of youth and energy, of leather and fresh sweat and vanilla. His was a distinct scent, comforting with its undertones of cigarette smoke and freshly laundered sheets, perfumed with longing and restless dreams. Climbing to the top floor, Claire hadn't heard footsteps behind her, yet now she felt his breath upon her neck. His scent was all around her, seeping into her hair, her mouth, her skin. Instead of feeling afraid, Claire closed her eyes and contemplated falling backward.

As she reached the top of the staircase, Claire turned around.

A young man, naked, but for a pair of black leather bikini briefs, a black leather corset, and a pair of combat boots, stood opposite her, two steps below the landing. Owing to this asymmetry, their eyes were completely level with one another. His hair was thick, dark, and wavy and his skin was smooth, nearly hairless. He wore a black mask over his eyes, Lone Ranger–style. The mask looked silly. Claire began to giggle.

Behind his mask, the man's eyes narrowed. Claire put her hand to her mouth. She didn't mean to insult him. His lips were full and ruby-red. The front of his briefs were laced. Above the briefs, a trail of dark hair ran from the man's navel downward. What was he doing dressed up like this? Was he an employee of the museum or a patron? Could he be a male prostitute?

"You laugh at me?"

The man spoke. Claire was startled. Speech seemed incongruous with his get-up. His voice was lovely—French-scented and husky. Behind his mask, his eyes were as dark as the bittersweet Callebaut chocolate drops she liked to buy at Fairway in New York. Before she could think about what she was doing, Claire reached up and untied the man's mask, pulling the satin string that hung down the back of his neck.

The cloth mask fell lightly onto the floor. Claire watched it fall. Then she lifted her eyes to the man's naked face. And felt her breath comes in shallow spurts as she beheld his beauty.

He was young, possibly her age. Any hint of menace fell away with his mask. His rich coloring hinted of Spanish ancestry, or perhaps Persian descent. There was something of the aristocrat and the mama's boy about him; he seemed nurtured, sensual, possibly even spoiled. It was easy to envision him curled up on his mother's lap, an adored child, sipping hot cocoa, listening to a bedtime tale. His posture was impeccable. His teeth were straight and white.

"I laugh at you?" Claire repeated his question back at him. He looked at her intently, his eyes serious and watchful. She saw herself in his dark gaze and caught the waif in black clothes reflected back in his midnight eyes. His shoulders were strong and fleshy; he was not as muscular as Byron but Claire found his body infinitely more inviting.

She shook her head. "No, I'm not laughing at you." She could not tear herself away from his eyes. She was falling into them. His skin was the color of burnt toffee. She saw his chest rise and fall beneath the laced leather corset he wore. Silky strands of black hair peered out from under his arms. A million questions danced on the tip of her tongue.

The young man looked at her inquisitively. He swept a lock of errant hair off of her face, traced the outline of her lips with his index finger. Claire closed her eyes. Soft, full lips pressed themselves to her mouth. He tasted of raspberries and cream and coffee. Claire fell into him, breathing him in, pressing her chest into his, grabbing onto his splendid shoulders. His hands were on her back, stroking her hair and the back of her neck. She opened her mouth and kissed him deeply. Small sounds were coming from the back of her throat, a song of sorrow and desire. She wanted to lick his vanilla toffee skin, taste his mouth forever.

Byron!

Claire's eyes flew open abruptly. What on *earth* was she doing?

"Married for only two months, Claire Seltzer found herself seduced by a strange man on her honeymoon in Paris. While her husband, Byron Wasserman, editor of the..."

"You come with me?"

Halting in the middle of her self-narration, Claire found herself gazing, panic-stricken, into bittersweet chocolate eyes, now molten. An eyebrow was raised in inquiry. Her thoughts flew in a flurry.

In front of her, in the stairwell of the Museum of Eroticism, stood a strange young man, half-naked, wearing a ridiculous outfit of black leather. Outside, she could hear the rain pelting the Place de Clichy, drowning the city of Paris. It was the eighth day of her honeymoon. She was alone in Montmartre. Her well-known husband was working out of the borrowed flat of his former lover, directing an editorial team in New York on what was sure to become the story of the summer. The coverage would likely earn him journalism's top prize. It would be one more badge of his extreme success, like the pretty young wife he had plucked from the junior staff of the *New York Times* and the child he was determined to make with her, as soon as possible.

Byron Wasserman's bride stood poised like a ballerina in first position on the landing of the topmost floor of the Musee de' L'Erotisme in Paris. The scent of vanilla toffee rose from the skin of her anonymous suitor. His lips were parted; his raspberry-coffee breath intoxicated and inflamed her. He held his head at a rakish, irresistible angle. His hands were poetry; his body was a Grecian urn.

The thought of her husband evaporated from her mind as suddenly as it had appeared. The unseen presence that winds and weaves its way through the streets and boulevards of Paris wrapped itself around her, drawing out her sorrow, converting it into art. A million songs flowed out of her heart; dozens of dances lifted lightly off her skin, framed pictures and skillful sculptures filled the marble hallways of her limbs. Her body became a museum. Warm, strong arms drew her into an embrace, lifting her, carrying her down the hall. Claire Seltzer closed her eyes and clung to the leather-bound stranger as if her life depended upon it.

TWO WRITERS

"EVERYTHING IS INTENSE FOR YOU. You never have a low-intensity day, do you? Things are magnified, larger than life, over the top. I'm not that way. I'm a writer. I sit in a room alone with my thoughts, weighing words. You are outward-oriented. You need to be filled up...you have a tremendous need to be filled. It is visible in your eyes and in your mouth. You have a rapacious mouth. You have a bottomless hunger."

It is late at night and they are both on their cell phones. He is in Boston, where it is substantially colder than New York. Imagining him there, she gets a Christmas feeling though it is only October—the comfort of wearing layers of warm clothes, wools against one's skin. Her Manhattan apartment is overheated and she is lying in bed wearing a white camisole and a pair of black underpants. They are from Victoria's Secret, part of her most recent anniversary gift from her husband, marking eighteen years. To say that the underwear is sexy is redundant. She dressed in preparation for his phone call, but it is not going as she planned.

"You're a writer... that's why you're *not* intense? Since when are writers known for their *lack* of intensity?" There is an edge in her voice. "*Number one*, you *are* intense, so stop pretending that you are a mellow, even-keeled person. *Number two*, in case you have forgotten, I am *also* a writer. I know that I'm not as famous or published as you are, but that's what I am. We're two writers."

Even if he is in denial about himself, even if he insists upon creating a barrier between them, what he says about her is true. Everything she craves is intense—hiking at high altitudes, surfing at daybreak, double espressos, psychosexual thrillers, Leonard Cohen, David Byrne, David Lynch, Pink Floyd, high boots, Dali, Picasso, Magritte, Nabokov, Amis, Hemingway, Nin, Mahler, Mozart, Hitchcock, Bunuel, Arbus, bittersweet chocolate, Irish cheddar, sour lemon candies, Kalamata olives, garlic, all-nighters, steam baths, loofah massage, acupuncture, fever, simultaneous orgasm, Rome, Paris, Venice, Cairo, Jerusalem, Barcelona, Amsterdam, New York, running until your lungs burn, dancing to the Doors, to the Stones, to Madonna, dreams that leave you gasping, dreams that leave you drenched in sweat, dreams that leave you exhausted.

And writing.

She rolls her eyes to herself in the mirror. This exasperating conversation has happened before in other seasons, in other cities. It's like a dance whose choreography is unvarying; it's like a destiny that she cannot escape; it's like a lyrical theme that winds its way through the concerto of their conversations; it's like the phases of the moon, like a recurring nightmare whose predictability is its most terrifying feature.

She is annoyed because she expects more from him. He's a literary superstar; why is he saying such stupid things? She fumes in silence, waiting for his response.

He doesn't address their shared identity as writers. What he says instead succeeds in pissing her off even further. "Don't read anything into us. You're already writing your epic about us. We are inconsequential. We are nobody in the context of history. And what we have is merely fun."

Fun. As in shopping for shoes. As in trying on makeup at the Chanel counter at Bloomingdale's. As in going dancing with girlfriends. As in getting a manicure. As in watching MTV. She feels a surge of clean, potent anger—remember, she is *intense*.

"Thank you for completely diminishing our—shall we say—relationship. Wait, did I use the wrong word?" She is sitting up now, furious. In the mirror on the opposite wall she sees that her hair is standing on end. The words "fright wig" come to mind. She runs a hand through her hair and shakes her head. "Oh, and by the way, I don't believe that what we have is *merely fun* and that I am just a diversion for you. I'm more than diverting for you and you are more than my plaything."

She stops to take a swig of water from her Poland Spring bottle. Why is he suddenly chastising her? This conversation makes no sense. "In case you've forgotten, let me set you straight—*I* am the married one, not you. *I*, not you, have something to lose. I love my husband and love being married to him. I am not looking to break up my family in order to make you my boyfriend. But I did think that being lovers entailed something more than *fun*." She has a sudden inspiration and seizes on it. "Or maybe I really am your ultimate Zipless Fuck."

He doesn't answer right away. *Score*, she thinks, but her sense of victory is short-lived. How disappointing that even when the boundaries are clearly drawn, even when the prospect of marriage is not even remotely on the horizon, there is no getting around the male-female *mishegoss*.

"Zipless Fuck," he repeats, laughing. "I like that." Non-committal. Avoidant. No wonder he is still single at the age of forty-two. She rolls her eyes again. "Listen." She can tell he is stretching. "I gotta go. My lecture begins at eight and I'm going to be incoherent if I don't get some sleep." The students at Harvard obviously deserve a coherent lecturer more than she deserves a proper response.

"Hmmm." It is maddeningly unresolved. She suddenly misses her husband, the solace of their companionship, the absence of these stupid adolescent-like conversations. When does he get back? Tomorrow night? She needs his dependable rationality right this minute.

She has already pulled herself away from David. *Zipless Fuck*, she thinks. *Well, fuck you.*

"Okay?" he is waiting for absolution. His voice is boyish, singsong.

"Okay, *what?*" She is, at this moment, the quintessential New York bitch, and proud of it.

"Sarah, we're just two people who like to sleep with each other. You know that you are my ideal woman. I worship your body…"

"I *am* my body," she cuts in. "Sorry, but it's a package deal." She is tired now and cranky and without any patience. The sight of herself sprawled on the bed in seductive underwear now mocks her in the mirror. "I find it really irritating that you assume I am running after you, trying to get something more than what you already give me." She suddenly realizes exactly what she is feeling. "I find you insulting."

"I'm sorry," he quickly replies. He is nothing if not a nice guy. He needs to think of himself as a good guy, not a cad. She can practically hear him thinking, *uh-oh…went too far…must retreat.* Knowing how invested he is in his nice guy image, she is hardly mollified by his instantaneous apology. Possible reactions, emotional and practical, present themselves to her. Alone in the dark of her bedroom, they parade across the blank screen of her mind. Her rapacious mouth is compressed.

"Look, it's late. Let's just say goodnight." The anger slips and she feels unaccountably sad. If there is love, or even affection, between them, he is doing his best to stomp it out.

"Goodnight," he says. The line is silent but neither of them has hung up just yet. She feels his presence, hears not merely his breathing but his heartbeat. The memory of his smell suddenly fills her nostrils, making her nearly sick with desire. If this were a conversation with her husband or parents, this is the point where she would say, "Love you." The words hover, unspoken.

"Goodnight," she replies and quickly clicks the red button, beating him to the end of the phone call.

The next day she drives her orange PT Cruiser around the city like a maniac, like a taxi driver on speed, racing other cars to the red light, pulling out before their drivers have had a chance to take their toes off the brake pad, giving everyone the finger, shouting, "Asshole!" to pedestrians. Well, it doesn't take a psychologist to point out the obvious—she is redirecting her anger at David toward innocent civilians. Even her toddler daughter Emily notices the change in her mother. "Mommy is mad!" she exclaims, clapping her hands when Sarah screams, "Motherfucker!" while leaning into the horn for about two minutes after getting cut off by a FedEx truck on West 96th Street.

Her husband returns home in the middle of the day and goes straight to his office, which is at Central Park West and 83rd Street. "Can you come home?" she begs.

He laughs, knowing exactly what she is getting at. "Sorry, sweetie, but I've already missed two days and there is an outbreak of strep. I'll see you around eight." Sarah's husband is Dr. Daniel Reinhart, or Dr. Dan, as every West Side parent and viewer of *Good Morning America* knows.

Dr. Dan—beloved, nationally-renowned pediatrician—had just been at a medical conference in Boston, ironically enough. Two weeks earlier, when Sarah mentioned that her husband would be presenting a paper at this event, David, her maddening lover and literary It-Boy of the moment, half-jokingly threatened to effect a "chance" meeting with Dan while he was in town. But in truth, David had been seriously considering this intriguing possibility and it was only because he was behind on delivering the second half of his new manuscript to his publisher that he didn't make good on his stated desire to meet his lover's husband under seemingly innocent circumstances.

Though David did not place himself in Dan's path, though he was holed up in his Somerville home with unwashed hair and beard growth and increasingly grungy sweatpants, he found himself conscious of Dan's proximity, found that during those three days he had an agitated, hyper-vigilant sense. The entire time that Dan was in Boston, David experienced a marvelous, tingly, magical feeling akin to what children feel on the last day of school.

While Sarah coolly regards the celebrity status of her husband, David obsesses over Dan, religiously watching his segments on *Good Morning America* though it makes him late for faculty meetings, or once, even class, though he has no children of his own. Since the start of the fall semester, David has also taken to Googling Dan every other day or so, checking to see if there is anything new to learn about this popular national personality who happens to be his lover's husband, reading way past the fan pages and *Good Morning America* references, going as far as to read the inane entries on page twenty, for instance, where the web listings have nothing to do with Dan himself, but with random people who have the first name Dan or the last name Reinhart or are about doctors in general, or with mornings or with America.

David's obsession began a year earlier when Sarah casually mentioned that her husband was Dr. Dan. She had been meticulous about keeping any identifying information about her family out of their discussions but when posters for *Good Morning America* began appearing in bus shelters around Manhattan—featuring a larger-than-life photo of Dan cradling a beautiful infant—it seemed appropriate to convey this piece of information to David.

David's reaction was volcanic, jealous, and entirely irrational. "What?!" he had erupted, jumping to his feet, looming over her lying tangled in his bed sheets, sounding, for all the world, like a betrayed husband uncovering proof of his wife's affair. "*Dr. Dan* is your *husband?* Why didn't you tell me sooner?!"

Shocked by his reaction, yet also amused, Sarah failed to understand that David mistook her withholding of this information as a challenge. David decided that Dan was a secret that Sarah had kept from him and became consumed with exploring the dimensions of his revelation. He dove headlong into the task of researching Sarah's husband; Dan became his new sideline, his hobby, his area of amateur expertise.

In the process, David began falling in love.

David now considers himself Dan's unofficial biographer. He has memorized his wardrobe, noting when he repeats a shirt or tie, taking stock of each haircut or a slight change in complexion or weight. He knows Dan's doctorly buzz words and phrases, loves the way he says the words "soothing bath," sometimes mouths his signature sign-off—"This is Dr. Dan wishing you good health on this good American morning" together with him.

Having pored over his bio from the *Good Morning America* website, he knows that Dan went to Columbia undergraduate and Harvard Medical School. He is quite smitten with Dan's fiftyish appeal and admires his blend of confidence, authority, wisdom, and cultural fluency. With his full head of salt-and-pepper hair, slight stoop, square white teeth, twinkling eyes and ruddy complexion, Dan is pleasant to look at, widely regarded as non-threateningly handsome by men and women alike. Watching him on television, David amuses and tortures himself by trying to figure out from Dr. Dan's demeanor how recently he had sex with Sarah.

Once, on a morning when Dan appeared unusually fatigued, David worked himself into a jealous fit by imagining him entangled with Sarah, making love for hours in every possible position. The images of

Dan and Sarah madly copulating would not leave his head. He couldn't concentrate on his work; he was truly tormented. In an effort to distract himself from his obsessive jealousy, David called up two old girlfriends of his who had since gotten married (actually, all of David's exes have since gotten married) and had mildly harassing conversations with them, about which he later fretted.

By mid-day, unable to resist for one more second, David finally called Sarah on her cell phone, catching her at the coffee department at Zabar's (her two pounds of Italian Roast were being ground, fine, for a Melitta filter) and interrogated her about the last time she and Dan had sex, not allowing her to hang up until she talked dirty (whispering, hand over the mouthpiece) to him and he came all over the manuscript he was editing, gasping loudly.

If David is overly aware of Dan, Dan has only a passing familiarity with David's name and work, knows, for instance, that he is a writer of two highly acclaimed short story collections based in New England towns, that he's been compared with Updike. What he wouldn't know is that David has been linked with various high-profile women—a *New York Times* columnist, a star faculty member at Brown, the glamorous twenty-something blond author, the glamorous thirty-something red-headed author, and a Latvian supermodel.

Though Dan hasn't read David's work, he has seen his wife reading his books, twirling her hair, thoroughly absorbed. Were the two men ever to meet, Dan would surely recognize David's face from his author photo.

It's not that Dan wouldn't enjoy David's writing. It's just that due to the extreme busyness of his life, Dan's reading these days has become streamlined, limited chiefly to the *New York Times* and the *Wall Street Journal, Time, The New England Journal of Medicine*, select articles from the *New Yorker* and a smattering of other medical journals, and the odd work of historical fiction.

Though his pediatric practice had consumed his time for the entirety of his marriage, his recent celebrity gig—only two years old— has rendered Dan almost completely unavailable, even to his family, which now consists of Sarah, their sixteen-year-old daughter Daphne, and Emily, their three-year-old. The obvious thing to assume is that Dan's scarce presence on the home front set the stage for Sarah's affair with David, the first in their strong and happy eighteen-year marriage.

Sarah has spent the past two years trying to figure out if this is a valid assumption because she doesn't take lightly what she has done, is shocked, in fact, when in the course of her daily family life she stops to consider that she is committing adultery. The coincidence of David appearing in her life just as Dan's television career took flight does make Sarah wonder if something other than desire dissolved her bond of fidelity.

Yet when David entered her life, she was happy and fulfilled and not fishing for new opportunities for adventure. She and Dan had reg- ular and occasionally steamy sex. After many years, she had recently given birth to a second child, a sister for her spunky thirteen-year- old daughter. Her life was filled with friends, vacations, books, trips to museums, gallery openings, films, theatre, cocktail parties, lectures, rarified dinner invitations, membership in an upscale health club, and intermittent writing. Dan's income provided a wonderful house- keeper, which meant that Sarah was free of many domestic chores and even of the need to spend too much time at home.

Minus the publication of the novel, the collection of short stories or the book of essays, which Sarah had always assumed she would com- plete by the age of forty, her life was charmed and full. David's sudden appearance, however, evoked a reflexive response in her, a unanimous affirmation, an understanding that he was meant to become an essential element in her life and could not be denied entry.

The basis of her relationship with David is a pure and powerful attraction that is elemental, spiritual, and, naturally, sexual. From the minute they first met two autumns ago at an author talk for *Endings and Other Stories* at the 82nd Street and Broadway Barnes & Noble, the pull was undeniable. Their attraction is nearly incestuous, sibling love, the oneness of twins separated at birth.

The day that Sarah and David first met, Sarah had not intended to hear him or any other author; in fact, she was wandering through the fiction section of Barnes & Noble in search of something to replace the work of that tall, handsome Indian writer—she can no longer remember his name now—whose novel was frankly disappointing, especially after all the celebrity hype he had received. Her plan was (after locating her new reading) to pick up a copy of *The Bell Jar* for Daphne and a new *Angelina Ballerina* for Emily, make a pit stop at the Korean shop on 84th for some Rice Dream and Bread Shop granola and then return home.

Removing books from the shelf, Sarah found herself doing something she rarely ever does—selecting new reading material largely on the merit of the author photo. It goes without saying that this method of acquainting oneself with new fiction is completely ridiculous; however, you must have noticed that if an author appears suave or sexy or fashionable or obviously European or simply looks the way one imagines a writer to look, then the book stands a far better chance of being read.

While Sarah felt it was shameful (and therefore crouched while so doing) to gaze so avidly at the author photo, in truth, many prospective readers openly check out the photo on the back jacket of the book before even reading the book's opening paragraph. These days, the author's alluring headshot is a key element in the success of a new writer's book. To deny this is useless.

Meanwhile, while Sarah was crouching down in the fiction aisle, leafing through a new novel by an author who looked a lot like Winona Ryder, she noticed legs striding past her, a rush of energy bound up in those passing legs. She looked up. A reading was about to take place. Women dabbed at their lipstick and wiped smudged mascara from beneath their eyes; men blew their noses into handkerchiefs; the Barnes & Noble staffers ambled by, keys jangling on neck chains, badges slightly askew, diligent, and on duty.

Standing up, Sarah peeked over the top of the bookcases and saw a tall, impossibly attractive man with black wavy hair and translucent eyes. From this distance, she could not tell his age, but it seemed to be around her own, which she would readily volunteer as "early forties." The author was talking comfortably with the Barnes & Noble staff, touching their arms or shoulders for emphasis, evoking laughter. A stack of books sat on a table to his left. He was the very posture of relaxed authority, one hand in the pocket of his beautifully tailored suit pants, the other at his side.

A sign on the table bearing the books stated his name—David Eastman—and the title of his book, *Endings and Other Stories*.

Sarah, who had skulked out of the house earlier in a pair of jeans and a faded Beatles t-shirt beneath a black zip-up sweatshirt (she had spent the previous hour crawling around the living room floor with one-year-old Emily), brushed her hand through her short black hair and ran a wetted finger along her eyebrows. She had never heard of David Eastman or his book yet knew instantly that he was the reason she left the house that evening. She fumbled in her sweatshirt pocket for a Chapstick and applied that hurriedly. Seeing the chairs filling up quickly, she walked to the third row and claimed an aisle seat. She sat down, breathing as heavily as if she had just run ten city blocks. Calming her breath, she lifted her eyes and took another look at this author.

She was wrong. He was not merely attractive—he was the most beautiful man she had ever seen. His skin was luminous, clean, and unlined, his teeth were straight and white, his eyes were flashing and long-lashed. He looked like Spanish nobility, though she had the distinct impression he was Jewish and probably grew up on Long Island or in New Jersey. His healthy, full hair framed his face, falling slightly over his forehead on the left side. His attractiveness was so blatant that it was embarrassing. She looked around herself in order to assess how many of the audience members were as smitten as she.

If David Eastman's effect on his audience was as extreme as his effect upon Sarah, there was a great deal of restraint going on at Barnes & Noble that evening. Having claimed their seats, the members of the audience sat patiently, leafing through the one or more books that rested upon their laps. No one seemed to be gaping at David Eastman or displaying any outward signs of intense attraction to him. People smiled pleasantly, yawned discreetly, listened to their cell phone messages. There was a convivial Upper West Side atmosphere of a free cultural event about to unfold.

Turning her attention to David Eastman once again, she tested his effect upon her. It had not diminished. She noticed now that she was sitting up straighter, losing awareness of her beat-up shoes and outfit. The other people around her disappeared until it was just herself observing him as if he were an exhibit at a museum or an image on her own computer screen. He gestured, he pointed, he ran his hand through his hair. He was alive with energy; she saw it coursing through his veins, dancing on his skin, rising out of his mouth. He was graceful and sensual; he was probably a beautiful dancer. His breath would taste spicy/sweet, with hints of cinnamon and cayenne; she could practically taste it in her mouth. She knew what he would be like in bed.

He was introduced by a chirpy Barnes & Noble staffer and promptly began reading from his story, *Boy at Nine*, about the sudden death of a mother. The story was elegant and mournful, rendered in impressions and fragments. Sarah was unable to stop tears from streaming down her cheeks though she knew with 100 percent certainty that no such tragedy had happened to the author; moreover, that the story was not only fiction in the truest sense but bore the taint of ulterior motive.

Listening to David Eastman read, Sarah knew that the sole purpose of this story was to seduce the reader into loving him by pitying his ostensibly wounded boy/self. Once seduced, one would be his loyal reader forever.

It was clear to Sarah that this skillful writer was clever and calculating, a master of manipulation. He was a narcissist, an egotist, irreverent, intrepid, yet terrified at the core. His eloquence, charm, and great beauty were his currency. Hearing him read his own prose, Sarah learned everything there was to know about David Eastman and desired him more than any man she had ever known.

After the reading, clutching his book to her chest, she walked up to the author table. She had a visceral urge to slap this author, yet she was also overcome by the urge to meld herself into his contours. The flow of her tears had left faint tracks on her cheeks. She felt both highly enraged and highly aroused. She let the line grow and then joined it, four people from the end.

When it was her turn at the table with David Eastman, she walked forward, head down, like a bashful bride on the way to the altar. Lifting her head slowly, she met his gaze. A current passed between them of such intensity that it was miraculous that all the electrical circuits at Barnes and Noble did not short at once.

David signed Sarah's copy, wishing her a life of good endings and great beginnings—his standard endorsement, riffing, naturally, on his book's title. Their eyes locked again and she felt herself take leave of her human body and become a creature of the wild, a predator, a tiger, in fact, blood lust surging through her, lined with dangerous stripes and lean muscles. She stood on her haunches, watchful, waiting. Her breath caught in her throat but others were waiting in line and she needed to get home to her celebrated husband, her infant, and her teen-age daughter who now were surely missing her, mysteriously and irre-sponsibly missing from home on a school night.

Leaving David's table, Sarah returned to her tamer self, step by step. Despite her pressing domestic obligations, however, she took her time leaving the store, stopping to browse through the New and Noteworthy table on the first floor. Several minutes later, as she was crossing Broadway and 86th Street, she was not surprised in the least when David fell in step beside her. They walked easily together, their gaits exactly matched. She felt the heat radiating from his body. She morphed once again and her stripes reappeared; she felt herself grow sleek and dangerous and irresistible. Sarah and David talked like old friends all the way to her apartment on Central Park West, between and 87th and 88th Street.

When they reached the corner, he grabbed her left hand, acknowl-edging her wedding band and brashly asked if he could see her again—he would be coming to New York several times over the next several months for book talks and lectures. By the position of David's upper lip, Sarah knew his envy of her Central Park West address, the hus-band and family that waited for her upstairs. For the first time in her life, she felt the power of her social and economic status. Wordlessly, Sarah gave David her cell phone number, which he wrote down in his date book. When it was time to say goodbye, he pulled her into the shadows and hugged her close for an indecently long interval.

David revealed himself most in that hug, reeking of need and overflowing with entitlement. There was a young boy's loneliness in that embrace, yet there was also a presumption that was unlike anything she had ever encountered; it was a pre-modern gesture of male supremacy or claim of ownership. The hug was something that might be pathetic, embarrassing, boorish, or Neanderthal coming from anyone else.

Coming from David Eastman, it was marvelous.

He was half a foot taller than she; her head reached the top of his shoulders. Through his clothes she felt his heat, smelled his male tiger scent, heard his heart thumping in his chest. His hands—warm, strong, muscular—encircled her small waist, working their way underneath her Beatles t-shirt, burning into her skin, marking her as his prey, claiming her as his own.

Pressed against him, Sarah was overtaken by the same desire that had swept over her earlier yet this second wave was so strong that it nearly obliterated two important considerations—that David was a complete stranger and that she was embracing this complete stranger under the nose of her husband and children, not to mention innumerable neighbors and her nosy doormen. This was the first—but not the last time—that her desire for David would make her heedless.

Reading her response, David smiled. He knew right there that he had successfully stolen another man's wife and the knowledge of his victory was as powerful an aphrodisiac as his lust for Sarah itself.

Over the twenty-three months of their affair, Sarah would often return in her thoughts to that night and marvel at how reflexively she received David as a fact of her life, wondering why it never occurred to her to spurn him. After eighteen years of turning down similar offers from other similarly attractive men, Sarah gave herself to this brazen, beautiful man without a second's hesitation. After a lifetime of taking seriously the biblical commandment against adultery, she was suddenly an avid and most willing practitioner.

"You are my first and my only," she has told him over and over again. "If we stop being together, I will not seek another lover. I know it is not the same for you and I don't even care."

Sarah's confession is the exact thing that the experts warn against—being honest with a man about your feelings. But this is not the classic situation of a single woman trying to snag a single man and turn him into her husband. Sarah has a husband whom she loves, whom she sleeps with and whom she intends on staying married to and David is the one lover she will ever have. She isn't looking for David "to commit." She isn't interested in "something more." She has not allowed herself to dwell on the question of what they actually feel for one another, whether there is love between them.

Their intermittent couplings—and frequent phone conversations—are all that she wants, no matter how infuriating.

Because of their innate attraction to each other, Sarah bristles at the word "affair" as it applies to her relationship with David. Affairs belong to others...they are sordid, cheap, pathetic, miserable, ill-informed, adulterous enterprises that are carried on at fancy hotels between married executives and their single assistants or on Hollywood sets between movie stars. She and David are lovers, yes, but they are not *having* anything. They are *being*. They are *doing*. The word "affair" sounds too institutional, too generic, too lacking in nuance and texture to begin to describe what is between them.

Imperfect though the word is, "an affair" is most surely the proper description for this...thing. For instance, if Dan ever found out about David, he would most likely be brokenhearted because his wife was "having an affair." If a *Daily News* reporter tailed Sarah on the day, two weeks ago, that she dropped Emily at nursery school and then headed down to David's studio apartment on 8th Avenue and 26th Street only to emerge two hours later, the resulting headline might be something on the order of "Paging Dr. Dan! Your Wife is Having an Affair! RX: Divorce!"

Though everyone else might term it an affair, what is taking place between David and Sarah is an organic and vital part of her life and because of this Sarah feels only unevenly guilty about the whole thing. What she regrets more than the infidelity is the deceit. Since she and Dan share so much with each other, Sarah irrationally wishes she could tell Dan about her friend David, with whom she has been having torrid, tempestuous sex for the past two years.

"I am *beat*" Dan sinks onto the bed, pulling off his Baruch Shemtov silk tie as he kicks off his Kenneth Cole oxfords. It is the evening of Dan's return from the conference in Boston and though he promised to be home by eight, it is nearly one hour later when he walks through the front door, spilling over with apologies. Used to his late hours, no one feels especially put out. Emily had been fed at six, Daphne grabbed sushi on her way home from school and Sarah had been reading *The Velveteen Rabbit* to Emily, cuddled beneath a blanket on the commodious living room couch.

Though he had always been reasonably well-dressed b.c. (before celebrity), Dan now dresses like a million bucks, thanks to Iggy, the image consultant afforded him by *Good Morning America*. His full head of gray hair, formerly reminiscent of Albert Einstein's mop, is now a glorious coif, gleaming with obnoxious vitality. His eyebrows are shaped (waxed every two weeks), his facial hair removed via laser, his skin is buffed and exfoliated, and his physique is toned from the three-times-weekly personal training sessions with Mad Dog, who used to be in Rikers Island (armed robbery) and was making two hundred dollars per hour within his first year of freedom from fitness-obsessed middle-aged people with too much disposable income.

In their recently renovated master bedroom suite, Dan's grooming products now overwhelm Sarah's. In their walk-in closet, his clothing predominates. Marco, the interior decorator, installed an electronic tie rack to help him manage his tie collection, which Emily loves to play with and Daphne shows off to her friends. The back wall of the closet contains a folding massage table. Dan receives massages on Monday and Thursday mornings at 7:45, in that window of time between his *Good Morning America* tapings, the kids' departure for school, and his own departure for work. The masseuse's name is Gypsy. Gypsy has a book contract with HarperCollins. His forthcoming book is called *I Knead You: Confessions of a Manhattan Masseuse.*

When her husband arrives home, Sarah has just reached the conclusion of *The Velveteen Rabbit,* which she is reading (as she always does) through her tears. Compassionate Emily reaches out a chubby little hand to wipe away her mother's sorrow and Sarah apologizes, as she always does, when she breaks down while reading. There are certain children's books that tug at her heart. *Charlotte's Web, The Giving Tree,* and *A Wrinkle in Time* are among them. No matter how many times she has read them to her daughters, they never fail to entrap her in their poignant power.

After Dan has finished kissing his wife and baby girl and braves the trip into Daphne's teen lair (clothes strewn upon every possible surface, some current popular band's music—Coldplay? Maroon 5? Blink 182? Green Day?—blaring, computer screen filled with instant messages, bras on doorknobs and towel hooks, random teaspoons and coffee mugs on windowsills, an armpit and bubblegum smell in the air) to give a hug to his eldest daughter, he heads for the bedroom. By his gait, Sarah can tell that hunger and fatigue are competing within him.

On more than a few occasions, Dan has fallen asleep without eating dinner, overcome by exhaustion.

Meanwhile, Sarah should be exhausted as well, having served as a solo parent for the past three days, having spent the previous night on the phone with David well past midnight. Instead, Sarah finds herself completely energized. Her anger at David inspired more than maniacal driving; she has spent the better part of the day writing a new story. Having read it through several times, making intricate changes at each reading, she is now delighted with her work.

At 4:00 p.m., with Emily happily watching *The Little Mermaid*, Marta preparing dinner and Daphne at a friend's house, Sarah escaped to her gym on Amsterdam Avenue for a six-mile run followed by a long, purging sweat in the steam room. The day felt magical and full. Her fury and frustration from the previous night morphed into her muse. The new story, she thinks, is a good one, possibly a breakthrough for her as a writer.

Now, watching her respectable husband disrobe before her, she feels a surge of lust. Dan stands to unbuckle his belt and Sarah slides up to him, pressing herself into his chest. He laughs, surprised, but not really because this happens rather often. Dan is the happy beneficiary of the never-ebbing wellspring of her carnal appetite. It is nearly nine in the evening. The bedroom door is locked. Dinner or sleep can wait. Sarah smiles at Dan, unbuttons his Brooks Brothers shirt, slides herself lower on him and finishes unbuckling his belt. He moves his hands to her hair, pulling her to him, closing his eyes. She kneels before her famous husband and doesn't leave until he cries out her name repeatedly: *Sarah, Sarah, Sarah, Sarah, Sarah.*

Sarah's intensity of nature is not lost on Dan, who is the first to admit his luck. He is a moderate, measured man whose success owes as much to his temperance as to his gentle intelligence and well-developed people skills. His passion doesn't flare as brightly as his wife's, but this is part of what makes them a good couple, marked for longevity. Two highly passionate people—Sarah and David, for instance—face the grave risk of burning each other out, not to mention causing a dangerous, destructive fire in the lives of those whom they love.

On more than one occasion, Dan has wondered at his ability to satisfy Sarah's rapacious appetite. On more than one occasion, he felt her palpable frustration at being bound up in the monotony of matrimony. On more than one occasion, he has experienced the less enjoyable aspects of her intensity—her exhausting need for long, often late-night conversations, her crying jags, her tendency to recount and endlessly analyze her dreams, her PMS, the red-hot flare of her temper, her sorrow at being a non-practicing writer, at having her wifedom and motherhood completely consume her existence.

On more than one occasion, Dan wondered if he was the only man in her life.

But not recently. Not, ironically, since David. An over-scheduled life is an interesting thing. It dulls your intuition, protecting you from knowledge that might destroy you.

Eerily, Daphne has asked her mother, more than once within the past few months, if she is having an affair. Sarah is not even remotely worried that Daphne has any concrete evidence for her suspicions as she has been meticulous in her discretion, still the question unsettles her. If Daphne questions her mother's fidelity, her evidence is entirely intuitive and there is nothing that Sarah can do to change that, other than blithely and laughingly reassuring her daughter. With the marriages of her classmates' parents unraveling at the speed of light, it is no wonder that Daphne is insecure about the soundness of her parents' union. With constant tawdry revelations of infidelity on the part of mothers and fathers whom she knows, naturally Daphne needs to inoculate herself by gaining complete reassurance from her mother.

"Are you worried about Daddy fooling around as well, or only me?" Sarah asked her daughter one evening as they were coming out of a Starbucks on their way to Banana Republic. Though they hadn't been talking about this matter that particular day, Daphne had just told her mother about the father of a classmate whose mother had been fighting cancer for the past five years, and who had been having an affair with her oncologist.

The news "really bummed me out," reported Daphne, who indeed appeared completely bummed out by it. Pale with freckles and black hair, Daphne had recently morphed from adorable moppet to urban sophisticate by growing three inches, taking up spinning classes and thereby losing her baby fat, and trading her ubiquitous ponytail for a chin-length bob.

Still, as she relayed the story to her mother, Sarah saw the anxious child beneath the glam exterior. "How depressing is *that*?" she kept asking. "How sleazy can you be?"

"God," said Sarah, struck by the true sleaziness of the situation. "How's Betsy doing with this news?"

Daphne took a long sip of her skim mocha latte while shrugging. "Shmeh," she replied, her invented word for "don't know but it doesn't look good." She waved her hand through the air as if to wave the news away. They walked in silence for a block and then Sarah asked her question. In response, Daphne gave her mother an arch look and said, "Dad would *never* fool around; he's too respectable."

Sarah smiled. "And me? I'm not respectable?"

Daphne rolled her eyes. "Mom, you *know* that you're a MILF." Which set Sarah's teeth on edge. This had been a sore point between them since two years earlier when a delegation of boys informed

Daphne that her mom was a "fox" the day after a school play. While Sarah pointed out that the boys' assessment probably had more to do with the fact that she was the youngest, least coifed, mink-clad, and Botoxed mother in the audience, Daphne would have none of it, shooting back that it was clearly the denim "teenage wannabe" mini-skirt her mother wore to the play that gave the boys that idea.

With Banana Republic looming on the horizon, however, the troubling conversation was dropped. Sarah, however, lingered on her daughter's comment and general suspiciousness. Daphne's intuition makes her watchful and a bit worried. It gnaws away at her maternal sense of self. It makes her feel as sleazy as Betsy's dad. It reminds her of what is at stake.

Following Dan's return from Boston (and her maddening phone conversation with David the previous night), Sarah spends virtually every waking hour apart from her children, Dan, and the treadmill crafting and re-crafting the story she began. The story, *Portrait of You as a Young Man*, is rather brilliant, she thinks happily. It is her own vision of David's childhood, her flight of fancy concerning some key events that helped to create the forty-two-year-old man. The writing of the story is not in itself an act of vengeance, for there is nothing even remotely nasty about the work, in fact, it is highly sympathetic to its protagonist. It is something of a retelling of David's personal narrative, a corrective to *Boy at Nine*.

Three days pass happily in a haze of creative flow for Sarah. Her life flows seamlessly; the household runs, food is bought and cooked, Emily is bathed and fed and taken to her playgroup and swim class, the miles pass like clouds beneath her treadmill-trotting feet, pages fill magically with marvelous prose. Daphne spends her days in school and evenings barricaded in her room doing homework and talking to her friends on the phone and internet. One afternoon, she asks her mother for money and surprises her by doing a mid-week food shopping at Fairway. Dan sees his family in the early morning and late evenings; he and Sarah make love twice in one night and then not again for an entire week. After many years of marriage, that's how it goes.

The ratings of *Good Morning America* soar and Dan is apportioned much of the credit. He is taken to lunch by a literary agent and sits for a photo shoot for *People* magazine in his office on Friday morning. The office staff is beside themselves with excitement, especially because one shot requires all the receptionists and assistants to crowd around Dan in their medical scrubs. The weekend arrives and a bar mitzvah of dear friends consumes their time on Saturday from early morning until late at night. In preparation, Sarah treats Daphne and herself to manicures and pedicures at the new spa on 92nd Street and Amsterdam. She and Dan see a rare film, the new Czech documentary on the children of Prague in the era leading up to World War II, they have dinner at Barbara Walters's home, they go to the opening of an art exhibition in SoHo, and they begin to plan a summer trip to Italy.

Life feels dizzyingly, dazzlingly full.

And then Emily wakes up on Sunday morning with a strange, raised rash all over her body and trouble breathing and everything comes to a crashing, calamitous halt.

"Dan!" Sarah cries, having discovered their toddler crumpled on her carpet, crying in raspy, jagged sobs and her skin disfigured by a rough red rash.

"My self hurts!" Emily wails. "My whole self hurts!"

Deeply asleep two rooms away, Dan does not hear Sarah. "Dan!" she yells and kneels down next to her daughter. "Oh, my poor baby," she whispers, inhaling sharply.

Emily is curled up into a ball, breathing laboriously. Her skin is hot to the touch. "Ow, ow, ow!" she cries at her mother's touch. "Make it stop, Mommy!"

Scooping her child up, Sarah runs into her bedroom. The door had closed on her way out into the hall and she rams it open with her hip and shoulder. Emily is burning up in her arms. Dan lies beneath the down quilt, face sunk into the pillow. "Dan, get up! Dan, it's Emily!"

In a flash, Dan's professional reflex kicks in and he jumps out of bed. He looks at his wife and daughter, both breathing heavily. "Down here," he says to Sarah. "Put her down on the bed. Get my scope and the kit," he orders. Sarah runs to their bathroom to get his home medical kit.

Dan listens to Emily's heart, looks in her throat, takes her temperature. Sarah gasps as Dan raises their daughter's pajama top; Emily's chest is covered with the same rash that covers her face. She rubs her eyes, crying weakly throughout the examination. Sarah's eyes flit frantically between her husband's and daughter's faces. It takes Dan less than a minute to assess the situation. Their daughter has rheumatic fever and has likely been harboring strep for the past week. Her temperature, taken beneath her arm, is hovering near 104 degrees. "Get dressed," he tells Sarah. "We've got to get her to Columbia Presbyterian."

Rheumatic fever! Sarah's mind sifts through files of information as she pulls on a pair of jeans and grabs the first sweatshirt she finds. She shoves her feet into sneakers without socks. *A potential threat to the valves of the heart.* Sarah's own heart races. She herself has mitral valve prolapse, fairly common, a condition necessitating prophylactic antibiotic treatment prior to surgery. She herself is prone to infection of the heart valves. What if she passed on this genetic defect to her daughter, who now has rheumatic fever?

Dan is in the bathroom, splashing water on his face, brushing his teeth. Emily is lying on the bed in her Hello Kitty pajamas, making soft whimpering sounds. It is chilly outside; she can't go just like this, thinks Sarah in alarm, though she herself is sweating. She bites her lip and takes gulps of air to reduce her anxiety.

"Dan," Sarah yells toward the bathroom. "I'm getting Emily some clothes. It's cold outside."

Dan emerges from the bathroom with a towel over his head. He looks at his wife. "Sarah, wash your face," he instructs. "Better yet, jump in the shower. I'll get Emily's clothes."

Sarah nods and walks into the bathroom. She sheds her clothes, turns on the shower, and steps under the stream before the water is properly hot. She says words in her mind—"wash under arms and between legs," "scrub neck," "wash face"—and obeys her inner track. She applies shampoo to her own command, rinses and adds a dollop of conditioner. She sees her razor, thinks, *I haven't shaved for a week*, reaches for the razor, then shakes her head at her own vanity. Her poor child!

When she emerges from the bathroom, Sarah is so surprised to see Daphne in the room that she actually jumps. "Sweetie," she says, scrubbing her short hair dry with the towel. "Why are you up so early?" Daphne usually sleeps until noon on Sunday unless she has track practice.

Daphne's face is sleep-lined, her eyelids heavy with the memory of recent dreams. She hands her mother a set of velour clothes. They are her treasured Juicy Couture, a Chanukah gift from last year, properly shabby, the epitome of trendy chic among the teenage set and Upper East Side pampered mothers. "Dad woke me up to let me know what was going on. Wear this outfit. It's really comfortable. "

Reaching for the clothes, Sarah draws her eldest daughter to her, taking little panicky breaths. She feels her teenager recoil in embarrassment and lets go. Sarah composes herself and holds her eldest daughter at arm's length. "Oh, honey, this is lovely of you."

As Sarah pulls on the outfit, Daphne sits down next to her little sister on the bed. "Hey peanut," she says. "Hey cookie-face. What's happening?"

"Daffy," Emily cries, her nickname for her sister. "A big boo-boo is all over me." Daphne scoops her little sister onto her lap and holds her. Emily grabs the fabric of Daphne's t-shirt in one hand, sticks the thumb of her other hand into her mouth. At this, Daphne and her mother exchange glances. Emily gave up thumb-sucking over a year earlier.

"It's called regression," Sarah explains to Daphne, smoothing lotion over her face and rubbing her hair into a presentable shape. "Sometimes when something traumatic happens to a child they revert back to behavior they gave up."

"I *know* about regression," Daphne says, with a note of edge. "I *do* pay attention in some of my classes." Dan appears back in the room with a small red outfit and a Zabar's bag containing three water bottles, three Granny Smith apples, a box of apple juice with a straw, a box of animal crackers, salted nuts, and two low-carb chocolate muffins. He places Emily's clothes on the bed.

"Thank God for that," Dan said, kissing his eldest daughter. "Daphne, leave a note for Marta, please. She'll be worried when she discovers us gone."

Marta arrives on Sunday afternoon from her home in Jamaica, Queens. "What's on your schedule for today?" Sarah asks Daphne, unplugging her cell phone from the charger.

"Kaplan's," Daphne reports, smoothing Emily's damp hair. She is taking her SATs this March. "Then I think I'll hang out at Chloe's and study for our history quiz." Emily's eyes are closed; she appears to have fallen asleep in her sister's lap. Sarah has a brief, horrible flash of a child-sized coffin, an open grave. She closes her eyes. "Can I have my allowance, plus something extra for lunch?"

But I just gave you a twenty on Friday, Sarah thinks, then bites her tongue. *No fights this morning,* she decides. Dan, who is on the phone with the attending physician at the pediatric ward of Columbia Presbyterian, silently opens his wallet and hands Daphne three tens.

"Thanks," she says, avoiding her mother's eyes.

Sarah picks up Emily's clothes from the bed. "Come on, Emzie," she says to her sleeping child. "We're going to the doctor now. Let's put on some clothes."

Weeping weakly, Emily allows her mother to remove her pajamas and dress her in a loose set of pants and a shirt. Sarah pulls socks over Emily's sweaty feet and fits her feet into Velcro sneakers. "Daphne, grab her sweatshirt with the hood on the back of her door," Sarah instructs as the family prepares to go downstairs and hail a cab to Columbia Presbyterian Babies Hospital.

The morning passes in agonizing slow motion. Dan had arranged for Emily to be admitted instantly and so they bypass the Emergency Room, go straight to the pediatric ward, and get a corner bed in an otherwise empty room. The attending physician confirms Dan's diagnosis of rheumatic fever. He schedules a strep test, an echocardiogram, an EKG, blood work, and an intravenous antibiotic drip. Emily limply surrenders to everything, her eyes alternatively wide with a wondering fear or sagging with fatigue.

The EKG is done bedside, as is the blood test and strep test. Emily gags when the long stick is inserted into her mouth to swab her throat and then cries for some time about the "giant Q-tip." A quietly-concerned Jamaican nurse takes her temperature, creates a chart, and sticks it at the foot of her bed. Dan and Sarah hover anxiously, speak telegraphically, pull up chairs, and then find themselves unable to sit.

After about an hour, Dan and Sarah are told to take Emily for her echocardiogram, which is on another floor. They lift her onto a small gurney and carefully arrange her IV lines, coordinating the position of the movable pole. Downstairs, Doctor Dan and Sarah wait in line with mostly elderly people. The walls are industrial pale blue and the lighting seems unnecessarily harsh. The incongruously orange and green plastic molded chairs look like social outcasts and the people who are sitting in them appear to be unfortunate children whose parents forgot to pick them up after school. Emily dozes between crying jags, her breath raspy.

The lack of aesthetics in the hospital hallway has a paradoxically soothing effect on Sarah. *Thank God for Dan's influence*, she thinks for perhaps the millionth time in their marriage, never getting accustomed to this reality, never taking it for granted, never getting over that feeling of guilty awareness of all those families still waiting with their own sick children in the Emergency Room while she and her doctor husband breeze right on in with their own daughter.

It is the previous spring and she is lying in David's bed in his Victorian home in Somerville on the Thursday afternoon of a trip she took to Brookline to visit her brother after surgery. Her two-hour tryst will be factored into the time it takes to drive back to New York and by the time she reaches her husband, David will be far away in her mind.

It's an overcast, rainy day, perfect for baking, or reading by the fireplace, or watching old movies or making prolonged love. The bedsheets are tangled and David is half-covered, gazing at Sarah, who is completely naked, reclining at a right angle from her lover. They are taking a brief hiatus. Sarah is deep in thought, recalling a scene from the film *American Beauty*. It is the hilarious and horrible moment when Annette Benning's character discovers her husband masturbating in bed. The husband, played memorably by Kevin Spacey, at first denies his activity, then admits it, then uses it as a weapon against his cheating, manipulative wife.

Sarah has no clue why this particular scene has dropped into her head for consideration at this particular moment but she adores it—the honesty of it, the touching humor of it.

"Do you feel powerful because of your beauty?" David asks at this moment. Sarah pulls back from her thoughts. At first his words—intruders upon her reverie—make no sense so she repeats them to herself. *Do I feel powerful because of my beauty?*

To ask this question one would first need to assume that Sarah indeed thinks of herself as beautiful, which is something that might happen twice a year or so. While Sarah acknowledges her above-average attractiveness, she stops short of considering herself exceptional-looking. Having morphed several decades ago from tomboyish to striking, Sarah is fairly reassured of her appeal from reactions she has elicited from men since her teens. Disregarding the inevitable PMS-fueled conviction that she is hideous (and fat), Sarah truly doesn't long to be perceived as better looking than she already is and harbors a secret superiority to women who are overly concerned with their appearances.

Of course she acknowledges the obvious, that good-looking people have a competitive edge. And yes, it is true that the attractive do constitute an elite of sorts, as do the thin, the rich, and the famous. But to move from this fact to the arrogance of power and privilege is to embark on a journey that Sarah has never taken.

David watches her intently, barely breathing, his query hovering. Sarah laughs—this is a quintessential David question. Her self-obsessed lover has projected himself into his own fantasy of being her. He, of course, uses his own beauty (gained only in early adulthood and regarded by him with a sort of awe), as if it were an otherworldly power such as telekinesis. David is haunted by the memories of the heavy, ungainly, sweaty boy he had been, the one who sat at home reading nineteenth-century erotica (bought at a neighbor's garage sale) and writing tormented poetry while his classmates were out having fun, the one who got teased and cried easily, the one who was a constant disappointment to his mother.

Beauty came to David as an insurance settlement when he was twenty-three, abruptly and completely without warning, just compensation for the pathetic childhood and adolescence he had endured.

Nearly twenty years and two bestsellers later, David still regards his beauty as a prize, a birthright, a trust fund, a preordained fate. Yes, thinks Sarah, turning her lover's question over in her mind that chilly afternoon in Somerville, beauty is power and it is the power of David's beauty that brought her to this prolonged moment of adultery. Yet she has never regarded her appearance as anything other than a piece of her identity.

"Not at all," she replies with complete honesty. "Should I?"

"Yes," David replies, suddenly serious, pulling himself up, spreading her thighs, gazing somberly, reverentially at what he has uncovered. "Oh yes, yes, you should."

Sarah recalls this moment as a young resident with waves of blond hair swept back from his forehead rushes past her and her family as they wheel Emily back to her room following the echocardiogram. *The rushing resident looks exactly like an actor playing his part on a soap opera*, thinks Sarah. As he passes them, the resident turns to look at Sarah and she holds his gaze for a spontaneous second. Neither her proven attractiveness nor the privilege that comes from being a doctor's wife makes her feel powerful right now; she is just the distraught mother of a very sick child.

And her beautiful, self-absorbed lover is the most irrelevant fact of her life.

The echocardiogram had been terrible for Emily because her chest is sore and she squirmed, cried, and coughed throughout the test, making it take forever for the technician to get clear images of her heart. Desperate to get their child back to her room, Sarah and Dan promised their daughter outrageous gifts, sang every favorite song of hers, told funny vignettes, stroked her, praised her, called her brave. By the time the technician wearily dismissed the family, Sarah's Juicy Couture sweatshirt—on loan from Daphne—was soaked under the arms and at the back of the neck.

Walking through the hospital hallway, Dan, who normally looks just like the handsome and heroic lead doctor on a soap opera, is pale, with perspiration visible on his forehead and upper lip. He is further put out because the technician insisted on waiting to show the results of the echocardiogram to the cardiologist on call, annoyed because his position and power failed to get him past hospital protocol.

Sarah knows her husband well enough to understand that his annoyance is mostly a smokescreen for his fear.

"Are you Dr. Reinhart?" asks the young blond resident who just raced past them, backtracking from his sprint.

Dan turns, nodding his head. "I'm Bill Martin," says the younger man, extending his hand. "I'm working with Dr. Epstein. He dispatched me to personally deliver the report to you."

The manila envelope is handed over to Dan, whose face is masklike. He does not thank the resident and takes what is handed to him in a haughty, dismissive way. This is a side of her husband she has never seen and witnessing it now, Sarah feels woozy and wishes to apologize to the blond resident—*my husband is normally more gracious.*

Dan knows too much, she thinks. Dan knows all the horrible possible outcomes, the worst-case scenarios. He has facts, medical literature, patient profiles. He has articulated, detailed, well-founded fears.

Dan looks at the sealed envelope in his hands, which suddenly takes on an epic quality. An eternity passes as its presence asserts itself in that hospital hallway. Muted accents—Caribbean, regional New York, Hispanic, Arabic—mix and mingle in the air. Emily dozes in her gurney, mumbles a message, and turns her head from side to side as if emphatically disagreeing with something. Disembodied coughs echo in the long, antiseptic airway.

Bill Martin is standing close enough to Sarah so she can smell his scent, which is like the beach—a combination of Hawaiian Tropic, sweat, and chlorine. *I must be ten years older than him, no, fifteen,* she thinks. The soft sound of shuffling, slippered feet suddenly makes Sarah's eyelids droop. Illogical relaxation, like a narcotic, seeps into her veins. *Soon I will fall into a trance,* she thinks. *Soon, I will fall into Bill Martin's arms and he will catch me like a lifeguard, he will perform CPR, he will carry me with one arm slung across my chest across the sand.*

Dan waits one second, two seconds, three seconds before sliding his finger under the seal of the envelope. Sarah grips the IV pole, which she had been actively steering just a few seconds earlier. *If I could only lie down,* she thinks, struggling suddenly to keep her eyes open. *If I could just slip in next to Emily and take a nap.*

Dan exhales slowly while pulling the paper out of the envelope. His eyes dart back and forth over the print. He shuffles the pages. His gaze is resolute. Bill Martin shifts his weight, crosses his arms, and clears his throat. Dan turns back a page, re-reads its contents, and replaces the report inside its envelope. He looks up at his wife. "Her heart is fine," he says in a soft voice. "Emily's valves are all healthy."

Sarah closes her eyes, sinks into the wall, and hugs herself around her shoulders. Emily's heart is fine. When she opens her eyes, Bill Martin is gone and the smell of the beach is gone and tears are standing in Dan's eyes.

Once they return to Emily's room, Sarah is amazed by how quickly she adjusts to her new—if temporary reality. The room they are given is sunny and spacious and mercifully still empty. Even with the IV needle in her arm and beeping monitors bedside, Emily's sleep appears relatively comfortable. The starchy whiteness of the hospital sheets reassures Sarah, hinting of health and efficiency and caring nurses. She and Dan sink into their bedside chairs and close their eyes, basking in the restorative sunshine. Sarah slides low in her seat, allowing her head to rest on the upholstered back. Within minutes, she is asleep.

"Mommy?"

Sarah is walking on the beach with a tiny, talkative Daphne. Barely three years old, Daphne has been chatting for the past fifteen minutes about her favorite dog breeds and has just embarked upon a detailed discussion of Pomeranians "who are *so cute*, Mommy, with little foxy noses and stand-up ears and a curly tail and long, fluffy fur!"

The day is spectacular and the beach is sparsely populated. It is a Tuesday and school doesn't end for another week. Burly Russian men in boxer shorts rush into the surf, jump rope, perfect handstands, and toss Frisbees and balls to one another. Gap-toothed Russian women with pendulous breasts swinging freely beneath flowered sundresses lie prone on the sand, surrounded by stuffed plastic bags. A smattering of preschoolers play in the surf with primary-colored pails, shovels, sifters, and other beach toys while mothers, fathers, and grandparents hover watchfully nearby.

Though this was the day that Sarah was supposed to have lunch with Anne, her high school friend now turned power editor at Henry

Holt, the sparkling perfection of the afternoon rendered the prospect of a midtown meeting entirely undesirable…if not downright sacrilegious. Within half an hour of waking up, Sarah had canceled her sitter for the day and her lunch with Anne at the Union Square Café and was on the D train to Coney Island with Daphne…and had enough snacks for every commuter from Manhattan to Brooklyn.

"But next to Pomeranians my really favorite dogs are cocker spaniels. Not the kind that get big but the little ones like Lady from *Lady and the Tramp*. Their ears look like long hair, don't they, Mommy? Like long, curly hair? And next to cocker spaniels, my favorites are the wiener dogs—what are they called again?—because they have short little legs and they look like hot dogs and next to wiener dogs…"

Daphne skips and kicks sand while she talks, stopping every few steps to try out a new skill—a cartwheel, a ballerina turn, the opening steps of the Mexican Hat Dance. Sarah smiles when their eyes meet and interjects interested murmurs, "Really?" or "Oh!" or "Uh-huh," or "Yes, they're so cute!" Daphne's voice sounds like water tinkling over stones in a brook, like the highest notes of a piano. Her bathing suit is pink with a purple skirt and her normally pallid skin is made even more so by the thick layer of sunscreen Sarah has glopped on in the Coney Island bathroom. Her stick-straight black hair, pulled into two pigtails, pokes out of the miniature Yankees cap she is wearing.

Behind them, the giant Ferris Wheel of Coney Island looms like a Tyrannosaurus Rex, ancient and commanding respect; the Cyclone whooshes through space in an endless loop, delighted screams lift in the salt air and mingle with the scent of brine, suntan oil, and cotton candy. Sarah looks at her little daughter, thinking that she has never adored anything or anyone as much in her entire life.

"Mommy!" The voice sounds plaintive and petulant, causing Sarah to frown; it is no longer reminiscent of water tinkling over stones, of piano notes. Sometimes when she is on a talking spree, Daphne will pause to quiz her mother as to the last five words she has just said, suspecting (often correctly) that she might not have been listening. But truly, Sarah has been listening to every word Daphne has just said, prepared to parrot back her critique of miniature poodles who are "like little stuffed animals, except they are real and really cute!"

Sarah spins around to seek Daphne's eye but cannot find her anywhere. Cold dread sits in her bowels. "Daphne," she calls, then screams, scanning the wide beach for a splash of pink with a slash of purple. The Russian men continue their play; their wives lie immobile like slabs of cow's liver at the butcher shop. The parents and grandparents keep up their surfside vigilance, not bothering to even look at Sarah.

A lifeguard! There must be a lifeguard at the beach! Sarah turns backward, toward the carnival, seeking the tall wooden structure, the tanned and muscular young man, the static of the walkie-talkie. She is confused to find that there is not a single chair tower on the beach as far as her eyes can see. Is that because the season has not opened officially?

"*Mommy!*" comes the voice again, insistent, upset, on the verge of tears.

Sarah turns back again and looks out over the swirling, frothy sea. "Oh God," she moans, sinking to her knees, her life at an end.

"Mommy, wake up!" Sarah's eyes snap open. Daphne is nowhere to be found but Emily, her little Emily, is right before her, safe, if sick, in her hospital bed. There is no menacing sea, no bathing Russians, Daphne is not three but sixteen and, judging from the time, which is now after 2:00 p.m., finished with her Kaplan class and studying at Chloe's house. Dan must be at the cafeteria or out for a walk or talking to a doctor. The Zabar's bag in on the floor, near his chair, which has a folded *New York Times* book review and magazine on it.

"Emz," Sarah says, pulling herself out of her nightmare, out of her seat, over to her youngest child. "Emzie, I was having a dream, a dream about Daphne when she was your age…" Emily's rash is still as prominent as ever, her eyes bright, her skin warm but not burning. The drop in her body temperature is not because of the magic of the antibiotics, which can take up to three days to kick in, but due to the acetaminophen she has been given. Symptom relief, administered to lower a dangerously high fever, nearly 105 when Emily was admitted, is necessary. Sarah quietly thanks the scientist who invented Tylenol.

"I'm thirsty, Mommy," croaks Emily.

Sarah jumps back from her examination of her daughter. "Of course!" she cries, retrieving the sports-top water bottle in the Zabar's bag. "You must be completely parched!"

Emily grabs the bottle her mother hands her, gulping the water while the plastic bends inward. When she pulls her lips off the sports top, one-third of the bottle's contents remain. Emily leans back on her pillow and hands Sarah the bottle. She smiles at her mother, yawns, and shuts her eyes. Within a minute, she has fallen back to sleep.

The day passes in a haze of abbreviated conversations with Emily, who wakes up primarily to quench her thirst, visits from nurses and Dr. Epstein, aborted conversations with Dan, phone calls from every single family member, including her sister Tanya in Jerusalem and several reassuring conversations with Marta their housekeeper, a quick trip down to the cafeteria for coffee and Haagen Dazs ice cream—the only food she craves—and half-hearted perusals through the Sunday *Times* and the myriad Sunday afternoon television shows and movies.

While she slept earlier, Dan had gone outside to buy disposable pull-up diapers for Emily so he and Sarah would not have to carry her to the bathroom. Having toilet-trained herself at the age of two, Emily would have normally reacted with indignation to this return to babyhood but either from fever or exhaustion or precocious maturity, Emily reacts philosophically to the pull-ups, informing Anny, the nurse, that they help her "get better by not having to walk to the bathroom on the cold floor."

Sarah instantly warms to Anny, who works the 7:00 a.m. to 7:00 p.m. shift on Sunday, Monday, and Tuesday. Quiet and watchful, she exudes a true empathy and devotion to her tiny patient. At Sarah's inquiry, she tells her that she thought she would be a doctor, even had applied to medical school, but felt called to comfort the sick in the way that only nurses can. Her two children, now twin fourteen-year-olds, are back in Jamaica, being raised by her mother. Listening to her lilting speech, Sarah feels comforted, blessed, grateful.

"How're you doing?"

It is 6:30 in the evening and Dan has just returned from a meeting with his agent, who leaves for Paris the next morning. Earlier in the day it had been uncertain whether he would be able to keep his 3:00 p.m. appointment, but once Emily was settled into the room, Sarah insisted that Dan make his meeting. She would be stationed at Emily's bedside and could reach him by phone or beeper. She has too much pride in her maternal competence, too much practice as a supportive wife to allow Dan to derail his commitments.

The color that had fled Dan's face earlier is now back with a vengeance and Sarah realizes that Dan has showered and dressed during his time away from the hospital. It is even possible that he squeezed in a quick workout and at this thought Sarah becomes vaguely jealous. Dan now enters the hospital room in a rush of energy and purpose and after-shave and Sarah becomes conscious of her teenage outfit, her sticky armpits and unshaven legs, her sneakers, her bare face.

Dan kisses Sarah and she tastes red wine and something else on his breath. Something rich and flavorful, perhaps beef. The meeting had gone well, she can tell. Dan is fairly humming. Dan is very pleased. Their daughter will be okay; the drugs will take effect in a couple of days and then she will go home. The *People* magazine article is coming out next week. His ratings are sky-high. He has hot news to share. He is on top of the world and climbing.

Dan opens his leather portfolio and removes a contract, handing it to her. She sees black print, legal phrases, imposing letterhead—Richard Rosen Literary Agency. There is a sum written on a line and her eyes linger on it—it has many zeros and a dollar sign preceding it.

"A million-dollar contract," he says, grinning. "They want to give me one million dollars."

Sarah stares at the papers. Richard Rosen Literary Agency wants to give Dan one million dollars?

"For what?" she asks, feeling stupid, like she's missing some really obvious point.

Dan pushes with his finger on the contract, showing her the line that says *Bagels Under the Boardwalk: The Making of Dr. Daniel Reinhart, America's Favorite MD*. He watches Sarah's face, but she still doesn't get it. "It's my memoir," he says gently. "Farrar Straus wants to give me one million dollars to write a memoir. I told Ruby I would take the contract home and talk it over with you and with Mel." His lawyer.

"One million dollars for your memoir?" Sarah repeats, confused, for her husband is a doctor, a television personality, not a writer. Between the two of them, she's the writer, though she has never published anything beyond a few articles and a short story in an anthology twenty years ago. Besides, what would Dan's memoir consist of? As far as she knows, his childhood was completely unexceptional, his career rather unremarkable until the past couple of years when one of his patients' mothers, a producer at WABC, got the idea to interview him for a segment on breastfeeding and he became a media superstar overnight.

Bagels Under the Boardwalk? Dan hates bagels, finds them too dense and chewy, prefers bialys, muffins, croissants, or even cinnamon toast in a pinch, thinks Sarah. And what boardwalk? Dan grew up in Queens, played handball against the garage door of his garden apartment complex and ran through the spray of a lawn sprinkler on hot summer days. A contract from a literary agency? A one-million-dollar advance?

This is not fair! cries a little voice inside of her.

Dan continues grinning. "They want the book to come out in time for Christmas and Chanukah." It is now mid-October. "It will be about one hundred and fifty pages long and have ten pages of personal photographs. They've given me a ghostwriter. The manuscript is due in four weeks."

A one-hundred-and-fifty-page manuscript is due in one month from a man who has never even written a grammatical patient history. Ten pages of photographs. A ghostwriter. One million fucking dollars.

"It's called book-packaging," Dan explains to his wife. He lowers his voice. "You know that I can't write. I'm going to spend two hours every day talking to Jasmine and she will shape everything; she's a ghostwriter for Farrar Straus. Jasmine can also spend some time with you to absorb the flavor of our life. I know you won't mind. She's twenty-five and really smart. She graduated from Harvard. She's adorable and really high-energy. She dresses just like Daphne and her friends."

"Who dresses just like me?"

The scent of Tommy Girl precedes Daphne's arrival. She is wearing army boots, a short pleated skirt with a wide belt slung low over her hips, a t-shirt with the Cheerios logo, and a black cardigan. In her arms, she carries a stack of magazines, which she presents to her mother.

"Sweetie!" Dan stands to embrace his daughter. Sarah, frazzled by the intensity of the day and now stunned by the (unfair) news that her already-famous husband is about to become even more famous as an author, receives her daughter's hug with a pasted-on smile.

The minute Daphne enters her orbit, Sarah knows two things: that her eldest daughter has been smoking dope and that she was not with Chloe as she said she would be. Her lips are smeary and chapped, as if she has been kissing for a long time. Sarah glances at Dan to see if his face registers any awareness of these matters but he is coasting on the endorphins of his recent meeting with Ruby, his agent, and Jasmine, the adorable ghostwriter.

Sarah has idly suspected Daphne of using drugs recreationally for about a year (and occasionally lying about her whereabouts) but has never had concrete proof of either. As a child of the seventies, she herself smoked dope during her adolescence and lied continuously to her unreasonably restrictive parents; however, now that she is a reasonably restrictive mother and no longer a rebellious teen, Sarah is completely opposed to both.

Faced now, in Emily's sick room, with near-certain proof (red-rimmed eyes that avoid looking directly at her, a loose-limbed, heavy-tongued affect, perfume barely masking the marijuana smell in her hair) of the likely validity of her suspicions, Sarah is frustratingly unable to confront her daughter. Sitting at Emily's bedside, she tucks away the revelation about Daphne for a more auspicious moment.

Half an hour later, Dan leaves the hospital with Daphne, promising her dinner at Carmine's. Sarah glares at their backs as they stroll arm and arm out of Emily's hospital room. For Dan, Emily's crisis is already history. That night, Sarah stays at her daughter's side, sleeping on a cot. Her last conscious thought before passing out on the narrow bed is directed at Dan. *Media whore*, she thinks, smirking.

In the morning, Emily's fever is down and she chatters happily in her bed, eating her breakfast, unconcerned with the heparin lock and wires connecting her chest to the various monitors next to her bed. The three-year-old is awake by 7:00 a.m., watching cartoons that her parents typically forbid. In her joy at being able to watch cartoons, Emily forgets to watch *Good Morning America*; Dan promised that he would send a special greeting to her on the air. She cries briefly, then gets distracted by the arrival of hospital breakfast—the small carton of Frosted Flakes, the little container of apple juice, the chocolate muffin encased in crinkly cellophane wrap. Her rash is fading; she drinks several cups of water and apple juice and does not mind when Sarah or Anny change her pull-up. All seems to be proceeding according to the best-case scenario.

Marta arrives at 10:30, as she and Dan had planned, and Sarah leaves for a four-hour break, during which time she goes back to her apartment to get a change of clothes and call Marta to make sure that nothing has changed since she left the hospital. (Nothing has. Everything is fine.) From there she heads to her gym and spends a blessed hour running. After her steam room sweat and shower, wearing her regular clothes and makeup—in short, feeling like herself—she calls Marta again, gets the all-clear, and spends a carefree hour drifting in and out of the shops along Broadway in the 80s, buying a sweater at Montmartre, a new lip gloss at Origins, a pair of textured stockings and a silky camisole at Gap.

She is standing in line at Gap when her cell phone rings. Her caller ID recognizes David's cell phone. David! From another lifetime! Their last conversation was the maddening one from the previous week. Sarah stares at the phone as it plays its melody ("Hava Nagila") and weighs the benefits of talking to her aggravating lover right now.

She steps out of the line and walks over to the bra display.

"Hi," she says, hand over the mouthpiece. The neighborhood is landmined with hundreds of people who know her as herself or Dr. Dan's wife.

"I'm on my way to New York!" David says, shouting, and she can tell that he's calling from a car. "I saw Dan this morning and heard about your daughter! I can't believe she's in the hospital! How are you doing? I'm leaving Cambridge right now! I'll be in town in about four hours!"

What? Sarah throws her pile of clothing down on the bra table, gestures apologetically to a salesperson, and quickly strides out of the store.

"What are you talking about?" she demands, alarmed, walking down to Riverside Drive, where she can speak as loudly as she wants.

"Dan talked about your daughter this morning on his *Good Morning America* segment! He said that she has rheumatic fever; it sounds kind of serious! Is she okay? I'm sorry I was such an asshole last week! I'm coming to see you!"

Can he be serious? "David! You can't come to see me now!" Sarah sputters. "I'm on my way back to the hospital! Dan will be there later. My housekeeper is there. My older daughter is coming after school! My parents will be there! I'll be in the hospital for the rest of the day!"

"You're not in the hospital now, are you?" he asks. "I can tell you're on the street."

"I took a break for a few hours but I'm on my way back! I'll be there the rest of the day!"

"Listen, I called the hospital. Visiting hours are until 7:00 p.m. I'll get into town around 6:00. Don't worry about meeting me outside. I'll drop by when I get in!" he shouts. Sarah looks at her watch. It is now just shy of 1:30 p.m.

"You can't!" shouts Sarah. She crosses West End Avenue and runs down 86th Street toward the river. "David, have you lost your mind?

This is my family's emergency! It's crazy for you to simply show up! How will I introduce you?"

"Introduce me as your friend who happened to be in town and saw the news on television! I'll see you in a few hours. I need to eat something on the way. Bye!"

"David!" But he has hung up.

Sarah runs her fingers through her hair, gnaws at a cuticle, drawing blood, calls him back, furiously punching in his numbers. "Yeah?" He has his hands-free set attached but doesn't know it is her.

"David! Listen to me! You cannot come to the hospital! It's completely inappropriate!"

"Sarah." David is using his teaching voice, which serves to infuriate her further. "I've been doing a lot of thinking and I realize I haven't been as good to you as I can be. I've been selfish. I want to be more giving! I want to be more a part of your life!"

More a part of her life! "David!" Sarah snaps. "You can't be more a part of my life! Especially now!" Only a forty-two-year-old bachelor would think like this!

"Sarah, I know that you're worried about Dan finding out, but I'll be careful. He'll never guess."

Sarah stands on 86th Street, listening to her lover attempt to reassure her that her life is not about to end. She is about twenty steps beyond panic right now, so completely at a loss for words that she actually wants to cry.

She has a desperate thought. "Listen, what if I meet you somewhere else? What if you don't come to the hospital? You don't need to see my family! Isn't it me that you want?"

David laughs. "Sarah, don't worry. I'll be on my best behavior. I need to see you in the context of your family. I'll be there around 6:00, 6:30." The phone connection is broken.

Sarah paces up and down Riverside Drive, considering her options, one of which seems to be throwing herself into the Hudson River. In the recesses of her imagination lurks a scenario just like the one that is about to unfold, with David as the *Fatal Attraction*–type stalker threatening her marriage.

Regret over their affair pours over her like a thick and bitter syrup.

For the first time in more years than she can remember, Sarah trudges back to her apartment and drinks vodka straight up until the edge of panic is lifted and she is able to make it through the next several hours. She takes great care to mask her drinking binge, brushing her teeth three times in quick succession, replacing the Absolut bottle on the shelf in the liquor cabinet, washing and replacing the coffee mug out of which she drank the stuff.

A complete non-drinker, Sarah feels numb within fifteen minutes of her first sip and then really plastered within half an hour. She checks her watch and notes that it is 2:15. She told Marta she would return to the hospital at this time. She runs to the bathroom and splashes cold water on her face. Then she calls Marta and tells her in her most carefully articulated voice that she is running late, she fell asleep. Marta, all compassion, tells Sarah that she must sleep and not return to the hospital until she feels rested and strong. Emily's fever is a bit raised, but she is still comfortable and is currently taking a nap. Sarah promises that she will return within an hour.

During the time she is home, Sarah spends most of the time lying on her bed, staring up at the ceiling. Her brain is functioning but everything else feels anesthetized. She turns on Leonard Cohen and sings with him at the top of her lungs.

She waves her arms through the air while singing her way through the CD (*The Best of Leonard Cohen*), then talks to herself, arguing with an absent David, relishing her drunkenness, welcoming the escape, trying to figure out how obvious her state will be when she leaves her apartment. She berates herself vocally, repeating the word *stupid* about one hundred times, hitting the bed with her fists for emphasis. She rolls around from side to side, making yodeling sounds. Then, her rational, pragmatic nature kicks in and she stumbles to the kitchen (holding onto the walls every step of the way) and carefully cuts about thirty cubes of feta cheese with a butter knife, which she eats with halves of walnuts sitting cross-legged on the kitchen floor.

Brewing herself two cups of Zabar's coffee, Sarah drinks them, steaming hot, leaning over the kitchen sink in case she begins to puke. By 3:30, with food in her stomach and caffeine in her veins, Sarah's drunkenness is more manageable. She brushes her teeth again, stuffs three pieces of Trident peppermint gum into her mouth, packs up a couple of changes of clothes for Emily and one for herself, a bag of lollipops she bought for Halloween trick-or-treaters, and a handful of storybooks and goes downstairs to hail a cab back up to the hospital.

"May I come in?"

It is 6:30 that evening. The moment she had dreaded has arrived. David Eastman is standing in the doorway of Emily's room, an over-sized bouquet of balloons in hand. Every possible member of Sarah's family and circle of friends, it seems, is crammed into the hospital room at that particular moment—Dan, Daphne, Daphne's best friend Chloe, Sarah's parents, her best friend Ellen, her cousins Sid and Lucy, Dan's brothers Jack and Allen, her mother-in-law Estelle, their good friends Susan and Bill, Anny the nurse and Emily, of course, sitting up in bed, chatting excitedly with Chloe and Daphne, delighted to be at the center of this party.

Sarah had been sitting on the window ledge, keeping a lookout, laughing a bit too loudly at Jack's pointless stories when David shows up. He is wearing jeans, a blinding white t-shirt and a black Armani blazer; his hair is longish, brushing the collar of his jacket, swept back from his face. His lips are full and red and slightly parted. He is completely and utterly breathtaking.

The conversation ceases abruptly when he shows up and Sarah wonders if it is too late for her to fall backward out of the window to her death on the pavement below.

"Aren't you David Eastman, the writer?" asks Sarah's mother in a reverential tone. The acknowledgment of a celebrity in their midst makes everyone stand up a bit taller, pull in their stomachs, and slip into more sophisticated versions of themselves. Loving this moment, David beams Sarah's mother an easy smile and walks into the room, handing the balloon bouquet to Emily, whose eyes grow wide with wonder.

"Say thank you, Emily," admonishes Dan, who steps forward, somewhat quizzically, to shake David's hand while Sarah sits frozen on the windowsill like a pack of Birdseye winter squash. What is she supposed to say? She cannot remember. What is their alleged connection? She is completely mute, utterly paralyzed.

"Thank you," squeaks Emily, unable to move her gaze from David's face. David, meanwhile, grasps Dan's hand warmly. "Forgive my intrusion, but I saw you this morning on *Good Morning America* and was so moved by the way you talked about your daughter's illness that I decided I would stop by on my way in from Boston just for a minute." He takes a step backward. "I don't want to get in the way of your family; just wanted to extend my best wishes." He puts his hand on Dan's shoulder and lowers his voice for that extra measure of sincerity. "I watch you every morning, even though I have no children of my own," he confesses. "I just love your advice."

Dan's eyes crinkle in appreciation and recognition. He wags his finger at David. "I've seen your face before," he says, turning to Sarah. "Don't you have his books at home? I know I've seen his author photo."

With all eyes on Sarah, she slides off the windowsill and goes to join her husband. Sarah feels like a wind-up toy, her bones made of thin metal wire or glass. "Hello," she says formally, miraculously, extending her hand. "We met when you did the reading at Barnes & Noble two years ago." Her voice sounds to her like it is being broadcast from far, far away, possibly Pluto, the planet of unfaithful wives.

David smiles avidly. He is having himself a marvelous time. Sarah, who can barely breathe, wishes horrible things upon him—death, disease, impotence, acne, cellulite, flatulence, writer's block, obscurity, poverty, obesity. "I remember the occasion well," David reports to Dan. "Out of all the people in the room, I felt as if I were reading to her alone."

Sarah feels Daphne's eyes go right through her, read her soul as if it were an x-ray. Her mother, on the other hand, uses David's remark to jump right into this combustible conversation. "Oh, that's Sarah!" she says with a measure of maternal pride that would have been appropriate had Sarah been five years old. "When I used to read to my children, it was Sarah alone who listened."

I'm in hell, thinks Sarah, standing on her fragile bones, an idiotic smile plastered on her frozen winter squash face. *I'm in adulterer's hell.*

"David, I'm glad you've come," says Dan, leading him to a corner of the room. "D'you have a minute? I'd like to show a real writer a book contract that I'm considering." And with that, the awkward impasse is over and the room picks up its cheerful din until thirty minutes later when an apologetic Anny shoos everyone out, except immediate family, citing hospital rules and Emily's need for rest.

"Sare, I'm going to walk David down to his car; we have a business proposition to discuss," calls Dan from the hallway, saying goodbye to his brothers. David, who has been leaning against a wall checking email on his BlackBerry while waiting for Dan (somehow David understood himself to be a member of the immediate family), shoots Sarah a shameless smile, slipping the device into his pocket.

"It was great seeing you again," he says, striding over to Emily's bed where Sarah is sitting. She stares him down. Here is her lover of the past two years appearing—of all places—at her child's sickbed, captivating her mother, enchanting her toddler, chatting up her friends, conducting business with her husband, insinuating himself into the bosom of her family. Fury, disgust, and betrayal compete within her. His nerve is beyond anything she could have imagined.

She meets David's gaze, allowing a cool moment to pass before responding. With Dan standing just outside and her toddler daughter within earshot, she can hardly say what is on her mind—which is that he should get the fuck out of her life right that minute.

Instead, Sarah smiles sweetly and grips David's hand in a vise. He winces, looks surprised, even hurt. Sarah holds his dark, long-lashed gaze until he averts his eyes. She wants him to feel ashamed. He has used his secret power—his beauty and charm—to gain entry into her inner sanctum. And completely without warning! Was it only last week that he was lecturing her over the phone about his solitary, contemplative life as a writer and chastising her for her intensity? Sarah has never endured a day as wrought with intensity and drama as this day, and it was orchestrated completely by David.

"Thanks for having me," he says softly. As if she had invited him, or even assented to his presence! As if she had a choice! "It was important for me to see you...like this." He indicates the room with a sweep of his hand. *If he thinks he's going to get away with kissing me,* she thinks, but he turns, waves to Emily, and walks toward the door. "Bye, Emily! I hope you get better soon!"

Emily waves back happily. "Bye-bye!"

Tempted to give him the finger, Sarah turns her head away instead, only to see Daphne brush by David into the room, bearing coffee. "Whoops," he says, skirting her. She gives him a steely glance. He seems unperturbed. "You have a great family," he tells her. "It was nice to meet you."

Daphne says nothing, just walks toward her mother, rolling her eyes. Sarah waits until David disappears from view and then leans back until she is lying across the bottom part of Emily's bed. "Okay," Daphne says evenly, about two minutes later, when it is certain that both David and her father are out of earshot. "What is up with that guy? You obviously know him from somewhere and I doubt it was just a book reading."

In response, Sarah raises her hand to her head. Either from the vodka or nerves or both, she has a pounding headache. Emily is peeling stickers from her book and placing them all over her sheets and Sarah wants to tell her to stop but cannot find the strength to speak.

"So..." prods Daphne. Sarah looks at her daughter. She is 100 percent sober today and 100 percent suspicious. "We..." she tries. She closes her eyes again, lacking the strength to neither deny nor admit to their affair. Daphne is waiting for her mother's response, breathless. Sarah opens her eyes, looks keenly at her daughter, still lying on her back. "Okay...what's your theory?" she asks.

"Well...I would say that you used to be lovers. He's about your age and he looked at you like he knows what you look like without your clothes and you almost died when he walked into the room. He's really good-looking but he thinks he's God's gift to women." Daphne pulls back the safety flap of her coffee and takes a long sip. "He's probably one of those famous guys who's not as talented as everyone thinks he is. He's kind of like a rock star that way."

Whether out of sheer relief or amusement at her daughter's caustically accurate assessment of David, Sarah begins to laugh and laugh, rolling over on her side to catch her breath. "Oh, oh, oh!" she gasps, finally. "Omigod, that was really horrible, wasn't it?"

"So, I'm right, aren't I? You *were* lovers," presses Daphne, triumphant. Sarah looks at her teenager, the one with whom she needs to have a stern talk. Calm reality reasserts itself. She is the mother. There is no earthly proof for her current sexual involvement with David Eastman, despite Daphne's intuition, despite his weird appearance at Emily's bedside.

"Mom?" Daphne persists. Sarah sits up and gives Daphne a secretive smile. "That's for *me* to know," she says, poking her daughter in the stomach. "Besides, I've got some questions for you, young lady, concerning your whereabouts and activities yesterday."

Daphne opens her eyes in surprise and takes a quick sip of coffee. "What do you mean?" she mumbles in an unconvincingly off-hand way. Sarah looks at Emily. This is really not the place for such a chat but she can't back down now.

"Daphne," she says in a lowered voice. "When you came by yesterday, you were stoned. It was kind of obvious. Daddy didn't notice, but I could tell right away."

Daphne looks at her coffee cup intently. Sarah remembers the surreal landscape of sixteen, the constant lies to her own parents, the furtive experimentation, the confusion. "Daphne, is something the matter?" she asks gently. "You know that you can talk to me about anything."

The minute the words leave her lips, Sarah knows that what she says is patently false. There are some things that simply cannot be discussed. Besides, adolescence is an adult-free zone. Sarah and Dan are the aliens. Their job is to beam unconditional love from the mothership but they can only orbit around their daughter while she drifts, lost in space.

Yet Daphne casts anxious eyes at her mother, bites her lip, and begins to cry. Sarah puts her arm around her oldest daughter, who does not shrug it off for once.

Emily looks at her sister with great concern. "Daffy!" she says sweetly. "Don't worry, I'm getting better!" At which both Sarah and Daphne have to laugh.

"Mom?" Daphne lifts her guilty eyes to her mother.

"Mmhhmm?"

"Do you think that kissing someone who is married counts as adultery?"

A sliver of sheer dread pierces Sarah's heart. The sins of the mothers are visited upon the daughters. She looks at her child carefully. The justice is too perfect, biblical, enough to make her believe in hell. "Daphne..." she says, inhaling sharply. Daphne's eyes are large and woe-filled in her ashen face. They seek out Sarah's and Sarah holds her gaze for one eternal, naked moment.

"Yes," she whispers to Daphne, touching her cheek. "But not for you. Not at your age." Daphne studies her mother and learns everything and nothing.

"Don't tell Dad," she whispers back and Sarah nods, a bitter tear trickling down her own cheek. The two sit silently for a moment while Emily sings her version of a popular commercial in a sweet, soft voice. There is the muted sound of Monday evening in the hospital, the padding of rubber soles down the hallway, the swish of fabrics, the changing of shifts, the remains of the day. It is as peaceful as a lullaby.

Thus becalmed, Sarah and Daphne float apart on separate yet synchronized clouds to contemplate their respective affairs until their attention is redirected by the reappearance of Dan, who leans into the doorway like Fred Astaire, jaunty, juiced, as jubilant as if he had just discovered the secret to eternal life.

"Sorry to break up this beautiful instance of female bonding but I thought I would let you ladies know that I've got myself a new ghostwriter for my book!" he announces with a flourish, practically tap-dancing his way into the room. "David Eastman has agreed to write *Bagels Under the Boardwalk* with me!" Dan beams at his audience proudly, as if expecting applause.

Sarah and Daphne exchange dubious looks, share a moment of pregnant silence, and then collapse in helpless, hysterical laughter, even as Dan watches, utterly and completely mystified, confirmed in his suspicion that he will never understand women, especially those nearest and dearest to him.

As for Sarah, each guffaw that wrenches its way out of her gut threatens to asphyxiate her. She laughs until it hurts, certain that her heart is going to stop beating at any second.

The following morning, Sarah wakes with a jolt at 5:00 a.m., takes stock of her surroundings (she is still in Emily's hospital room, on the folding cot) and then sinks into a horror-drenched analysis of the nightmarish and absurd events of the previous day.

David's nerve is matched only by Dan's naiveté, thinks Sarah. Sure, he's charming, handsome, and famous, but isn't her husband even slightly suspicious of David's unsolicited appearance at Emily's sickbed? Why would a famous writer, who just happened to have met Sarah a couple of years earlier, suddenly show up to visit their ailing three-year-old? Even if Dan has failed to wonder about the relationship between David and his own wife, wouldn't he be concerned that David poses a threat to himself by being a groupie??

How could Dan dive in so heedlessly to this collaborative relationship with David? And what of the adorable Jasmine? Like Sarah's phone conversation with David the previous week, this latest turn of events makes no sense.

At seven, Anny informs Sarah that if Emily continues to improve, they can leave the hospital the following morning. Dan is en route to the hospital with Sarah's laptop and the news gives Sarah a deadline: today is the day that she will finish her story from the previous week, *Portrait of You as a Young Man.* The fury that served as her muse the previous week has only intensified to create a turbo-charged motivation for finishing this work.

Justice does she pursue.

When Dan arrives, bearing twin cappuccinos from the Starbucks across Broadway, he is overflowing with the desire to deconstruct Monday's magical visit from David Eastman, that fortunate accident that will catapult his book to mega-stardom. It is the ultimate marketing ploy, a match made in media heaven. It depresses Sarah to think how divergent their realities are. For the first time in their marriage, she feels smarter than and consequently sorry for her husband.

"The minute he told me that he thought my television segments reached beyond the parents-of-young-children market, I realized that he was onto something," reports Dan, all boyish excitement. "He's been watching me for two years; he actually knows who I am. This Jasmine whateverhernameis is a pen-for-hire who has never seen me on *Good Morning America.* A book like this requires a hand-in-glove relationship between the author and the writer and, well…let's just say that it feels like David is already a part of my life."

More than you know, thinks Sarah. Listening to her husband prattle on, Sarah practices the wifely art of listening, perfected over the past eighteen years. Though she appears every inch the patient, supportive spouse to Dan's undiscerning eye, she has been able to retain a love and respect for her husband during the two years of her affair with David (whom she is now certain she has never loved), she knows at that minute that something vital has ruptured in her relationship with her husband and she mourns it instantly.

"And then when I asked him, he was at first reticent, though obviously flattered. I've already put a call in to Ruby. We will draft a new contract and hopefully sign today or tomorrow. David said he will be in town for a few more days."

"Hmm," Sarah says, nodding, suddenly envisioning David in his Chelsea flat. She remembers the last time they were together, recalls rushing uptown afterward, the taste of David in her mouth, salty and sweet. She remembers how obvious and self-conscious she felt, as if all the gay men at the 23rd Street subway station somehow knew what she had been up to.

"He is going to contact *People* and propose a personal sidebar to the article they're running on me," relates Dan with awe, unable to believe his good fortune. "One of the feature editors is a previous girlfriend." *The entire world is his previous girlfriend*, thinks Sarah poisonously.

While Dan sails through the latest marvelous chapter of his marvelous life, Sarah's thoughts turn inward. Her affair with David is over, of course, especially as he is now Dan's new best friend, co-writer, and potential lover, for all she knows. What he has done is unbelievable, admirable in its hubris, magnificent in its drama and career-building potential, of course, but truly inexcusable, endangering her marriage and her entire family's stability, violating an unspoken agreement.

"You are a freaking psycho, you know that?!" Sarah yells into her cell phone two hours later, racing around the track at Riverbank, the New York State park built, scarily, on top of a water treatment plant next to the West Side Highway. Riverbank is a place where she knows no one, not the dignified Harlem matrons walking in pairs, not the undernourished, artsy Washington Heights residents running anemically, not the unemployed thugs hanging out on the side of the track astride undersized bicycles.

Immediately after Dan had left the hospital, Sarah called Marta, asking if she could come to the hospital earlier than they had planned, perhaps by nine instead of two? Having been up since 6:00 a.m. baking chocolate chip cookies, Marta is delighted to be able to deliver her goods immediately and have the pleasure of feeding Emily, whom she loves like one of her grandchildren. Having secured an escape hatch, Sarah writes furiously on her laptop at the foot of Emily's bed while her daughter watches Regis, twirling her hair. When Marta shows up, she slams shut the computer, kisses her daughter, hugs her housekeeper, and dashes from the room, running the half-mile to Riverbank.

At the park, safe in her anonymity, Sarah unleashes her rage on David, barely stopping to wonder whether she is calling at a convenient time, whether he is answering his cell phone in the privacy of his apartment or in a meeting with his editor or at the gym or eating breakfast or lying in bed with another woman or while sitting down for his first meeting as Dan's ghostwriter.

"What was yesterday about? I'd really like to know how you had the chutzpah to show up in the midst of my family medical crisis and become the toast of the town, Dan Reinhart's ghostwriter, or is it co-writer, Mr. Eastman?"

Sarah is breathing fire, spitting as she speaks. Bitterness and disappointment well up in her. Their affair—yes, she admits now that it was an affair after all—was not about the fusion of two spirits destined for one another, about siblings separated at birth, about the creation of a rare and vital compound, etc., etc. Their affair, like most, was about desire. And selfishness. And timing. And need. And acquisition. And vanity.

There was nothing eternal between them, not a trace of transcendence in their lovemaking. They borrowed each other's bodies; they filled each other's time. He never loved her, he never loved her, he never loved her.

I have known this all along, she thinks, blinking back her tears, wrestling with the grief that crouches, like a lion, at the door of her soul. *But I never let him penetrate my heart or dwell in my dreams even as he branded himself upon my flesh.*

"Sarah," David tries. Obviously, he has screwed up with her, but wasn't that his intent? Like so much in his life, yesterday had unfolded naturally, the consequence of a spontaneous decision. Yes, what he had done was brash, but hadn't the time come to edit Sarah out of his life? He had tried the previous week and she got furious with him. How do you apologize for hurting someone when it is the only way to get what you want?

Sarah's phone call catches David at an Oren's Coffee down in Chelsea. He has been up for hours, walking up and down Eighth Avenue in an effort to outpace his guilt. He is nursing his third cappuccino, see-sawing between remorse and joy. Leaving the hospital the previous evening, he spent the better part of the night in a state of magical disbelief, marveling at the unforeseen fortune that had landed in his lap.

The guilt had arrived only with the morning.

David would miss Sarah. He thought highly of her, in fact, would like to marry someone very much like her someday. As a lover, she meshed perfectly with him and was refreshingly independent, managing not to fall slavishly in love with him as had most of his previous lovers, sustaining the ability to view their affair as an end in and of itself. She was smart. He adored her body. He considered it a coup and an honor to be with her.

He had known, of course, that she felt terribly guilty; he saw it in her eyes when he was inside her, a flash of shame hidden in the fathomless pool of her desire. The knowledge of her guilt and its manifestations (she would not, for instance, allow herself to come for the first couple of months they were together) made him jealous and fueled his obsession with Dan, the better man, the object of Sarah's loyalty and love.

Though he would have access to Sarah by proxy through his status position as Dan's co-writer (name on the cover, a nice advance), she was lost to him; she had locked him out of her heart. The look in her eyes last night was so fierce that he realized he had underestimated her strength. The look in her eyes last night threw his equilibrium; it was his mother's look, her fury and her disappointment.

"Don't say that you're sorry, because you're not," says Sarah toward the end of their conversation. It is nearly one hour later and she is depleted, physically and emotionally, spent of her anger, overwhelmed by a sadness that feels familiar that has accompanied this relationship from the start. She realizes that she had wanted to love David and that she wanted his love as well, not as a corrective or supplement to her marriage but as an affirmation of love itself, of the triumph of good over evil, of the existence of God, of the transcendent nature of the human spirit.

What is left of their affair tastes like ashes in her mouth.

One hour into their phone conversation, David has ended up on a pier jutting out over the Hudson River just south of 14th Street and the Nomadic Museum. He feels afraid but he also feels free. The day is exquisite and unseasonably warm. The water of the Hudson sparkles with sunshine, runners in the skimpiest of shorts and shirts race past him, rollerbladers and cyclists pass before him—slashes of pure motion on a static backdrop—young women in light dresses stroll alone or with men, the breeze of the river blowing their cotton or rayon shifts to the lovely contours of their bodies.

The day is utter perfection. It occurs to David that September 11 was such a day. He had been in New York to meet with his editor that day, having driven down from Somerville the night before. He remembers the hell, the mad illogic of the devastation, the profanity of mass murder against the backdrop of flawless weather, bodies falling, bodies lost, lives shattered, the troops passing beneath his window, headed uptown on Eighth Avenue, a retreating army of pedestrians, the smoke, a sacrificial offering to a Moloch-like God.

David is seated on a bench facing downtown. Far away, in New York Harbor, he can see Lady Liberty. He is forty-two years old, at the height of his powers, his potency, his attractiveness to women, and (as the last twenty-four hours had proven) to men. He is a famous, critically acclaimed writer of fiction. He lectures at Harvard. His students adore him and his peers admire him. He is in sterling health. For the past two years he has been sleeping with Dan Reinhardt's sexy wife, Sarah.

It's a damn good thing that he is co-writing Dan's biography because this little tidbit of information has the power to dominate headlines for weeks, the power to bring them all down.

"I wanted to love you," says Sarah simply. "I wanted you to love me."

They stand on the shore of the same river, nearly seven miles apart. The breeze of the Hudson has dried Sarah's tears. David is moved by her sorrow. It is exactly two years since they met.

"I will miss us," replies David and the poignant, searing truth of this admission stings him deeply. Freedom is at hand, beckoning to him on the horizon, yet he suddenly feels a pull homeward, the metallic taste of loss, a bolt of panic. Being David Eastman, he will move past this moment, yet being David Eastman, he will never forget it.

The conversation at an end, Sarah walks back to the hospital. Now that it is over, she ponders the beginning of the affair. How did it come about? There had been so many others who also made her heart race. There is now Bill Martin, if she so wishes. She could easily seduce him or allow him to seduce her, meet him in a downtown club, something trendy with the word "bar" in its name, have a margarita or two, and follow him home.

There had been so many others but none were like David.

It is over; it is over. Too soon to analyze its true legacy, Sarah instead focuses on the story she had begun last week, the corrective to *Boy at Nine*, her first true writing in two decades—*Portrait of You as a Young Man*. Returning to Emily's room, she intends to relieve Marta but is instead given strict instructions by her housekeeper to go somewhere else to finish her work. Meekly, gratefully, Sarah packs up her laptop and relocates to the Starbucks across the street, settling into the organic task of writing, too long delayed, now joyfully reclaimed.

Sarah works smoothly, with perfect focus, for several hours, breaking away only to run to the bathroom or replenish her grande-sized coffee. It is an ecstatic, monastic experience. She has everything at the ready—a bottle of Crystal Geyser water, her anger, and her insight. The story is good, even better than she thought it was last week. Waiting behind it, like customers patiently lined up for their lattes and frappuccinos, are a multitude of tales waiting to be written.

Her story is good; she is about to emerge as a writer, even if David beat her to it by publishing two books already, even if she's only been the secret lover of a celebrity author and the wife of a celebrity doctor, whose soon-to-be-published book, ghostwritten by her ex-lover, will get more publicity, make more money and sell more copies than her critically-acclaimed work ever will.

One day, she thinks, biographers might piece together the story of her and David Eastman, fleeting early twenty-first-century literary sensations. One day, a literary scholar might be moved to make sense of her life. She might discover Dan's inconsequential yet best-selling book, translated into twenty languages, and David's shared byline. She might posit that Dan and David were also romantically involved. She will determine whether Sarah's affair with David constituted a literary partnership or an epic romance or if they were largely insignificant within the context of social and literary history.

Sarah is forty-three and she is about to emerge as a writer. Within a couple of months, her story will be joined by a handful of others, bound carefully into a collection, and submitted to serious editors at venerable publishing companies. Dan's literary agent will represent her. There will be a small bidding war for the publishers to recognize the potential success of such a work, the promotional value of the attractive author who is also the wife of a famous television personality, the inspiring example of midlife success for women everywhere, this rare example of someone who acquired that elusive attainment known as "having it all."

The marketing department of Sarah's publishing house is able to foresee not only respectable book reviews but also a full complement of feature articles, profiles, and interviews. They envision spots on *Oprah, Ellen,* and *Regis*. They assess Sarah's media value even without knowing the most media-worthy detail of her life.

On a chilly October evening, exactly one year later, Sarah sits behind a podium at Brandeis University, waiting to deliver the keynote address at an annual women's literary forum. She is joined by a twenty-something author who has just written a memoir that has become the battle cry of her generation of women and a woman in her seventies who just revealed, in the pages of *her* memoir, that she had had a romantic relationship with Golda Meir.

The room is packed with academics, writers, students, and family members. There are also members of the press in the audience—a *Boston Globe* reporter, a writer from the *Christian Science Monitor*, an *NPR* morning show host, a columnist from *Vanity Fair.* On a table at the back of the room a representative from the local Barnes & Noble mans a table stacked with copies of her short story collection, *Portrait of You as a Young Man* (published last month), as well as the works of the two other authors.

As predicted by the publishers, Sarah's book has made a huge splash. She is now the new literary It Girl.

The year has been horrible, wonderful, and transformative. Daphne's adulterous kiss turns out to have been with her physics teacher, Mr. Roberts, who is dismissed once Daphne goes to her principal in a moment of outraged clarity. Though she never has sex with her thirty-four-year-old teacher, it is not for his lack of trying to seduce his smart, sexy sixteen-year-old student. When Dan and Sarah find out about the near-affair (the principal calls them with a tearful Daphne in his office and they drop everything and arrive at the school within minutes) the crisis binds them together. Daphne enters five-days-a-week therapy, the school avoids a media storm, and Sarah and Dan do not breathe a word of this incident to anyone.

Emily breaks her foot two months after her bout with rheumatic fever and spends six weeks clunking around the apartment in a cast, driving the downstairs neighbors crazy and nearly resulting in a lawsuit. When her foot heals, she goes through a phase of only wanting to wear her yellow rain boots, which Dan and Sarah permit until she develops a fungal infection in her right big toe. Marta, their devoted housekeeper, decides that she will leave within the year to open up a

Portuguese restaurant in Queens. Though Dan and David are in continuous contact with each other, their meetings and writing of the manuscript take place outside of the parameters of Sarah's home and her personal life.

Respecting Sarah's wishes, David stays largely out of her life. It is only as the publication of her book looms that she relents to his periodic overtures (he calls her at least once monthly on her cell phone "just to say hi;" she never answers or returns his call) and agrees to meet with him in Harvard Square on the day she is scheduled to speak at Brandeis.

While *Bagels Under the Boardwalk* is still selling millions of copies around the world, David's collection of stories had come out the previous spring, meriting mixed reviews. In his private, middle-of-the-night musings, David feels the limits of his power and wonders if his star is about to fade. Within the intimate confines of their lunch together, he is moved to admit his fear to Sarah.

Now carrying on a tepid affair with the wife of a religion professor, David still excites her. During lunch at Algiers their hands brush together, their knees touch, color rises to their cheeks. Sarah stares at his lips, remembering them on her neck, on her breasts, between her legs. She feels a tremendous kinship with him, a warmth, a nostalgia. They are, after all, siblings of a sort. Their parting hug on the street is passionate. David's skin is hot through his clothes; his Somerville house is only ten minutes away and Sarah is not due at Brandeis for several hours.

But it is over. They gaze into each other's eyes. David will marry eventually, have children, and engage in numerous extramarital affairs. Sarah will never take another lover. David Eastman was her one and only.

The Brandeis auditorium is filled with the electric excitement of a memorable cultural event about to unfold. The chair of the department takes the stage and the room quiets down. The program is underway.

Sarah studies her audience during the introduction. This is her first appearance at a university and she is honored to be reading at such a venue. She hears flattering words being applied to her, snippets of her reviews quoted, and the names of important publications cited in conjunction with her work. She thinks about her two-decades vow of silence as a writer, the extraordinary reversal of the past year. She wants to impart something eternal and invaluable to those who have come to hear her. She wants her prose to have the power to transform their lives.

She sees David sitting in the audience and her breath catches in her throat. He is impossibly beautiful. Her gaze lingers on him lovingly, and then he vanishes before her eyes, slipping back into the phantom world, her muse, her invention, her dream lover.

THE JERUSALEM LOVER

1

It is a chilly morning in early March. You are sitting at Café Rosa in Jerusalem, reading your usual pile of newspapers, magazines, and dog-eared paperbacks, nursing a mug of tepid tea. Café Rosa is located in the Valley of Ghosts; it is the main thoroughfare of South Jerusalem, invariably and somewhat inaccurately termed trendy or upscale or affluent in the international press. It is, in fact, the pulse and soul of the German Colony, studded with eateries, hardware stores, clothing shops, food markets, jewelry boutiques, kiosks, and cafes, known more commonly by its Hebrew name—Emek Refaim.

You are a creature of habit and it is your habit to arrive at Café Rosa every morning at 8:00 a.m. and remain for a couple of hours, after which it becomes unseemly, slothful and perhaps even suspicious for a solitary man to remain reading in a coffee house as if he has no work, no obligations, no human ties.

This morning, though, you are heedless of time, reading the iconic work of a twentieth-century Jewish philosopher, a paperback edition, published locally and recently re-released after an initial printing some fifty years earlier. So engrossed are you in your reading that you barely notice the table to your left being occupied by two American teen-agers—a boy and a girl—who bear a striking physical resemblance to one another.

After a short interval of chair scraping and the resting of their respective book bags under the table, your young neighbors attend to the matter of breakfast. The boy scans the menu and orders a hearty

Israeli breakfast platter while the girl places an elaborate order for coffee; there is much discussion in American-inflected Hebrew, with agitated hand motions. It seems that the girl wants to make sure that her coffee is decaffeinated with skim milk and artificial sweetener. She is anxious that her order might get mangled. In the lull between placing their orders and the arrival of their breakfasts, the students unabashedly turn their attention to the work you are reading as if they were browsing in a bookshop and you were merely the shelf upon which it rested.

"Do you believe in the covenant?"

It is the girl who poses the question; she is a delicate version of the boy, with languid feline eyes, brown hair in a pixyish bob, and pink cheeks. You look up at her question but she is addressing the boy. You might as well be invisible. "As in between God and the Jewish people?"

The boy has been checking text messages on his cell phone. He slips the device into his pocket and regards the girl. It is clear now that the two are twins, most likely college students spending a year studying at Hebrew University, citizens of an American city rich in history and lore, a city that hosted the likes of Benjamin Franklin or Thomas Edison or Mark Twain. The boy's cheeks are not pink but they are smooth and full and his haircut mimics the girl's. Where he differs from his sister is in the color of his hair—it is a rich and complicated cocoa brown—and in the haunted nature of his gaze.

The girl awaits her brother's response. She wears a red band around her right wrist and has numerous piercings along the perimeter of her left ear. Her low-slung chinos reveal a small *hamsa*, the Middle Eastern good luck amulet, tattooed onto her lower back. Her eyes are greenish to her brother's gray. Between the two of them, she is the trusting soul, he the skeptic. She falls in love easily, nurtures numerous fascinations, and has had her heart broken several times in her young life. Flesh of each other's flesh, he is the observer, the critic, the inadvertent breaker of hearts.

The boy turns the question over in his mind. He is distracted. There is a shadowy message he has received, a warning. He peers beyond his sister's face to his dream of the night before but the memory proves elusive and his sister is waiting. What does she want from him? Oh yes...the covenant...his opinion of the covenant between God and the Jewish People.

A sliver of last night's dream insinuates its way into his consciousness. He looks at his sister desperately. Her question is a key. Whispered prophecies come to him late at night. They confirm the teachings of his tradition—everything he tried to run away from as a teen—the *brit* with Abraham, his own covenant, branded upon his flesh. These intimations furnish an ending for the narrative that has wound its way through the pages of human history leading up to this present moment of the fulfillment of an ancient promise, the glorious nation that has sprung up, miraculous and messy, in the modern Middle East.

To ask about his beliefs is irrelevant for he cannot properly be termed a believer.

He is a seer.

Yet he tells his sister—in a voice that is prematurely weary—"The covenant you are talking of is entirely man-made. It is the hope of the Jewish people, their sustaining, primal myth of chosenness. The idea of a covenant with God forms the faith of the Jewish people but faith does not make anything real."

The girl opens her mouth as if to argue and then their breakfast arrives and the conversation is forsaken.

You would marvel at the coincidence of this conversation happening in such close proximity to yourself, echoing your innermost quest, but after several months in Jerusalem you are beyond the concept of coincidence. Being here, you have learned that what you suspected all along is true: unseen forces operate in our daily lives. For instance, it is on this morning that you first see Rachel sitting diagonally across from you and your paper-strewn table.

Sitting alone like you she wears an air of melancholy, her thick auburn hair falling heavily around her delicate face. She wears the pallor of one who is not naturally fair but weary, one who has recently emerged from a devastating illness. She is thin, without a hint of muscle, the thinness of neglect. She is studying the menu as if it were a mystical text, squinting to read the meaning between the lines. You are mesmerized, watching her. There is a dull quality to her hair and you imagine that she smells slightly rancid, unwashed. Her nails, you think, must be jagged. Her feet, resting inside unseasonable sandals, are dirty.

She will now scratch her left arm, you think to yourself, and she scratches her left arm. The waitress will now arrive, you think to yourself, and the waitress arrives. She will point to an item on the menu, you think to yourself, and she points to an item on the menu.

You have been in this moment before. But it is not over.

Half-rising in your seat, you know to look toward the street where a young woman approaches the entrance to Café Rosa in an obvious wig and large sunglasses. The gray-eyed boy stands as well, recognizing the vision from his own dream. His mouth is open. His sister follows the line of his vision and turns her head toward the front of the café.

Something about the approaching woman is wrong. Her wig is not the kind worn by the ultra-Orthodox women of Jerusalem. Her coat is too large. She is walking very quickly toward the cafe. The young Ethiopian security guard rises from his stool as if to greet her. He is Samson in the temple of the Philistines. The girl stands, as if hypnotized, pushes over her chair, strides to the front of the cafe, and shouts in Hebrew: "*M'khabel*!" Terrorist! The café is a montage of panicked faces and darting movements downward, screams and whimpers, shouted pleas to heaven—*Elohim!*—broken glass, smashed plates, the stench of fear and then the awful explosion, the end of the world.

11

Exactly four months earlier, Rachel Rosensweig walked through the tastefully ornate abode belonging to Martin Holloway, the president of Columbia University, flanked by two faculty wives whose names she was forever confusing or simply forgetting. The one to her left, married to the famous astronomer, was it Doris or Barbara? And the one to her right, married to the chair of the history department, was it Lydia or Margaret?

If I cared, even remotely, I would remember, thought Rachel, finally excusing herself and setting off in search of the bar.

In the wake of a fall semester filled with unprecedented incidents of bad press for the university (a Pulitzer-winning literature professor accused of plagiarism, the discovery of rampant cocaine use in a mostly freshman dorm, the appearance of swastikas in the bathrooms of Butler Library on the day that the Israeli ambassador was scheduled to speak, a suicide on East Campus), President Holloway was eager to create good cheer, lift faculty morale, and demonstrate his return to the reins of power at the university.

This pre-Christmas cocktail party was essentially a public relations maneuver and a fairly transparent one at that. Despite the jovial atmosphere in the room, the tasteful string quartet in the corner, the mute cocktail waiters carrying trays of delicacies, the easy smiles and melodious laughter, the subtle flirtation, the flow of wine, and the admiring glances at the décor and architecture of the president's palatial home, cynical thoughts were being harbored by practically everyone in attendance.

"Red wine, dry," said Rachel, standing before the bar, which was the same height as her shoulders. A petite woman with thick auburn hair and large brown eyes, she looked girlish and boyish all at once. She wore a brief black skirt, a black t-shirt, sheer stockings, and high black boots. To her left stood a slender young man, Indian, wearing an embroidered tunic of mustard yellow. He was tall for an Indian, she thought, and rather good-looking. She turned to look at him and he looked back at her boldly, without a hint of a smile. Taken aback, she quickly turned away, receiving the wine glass being handed to her. Fixing her gaze on the drink, she took a careful sip, stepping away from the bar.

"So, Professor Rosensweig, what is your opinion on this matter?"

Professor Stiles's voice boomed across the room suddenly turned silent. A Shakespearean scholar, Bob Stiles was a theatrical presence in his own right. Every head turned toward the sound, eager to catch a whiff of drama. In the center of the room, President Holloway stood statue-like, his face frozen in a rictus. A circle of academics, male but for Shoshanna Ratner, a celebrated Women's Studies scholar, had formed around the president and they now all faced away from him. *Let it not be about Israel*, prayed Rachel, holding her breath, watching an invisible spotlight fall on her husband, Elisha Rosensweig.

A renowned scholar of Hebrew literature and language, Elisha Rosensweig was at the epicenter of Columbia's public relations problems this past semester and his inclusion in President Holloway's soiree was reason enough for others to attend. Skirting political involvement for his entire career, Rosensweig had emerged, following 9/11, as a stinging critic of American foreign policy, publishing essays and later a book that laid the blame for the attacks on America herself. While the book hinted at a sinister alliance between the US and Israel, it was not until the beginning of the war in Iraq that Rosensweig turned his full-time attention to publicly flogging the State of Israel.

What began as a criticism of policies (the building of the security fence, the IDF's policy of demolishing homes belonging to family members of Palestinian terrorists following attacks against civilians, Israel's Jewish-only law of return) quickly morphed into a full-time anti-Zionism, culminating in an article he had written at the beginning of the fall semester—and published in *The Times* of London—which used the word "apartheid" to refer to Israel's policies toward the Palestinians and called into question the very legitimacy of Israel's existence.

While harsh criticism of Israel was hardly a phenomenon within academia, there was something about Rosensweig that succeeded in capturing the attention of the media, who had taken to stalking him like paparazzi. His every pronouncement—rational or intemperate—was reported and immediately posted on websites and blogs. Students either flocked to his classes or avoided him like the plague. He became the darling of the Edward Said Society at Columbia and spoke frequently and warmly of the friendship the two men had shared when, in fact, they had hardly been able to stand one another. Rosensweig's political views and status as an Israeli Israel-basher had turned him into a freakish celebrity, unseemly and undignified, the kind one sees on reality shows. Enamored of the limelight, he fed the media ever-tastier tidbits.

His latest offering had been delivered just two weeks earlier, on the eve of the festival of Hanukkah. Calling a noon press conference at the Broadway gate of Columbia, he renounced his Israeli citizenship as an act of protest against what he now regularly termed the "Nazi-like" State of Israel.

Rosensweig's most recent pronouncement seemed to shock even those who bore anti-Israel sentiments. At the press conference, Rosensweig stated that because "Israel was the new South Africa," he would refer to himself thereafter as a "former Israeli," that he sought to distance himself from any association with the state, that he would never set foot in the land again as a gesture of protest. He said that he would devote himself to promoting divestment proceedings against Israel in academic and religious circles.

The following morning, the search committee that had considered Elisha Rosensweig a front-runner for the position of chair of Columbia's first-ever Department of Israel Studies quickly and quietly dropped his name from their roster, going as far as destroying evidence that they had even considered his candidacy in the first place.

"I think," replied Rosensweig now, in his Hebrew-inflected voice, relishing the sudden quiet, the captive audience delivered to him by Professor Stiles in President Holloway's mansion on Morningside Drive, "that women naturally have a different relationship to numbers and we should not be shy about saying so."

There was a collective forward tilt in the room. "In fact," Rosensweig continued airily, "I would like to know more about how male and female brains process numeric data. But," he added, seeking out Rachel's gaze from across the gathering that had suddenly become paralyzed with suspense—this issue had dominated headlines since it was raised in the course of a conference at Yale last week—"I think that we cannot fall into the trap of assuming that men or boys are naturally 'better' with numbers. I don't know what better means. Besides, it could be that there is a feminine approach to numbers that is superior but has been squelched by centuries of male mathematical supremacy."

"Hear, hear!" cried Douglas Elkin, a professor of sociology, raising his wine glass in a toast.

"Hear, hear!" boomed back President Holloway, grinning widely beneath his mop of unmanageable white tresses as the crisis passed and the entire room let out its breath in a collective sigh of relief.

The entire room that is, except for Rachel Rosensweig, who turned away from the sight of her notorious husband and strode into an elegant, adjacent drawing room. A tapestry depicting a vague Biblical battle hung against a walnut-paneled wall. Was it David returning from his encounter with Goliath? Jesus walking through the ancient city of Jerusalem? Jonah confronting the sinful inhabitants of Nineveh?

"Are you Mrs. Rosensweig?"

Before she even heard his words, she felt his breath upon her neck and spun around. It was the young Indian man. He was standing nearly toe-to-toe with her. His gaze was presumptuous. Regal and haughty, he was at least ten years her junior.

"Why do you ask?" she asked coldly, but not without curiosity.

"The way he looked at you, like he owned you." The young man looked directly at her breasts, then back at her face, daring her to rebuke him.

Rachel crossed her arms over her small breasts. Her traitorous nipples had hardened noticeably beneath her thin t-shirt. "Marriage is not ownership," she informed this stranger.

Digesting her words, the young man let his eyes roam freely over her small, compact form. Rachel started to feel enraged, uncrossed her arms and placed them on her hips, shifting her weight.

"Do you share your husband's political views?" he asked.

"No," Rachel replied hotly. What was it this man was after? She looked at him sharply, feeling the authority of her years, her status as the wife of a controversial professor. "Who are you?"

Dismissing her question, the young man pressed on. "Do you know that your husband has said that terrorist attacks against Jews are a legitimate form of resistance to Israel's occupation?" He thrust a computer printout of an article into her hands. Rachel grabbed the article. It appeared to be a downloaded version of an article from *The Financial Times*.

"What the hell is this?" she demanded. She had never seen this article before.

"It will appear in tomorrow's paper," he said. "Go home and read it. Your husband is quoted as saying that he would feel no remorse if you or your daughter were killed in such an attack."

Rachel tasted metal. Her blood pounded in her ears and her legs felt shaky. The cocktail party was in full swing in the room next door and the noise was suddenly unbearable.

"Are you all right?" the young man asked, not without compassion, putting his hand on her arm. His touch was hot. She felt it through her clothing.

"Fuck off," Rachel said with sudden vehemence, throwing off his arm, striding toward the elevator through the room where President Holloway was happily holding forth, blissfully unaware of the storm that was about to break with the dawn of the new day.

111

The line outside of Miller Theatre snaked up Broadway, ending at the tip of West 118th Street. Holding a ticket and shivering, Dan Seligman wondered why the theatre's public relations office couldn't get their act together. It was ridiculous, really, how they had failed to furnish press tickets or a press kit or even answer his emails or phone calls. The entire episode was either an exercise in stonewalling or sheer incompetence. Perhaps both.

Appearing tonight at Miller Theatre was controversial Columbia professor Elisha Rosensweig. His subject for the evening was "Israel/IsNOTReal." The copy on the fliers posted all over the campus promised a "provocative evening from a provocative thinker." One week before the appointed evening, the event had sold out.

Dan, who was on assignment from the *Columbia Spectator* that evening, was three months into his college career, a wide-eyed freshman hailing from Oakland, California, madly in love with New York. One year earlier, he had traveled east with his mother to see twelve campuses forming a protracted triangle from Maine to Chicago to Maryland. Columbia was the first stop on their trip. After spending six hours on the campus, Dan declared the college tour officially over. He would be applying only to Columbia University, he informed his mother. If he didn't get in, he would apply for a job there and spend every waking hour on campus auditing classes.

An exceptional student, Dan was admitted to Columbia on early decision and granted a freshman dorm in Carmen, the ugly-as-sin building fronting West 114th Street, designed for first-year students. His roommate was the son of a folk musician from New Hampshire and the roommate's friends became Dan's surrogate family. He loved every one of his classes, including the first-year writing seminar, considered a deadly requirement by every single member of the student body. Following the recommendation of his writing professor, he joined the *Spectator* as a feature writer.

This Monday night's event constituted Dan's fifth assignment for the *Spec.* His beat was loosely defined as cultural events that fell outside of film, dance, music, theatre, or art. Though the staff argued at some length over whether Professor Rosensweig's lecture was culture or news, the assignment was unanimously handed to Dan, who had been hearing wildly conflicting reports about him since virtually his first week on campus and had been curious to hear the man and draw his own conclusions.

The night was icy cold for early November and Dan could have kicked himself for running out of Carmen dressed only in a t-shirt, jeans, and a thin blazer. On his feet were his over-worn and much-loved Birkenstocks, bought in Berlin the previous summer. When a matron joined the line, wrapped in a fur coat, Dan forgot his anti-fur sentiments and coveted the dead animal with all his heart.

After an interminable crawl toward the entrance, Dan was inside Miller Theatre. He strode to the staircase, scoring a front-row seat on the balcony. On his way, he passed the audio-visual crew setting up their recording equipment. Stepping gingerly over the wires, he patted his microscopic tape recorder, nestled in his breast pocket next to his thin reporter's notebook.

A flow of humanity filled the theatre. Seats were snatched like life rafts on a sinking ship and students sat on steps and lined the back walls. In the front row orchestra, Dan made out the form of President Holloway, the provost Marlin Jennings, and numerous faculty members of the university. Opening his notebook, he began taking notes.

Within minutes, the program began, with an introduction from President Holloway about the value of an academic institution such as Columbia hosting events wherein controversial views were to be aired.

"What is a university, if not a universe of forces and ideas, often colliding?" he asked rhetorically and rather moronically, thought Dan. The mike was handed over to a young girl whom Dan recognized from the spate of anti-Israel protests on campus that fall. She was fair-skinned, freckled, and tall...saved from boring Midwestern wholesomeness by the ratty black *kafiyeh* wrapped around her curly red hair.

"I'm Claire Bernstein?" she squeaked into the microphone. "As founder and president of CSAZO?—Columbia Students Against Zionist Oppression—it is my great pleasure to introduce to you a modern hero? A man who is not afraid to stand up to the fascist regime of Israel? A noble truth-seeker who has risked his life to transmit his message and hope for peace? An important thinker who will reveal the racist policies and programs of the country that is the worst violator of human rights today?…Dr. Elisha Rosensweig!"

Dan swiveled his head around, eager to catch the audience's reaction. Claire Bernstein seemed to him a caricature of an activist—light on the facts, heavy on the moral outrage. Last year it was Take Back the Night; this year it was The Unpardonable Crimes of Israel. She probably spent her school breaks denouncing her parents' Zionism to their faces, screaming at them for being such *hypocrites*. Next year she might be marching with PETA and pouring buckets of red paint on fur-wearing women. Who could take her seriously?

"Free Palestine!" screamed a girl directly behind Dan. The theatre reverberated with lusty applause as Claire Bernstein sashayed off the stage, passing the lumbering Elisha Rosensweig who paused to hug her before assuming the podium himself, powerful, erect, electric. He gripped the sides of the lectern as he scowled out at his audience. Learning over the railing, Dan saw President Holloway, returned to his front-row seat, clapping vigorously, his face a mask of sheer and abject terror.

IV

Within minutes, ambulances arrive and the survivors are taken to the emergency room of Hadassah Hospital on Mount Scopus in shifts, the seriously wounded trundled off within seconds. Hasidic men in bright yellow vests, members of ZAKA, the rescue and recovery unit, step gingerly yet efficiently through the devastation, collecting human remains. You are prostrate on the floor, having passed out at the sound of the explosion. There is a rough shaking of your shoulders, the word "Hey!" yelled urgently and repeatedly. You open your eyes and they pull you to a sitting position. Somehow your glasses are still on your face, unbroken. You are fine, you insist repeatedly to the Israeli paramedics who ignore you, bundling you onto an ambulance with other lightly wounded survivors.

Ani b'seder, you state uselessly, letting them know that you are not in need of medical help, craning your head as you walk, looking for the woman with the auburn hair. Rachel.

At the hospital, you are led to a seat, made to sit. You are fine, as fine as one can be who has just crawled out of a hellhole of blood and body parts and shattered glass. You are fine. You are whole. You are alive.

The gray-eyed boy sits across the room, wrapped in a blanket, staring at the floor with unblinking eyes. By his feet are two book bags. His cell phone rings and rings with a popular melody but he does not answer it. An elderly couple—the man with a bleeding head wound, the woman with a blood-soaked arm in a makeshift sling—are escorted by a nurse directly into the emergency room. A young woman, clutching a toddler in her arms and sobbing uncontrollably, is attended to by a volunteer. Frantic relatives and friends arrive by the second.

You stand up and look around the room for a hint of russet. A young nurse appears beside you and asks questions you cannot understand. You are led inside a room where briskly efficient physicians examine you. *I must be in shock*, you think to yourself. This is what it must feel like, a terrifying absence of feeling, the sense of being exiled from one's self.

When you are released from Hadassah Hospital, you weave your way through the throngs of journalists camped outside, keeping your face down, waving away requests with your hands. You hear the snapping of shutters; questions are shouted at you as you pass. The press is looking for angles on the morning's suicide attack. They will get information on the fatalities from the police but they want to know about the survivors as well. Foreigners who come close to being killed in a terrorist attack always make for good copy and create an opportunity for a freelance article to appear in a foreign publication, as well, offering a harrowing, personal account of the survivor and a career boost for a local journalist.

Famous foreigners are especially sought-after sources, particularly those who can speak in sound bites, as writers often can.

But the last thing you want is to speak to a reporter, to recount what you saw. Nor do you wish to give voice to your shock, your amazement at walking away unscathed. Thankfully, your appearance is unremarkable and your fame is so recent that even those who have read your new book would have a hard time linking your face and your name.

You feel leaden and weightless at once, lifted out of your body and more rooted than you have ever been. You feel the very tenuousness of your bodily existence; feel yourself poised between the present and the hereafter, heaven and earth.

If ever you needed a sign, this was it.

God is with you.

Leaving the hospital, you find that you are possessed by a ravenous hunger. You walk from Mount Scopus into the center of town, seeking the falafel stand on King George Street, the one that's been there forever, eschewing renovation, beloved by native Jerusalemites and tourists alike. Holding your oversized shawarma wrapped in warm lafa, you head toward Independence Park.

Slowly, almost leisurely, you make your way through Yemin Moshe, the community of stone-built homes overlooking the Old City. Awash in the Jerusalem sunlight, open only to foot traffic, the interior of Yemin Moshe has a timeless quality, like Jerusalem itself. A beautiful young woman, speaking French to her child, steps briskly around you, holding a long-stemmed sunflower in her hand. A teenage schoolgirl walks by, knapsack bouncing on her back, ear pressed urgently into a cell phone. An old man with a grizzled face and a large black yarmulke covering his head approaches and stops directly in front of you, placing his bag of groceries on the stone walkway. Looking intently at you, he touches your cheek and speaks in God's sacred tongue. Picking up his bag, he resumes his journey.

Jerusalem is awash with holy men and lunatics, sometimes in the body of the same person. The old man has told you to recite the *gomel* blessing this Sabbath in synagogue—the blessing that one recites after being spared from death.

The aura of one who has eluded death clings to you. The footprints of angels are visible on your shoulder.

In the evening, you walk past Café Rosa. Every trace of what has taken place earlier in the day has been removed and glassworkers are busily replacing the front panes of the café. The red-stained sidewalk and street has been scrubbed clean. People walk around the workmen, on their way home from work or heading out for the evening. A photographer stands at a discreet distance, snapping pictures. A white poster board is propped up on the opposite corner, a makeshift memorial. The owner of the café paces through the interior, smoking urgently, speaking on his cell phone, pausing to lean into a chair and weep loudly. An old Yemenite woman comes out of the shadows, starts shrieking and rolling her eyes, casting her hands heavenward.

"*Hashem Yinkom*," shouts a man, passing her. May God avenge us!

Watching from across the street, on Emek Refaim, you start to shake uncontrollably. Wordlessly, a *chayelet*—a young female soldier— leads you away, walking you upward along Rehov Masryk toward your apartment in Abu Tor. The night is darker than any night you have ever seen.

You are sick along the way, twice, three times. You retch into the gutter, into a bush, an alleyway. The soldier waits for you, holds your arm firmly when you are done and helps you walk. You reach your apartment and she brews you a cup of tea and places a cool washcloth on your head. You cannot stop trembling. After you drink your tea, she undresses you, as a mother might a sick child, leads you to your bed and lays you down to rest. She sits in a chair beside you, quietly vigilant. You try to see her face, but your vision is blurry from tears. As you fall asleep, tumbling backward through heartbreak and history, you think of the boy and his missing sister and the woman with the auburn hair. Rachel.

Rachel arrived in Israel in the midst of a freakish January snowstorm and the El Al plane had to circle Ben Gurion International four times before it could make its scheduled 4:00 a.m. landing. She had come alone, with a shoulder bag and small suitcase, having shipped all her worldly belongings via ship in a container that was scheduled to reach the port in Haifa one week later.

Since her first visit at the age of eighteen, Rachel had been in love with Jerusalem and Elisha was its self-proclaimed poet. He wooed her with couplets from the Song of Songs, calling her *my sister, my beloved*. Golden-tongued and nimble-fingered, he built a tower and set her inside to be his princess. Whispering ancient Hebrew verse into her velvet ear at midnight, he made her body his lyre. Gasping in delight at her unpracticed touch, he proclaimed her more skillful than the young virgin summoned to arouse the aged King David.

Their bed became Jerusalem, their marriage a covenant that transcended time and place.

And now, across the ocean of time and heartbreak, the city beckoned to her, calling her home.

With her red-brown hair pulled back in a ponytail, dressed in jeans, sneakers, a t-shirt, and a zipper-down sweatshirt, Rachel looked virtually indistinguishable from the scores of college kids who traveled on her flight, returning to their year-abroad study programs after Christmas break. During the flight, Rachel had spoken to no one, had refused the airline meals, only drinking bottled water and nibbling on M&M's.

Her face was bare of makeup, a practical measure undertaken to prevent smeary trails of melted mascara from running down her cheeks. When she wasn't eating chocolate or drinking water, Rachel was weeping.

At the age of forty-three, Rachel was uprooting herself, leaving her home, her country, her daughter and her marriage of twenty-two years. She had met Elisha when she was a student at Barnard and became his lover and then his wife. They married when she safely graduated. He was eighteen years her senior. He had been her hero, her savior, her mentor, her god. He had been the wise professor, prematurely mature, beloved by his students and respected by his colleagues. He had a gentle wit. He eschewed materialism. He was charmingly cosmopolitan, forgivingly forgetful.

For the majority of their marriage, Rachel and Elisha had lived modestly and happily on Morningside Heights in a walk-through apartment on Claremont Avenue owned by Columbia University and given to faculty and graduate students. Their daughter Anya was born in 1985. Anya went to Columbia daycare and later, a private school built by the university and subsidized for faculty families. The apartment had six rooms—commodious for Manhattan—but they were small. Elisha kept meaning to campaign for a larger apartment, perhaps on Riverside Drive, but never got around to trudging down to the housing office and stating his case. Caught up in his coursework, his publications and the building of his brilliant academic career, the necessary paperwork was never filed.

Still, the apartment had ample space for Rachel's studio, which she set up in a converted maid's room. Rachel was a painter of large canvasses. While Anya was small, she painted during her naps and in the middle of the night, arranging the completed works along the long walls of the Claremont Avenue apartment. Visiting friends, students, and academic colleagues reacted uniformly—and enthusiastically—to her work, urging her, even insisting, that she exhibit or at least enlist the help of an art dealer.

A stubborn purist, convinced of the corruption of the art marketplace, annoyed by the rapid transformation of SoHo from industrial neighborhood to art mecca, scornful of the sudden rise to the celebrity status of mediocre artists, Rachel refused to show her work for the better part of the marriage, relenting only when Anya stood ready to graduate from high school and the specter of college tuition loomed.

Her first show, at a small gallery in Chelsea, drew admiring reviews from *Time Out New York*, which hailed her as an important new talent. The *Time Out* review drew the attention of the *New York Times*. *New York* magazine followed with a feature article about Rachel, which focused on her emergence as an artist in mid-career and on her marriage to Elisha.

The tone of the *New York* article was breathless and hilariously off-mark according to everyone who knew Rachel and Elisha. It made this quintessentially unfashionable Upper West Side couple seem like the toast of Manhattan; it idolized their lifestyle, featured their teen daughter as the heiress to the artistic and intellectual thrones her parents occupied, and celebrated their lack of interior décor as deliberate minimalism, their modest possessions as conscious anti-materialism.

"From shabby to chic!" exclaimed Elisha again and again, delighting in showing the article to guests at dinner parties, roaring with laughter as he pointed to the soft-focus photograph of the family, bathed in sunlight, sitting on the rotting living room couch, the ancient end table looking like an important antique, the threadbare curtains framing this suddenly photogenic family, erasing wrinkles and gray hairs and paunch and acne. Sitting on either end of Anya, Elisha and Rachel looked like an archetype—the distinguished older male scholar and his pretty, young artist wife.

"Ah, the alchemy of journalism!" he intoned in exaggerated lofty tones, extending his arms to either side to indicate the dissonance between the image on the printed page and the squalid reality, shaking his head in admiration and disgust at the editorial sleight of hand that had been employed in his apartment's—and family's—favor.

The article appeared in the spring of 2002 and marked the last sustained moment of normalcy in their shared life.

Cocooned within her narrow airborne seat, lifted above the surreal landscape that had characterized her marriage over the past three years, Rachel pondered Elisha's metamorphosis, hoping for the insight that had thus far eluded her. The change came slowly and deceptively. The first sign was argumentativeness, a new characteristic that everyone mistook to be a sign of middle-aged eccentricity. Then came extremist pronouncements, stunning in their illogic and passion.

There was a long stretch where it seemed to Rachel that if the problem was Elisha's political point of view, then the solution was to have apolitical conversations, focusing on matters such as art, family, friends, and Columbia gossip. During this period, it was still possible to laugh at Elisha's views, rolling one's eyes as if he harbored a fondness for a bad rock band or suddenly adopted an idiosyncratic style of dress. Yet, while she and Anya grew skilled in the art of avoiding certain words and subjects, there was no stopping Elisha from spewing forth his hateful ideology in the presence of unprepared friends or guests.

"Okay, Elisha...that's enough," protested their dear friend Nomi Ben Avraham, a professor of history at Dartmouth, smiling indulgently at the man she had known for two decades. The Sunday brunch had been a congenial, lighthearted affair until someone mentioned the previous day's terrorist attack at a nightclub in Tel Aviv and Elisha, snarling, referred to the teenage victims as "vermin."

"Really, with Jews like you, Hamas might as well go out of business!"

"Don't you *ever* call me a Jew!" Elisha had shouted, pounding the tiled tabletop, causing the loose tile—and everyone assembled—to jump. Rachel was sure that she felt her heart pause for a moment, actually failing to beat in reaction to her husband's words. In that airless, bloodless moment everything changed. Her friends sat like monuments, stunned, silently bearing witness. Her daughter Anya jumped to her feet and ran from the table. Rachel's heart expelled Elisha in an involuntary spasm, resuming its rhythm, scarring over the place he had occupied with the words *y'mach shemo*—may his name be blotted out.

Looking back, Rachel realized that she—and everyone around them—had indulged in denial for a dangerous period of time and when the danger was undeniable there was nothing left to salvage. The only person who had sounded an early warning was Dr. Manfred Sandler, professor of psychology at Brandeis University—Rachel's father.

"His views are not political; they are pathological," the eminent psychologist had told his daughter after witnessing one of Elisha's outbursts. It was shortly after the first anniversary of 9/11 and Dr. Sandler was in Manhattan for his monthly visit with his daughter's family. Anya had just told her grandfather about an assembly at school where the father of her friend, Jared, had shared his story of escaping from the north tower the previous year by running down eighty-seven flights of stairs as they crumbled beneath his feet. His survival, Jared's father had said, had to do with the lucky fact that he wore sneakers to work that day because he woke up late and couldn't find his shoes.

"Or perhaps because Mr. Schwartz had advance information from the Mossad that he would need to run," remarked Elisha from behind the *New York Times*.

Anya looked at her mother. This was perhaps the tenth time that week that her father had made a comment along those lines, either in direct response to something they had said or in a disconnected, general way. Rachel turned to her father. He put a comforting hand on her arm, shaking his head ever so slightly. *Later*, said his expression. "Come over here, you," he commanded suddenly in his oratorical voice, pulling Anya into a bear hug. "Mmmmm! That'll keep me warm up in Boston!" The girl giggled happily as Rachel went to get her father's coat on wobbly legs.

Rachel and her father walked in heavy silence as they walked down Claremont Avenue toward Riverside Drive. "What a sick thing to say, especially in front of Anya. Is this his idea of a joke?" Dr. Sandler's voice contained equal amounts of anger and disgust.

Rachel shook her head. "He's dead serious," she said. "He manages to sneak in these comments at every possible opportunity...and there's no arguing with him, either."

Dr. Sandler was quiet. A group of cleaning women spilled out of the Interchurch Center, chattering amicably in Spanish. The night watchman called after them and they responded with gibes and peals of high-pitched laughter. "Would it help if I spoke with him?" he asked, finally.

Rachel looked dubiously at her dad. "I think we both know what a disaster that would be." Dr. Sandler's relative proximity to his son-in-law's age had promoted a collegial bond between the two academics for the majority of Rachel's married life, yet that very closeness would work against them now, she knew.

Dr. Sandler sighed and pulled his arm tightly around his daughter. "Then you, my dear, need to find someone to speak with…aside from me, of course. You might have some big decisions to make."

The decision was three years in the making. If it was an illness that overtook Elisha, there were periods of remission including a nearly yearlong stretch, in fact, when Elisha's rhetoric reverted to normal and they were all able to resume a semblance of their regular lives. And there were isolated weeks and months of household harmony. But it all came to an abrupt halt in the spring of 2004 and from then on, it was a dizzying downward spiral.

Rachel resolved to leave the marriage with the publication of the *Financial Times* interview that Christmas and was on the plane to Israel within a month.

So, what was it like, Rachel asked herself now, tracing her reflection in the window of the airplane. Was it like discovering that your husband is a bigamist or a cross-dresser or a child molester? Was it like losing a loved one to Alzheimer's, having their familiar personality slip away inch by inch until the former person is completely gone?

No, decided Rachel firmly. What happened to Elisha defies the rules of reality and resembles an episode of the *Twilight Zone*. A woman goes to sleep at night and in the morning her husband is replaced by a pod-person, a robot supplied by the evil engineers of Stepford, an alien from another planet whose master plan is to destroy Earth and all its inhabitants.

VI

3:00 a.m.

Dan Seligman was awake, lying in his narrow dormitory cot, unable to sleep, reviewing the events of earlier that evening at Miller

Theatre. Elisha Rosensweig's presentation was, in equal parts, horrible and absurd. What purported to be a radical political critique veered quickly into an anti-Semitic rant. There's no point in trying to sleep tonight, he realized, flicking on his bedside lamp. Reaching a long arm onto the floor, Dan retrieved his reporter's notebook and, pulling himself up onto his side, thumbed through it, checking phrases he jotted down against with the tape recording he had made.

The tiny tape recorder rested on the bed and he pressed the buttons clumsily, chasing a phrase, overtaking it, backtracking, finding it, clicking *play... fast forward... play... rewind... play... stop.* Really, he would wonder at his sanity if he didn't have proof of Rosensweig's outrageous utterings: "sneaky Jewish SS, also known as settlers;" "the obese Jewish war criminal Sharon, bloated from guzzling the blood of Palestinian children;" "the Jewish myth of superior intelligence is disproved by the stupidity of the occupation"…and ever more pungent phrases.

In the course of Rosensweig's presentation—which presented Israel as an ill-gotten country, stolen from the indigenous Arab population of Palestine, financed by Jewish bankers, a figment of the imagination of some international cabal akin to the infamous and mythological Elders of Zion—he painted indigenous Israelis as the Middle Eastern equivalent of the KKK, clamoring for the opportunity to lynch Arabs, hanging their bodies from date palms and olive trees. The immigrant Israelis were either "fat slobs from Brooklyn" or "criminal scum from Europe that the continent is only too happy to part with." Israeli schools were breeding grounds for Zionistic supremacists, the next generation's stab at world domination.

He flipped through pages hurriedly. What was it that Rosensweig had said about halfway through his presentation that made his skin creep? It was somewhere after his story about the Palestinian woman going into labor while waiting to cross over a security blockade—a terrible thing, to be sure—yes, yes, here it was:

"The greatest problem of the modern world is that the Jews have been given too much power."

Sitting in the balcony of Miller Theatre earlier that eerie evening, Dan found himself sweating profusely, breathing in small, shallow gulps as he attempted to bring an impartial journalistic perspective to the circus before him. Craning his neck, leaning over the railing to gauge the reaction of the Columbia faculty in attendance, he was stunned to find the audience beaming approval and affirmation to its deranged presenter. Amazing. Even more amazing, he counted a handful of Jewish professors in the audience. Was it possible that they missed the hate speech against themselves, the point at which "Israeli" became interchangeable with "Jewish"?

Why had it become acceptable—even commendable—to say heinous things about Jews if the context was Israel? When did this social convention click into place? Had a movement been growing underground, gaining momentum while he remained blissfully unaware? Did an acceptable number of years elapse since the Holocaust, lifting the lid off a self-imposed lock, releasing beliefs that had to be suppressed for several decades, out of a sense of etiquette?

Dan smelled an acrid, metallic scent wafting up from his chest... the scent of an animal in distress. *Maybe I'm not cut out to be a journalist,* he thought, wiping his damp palms against his blanket, turning on his side. *Maybe I'm too invested in my own Jewishness, too unapologetically Zionistic, too fond of my summers at Young Judea. Maybe I'm just a small-town Jew boy shocked by the sophistication of academic discourse.*

He checked the time. 3:15. It was impossible to call anyone at this hour; even his parents on the West Coast were asleep by midnight. And yet he badly needed to talk to someone. Half his dorm was awake at this hour but this was not something he could talk about with stoned strangers or even his newfound friends. Cal, his roommate, would have been a great sounding board but he was up in Maine doing some environmental project. Dan lay motionless on his back, feeling completely cut off from humanity.

Somewhere in this world it was daylight, he knew, and his call would not be robbing a friend of sleep...but where? Reflexively, he counted forward seven hours: 10:15. Israel! It was already morning in Israel and he could call Jon Resnick, his friend from Oakland who was studying in Jerusalem for the year.

With a surge of joy, Dan jumped up and scrounged in his night table for his international calling card, retrieving Jon's number from his computer with his other hand. He grabbed his cell phone, flipping it open. *Let there be time left on the card,* he prayed silently, punching in the calling code, then Jon's phone number. *Let Jon have his phone on him. Let him be free to talk.*

There was a pause and then the automated voice informed him that he had four dollars left on the card and could therefore talk for one hour and ten minutes. His heart leaped in hope. Another interminable pause and then Dan heard the ring of Jon's cell phone once... twice... thrice.

"Hello?" came the voice of his childhood friend from halfway across the world.

"Jon!" shouted Dan, awash with relief. "Hey Jon...it's Dan Seligman calling from New York!"

"Hey!" came the happy, surprised voice of Jon. "Dan! It's so good to hear you, man! Isn't it the middle of the night or something? Are you okay?"

Dan ran his fingers through his hair. A lump had formed in his throat and tears threatened to spill out of his eyes any minute now.

He took a deep breath. "Yeah…I'm okay, but I really need to talk, Jon. Something happened tonight at Columbia. D'you have a minute? Are you in the middle of anything?"

From across the ocean, two continents away, Jon recognized the catch in his friend's voice and sat down, placing his knapsack on the floor. His class in Biblical Anthropology would begin in twenty minutes and he was about to leave to jump on a bus to the Mount Scopus campus. "Dan, I'm with you," he said, motioning to his sister that he would be a while and that she should go ahead to class without him.

Suzanne picked up her book bag and gave her twin brother a wave, the red bracelet sliding down her slender wrist. "See you at seven," she mouthed, reminding him of their dinner appointment with their father's aunt at the King David Hotel that evening. Nodding, Jon waved goodbye to his sister.

Heading out the door, she turned and blew her brother a kiss.

VII

In the week following the bombing at Café Rosa, you are walking together along Derekh Beit Lechem in the south Jerusalem neighborhood of Baka, when you catch a glimpse of rust-colored hair, your heart skipping a beat.

It is she, you realize, Rachel, whose forlorn form figured in your delirious dreams over the past week. Though you had seen the heartbreaking articles following the attack, known from the photographs of the victims that she was not among those who perished, you had a fluttering fear that terror had driven her from Jerusalem and that you would never see her again.

Yet here she is, walking toward you with an uncertain smile riding upon her full lips.

"I've seen you," she states, approaching. "I know you from somewhere else."

Café Rosa, you wish to tell her, but the words are stuck in your throat. A torso with the tattoo of a hamsa lies on the floor to your right. You lift your head and stare at the tattoo, unable to comprehend its meaning. The floor is sticky with blood and bejeweled with broken glass. A hand rests atop a table, palm upward, beseeching. The ceiling is spattered with human remains, dripping downward. There are other horrors you cannot name; they do not belong to the world that you know. The air is thick with the scent of death.

The woman's eyes grow wide. You see her mouth form the shape of an O. You want to confirm the truth of what she says—that she does indeed know you from somewhere else—but the name of that other, faraway place has vanished from your mind and in its place there is only the nightmare of Café Rosa. A bloodied child screams, "Ima! Ima! Takumi! Ima!" pounding the back of an immobile woman with small fists. The American college student stands on a chair in the middle of the café and waves his arms like a conductor, commanding an orchestra of invisible avenging angels in *tohu va vohu,* the symphony of primordial chaos.

The walls of the café weep as the souls of the murdered lift heavenward. The flowers lining the windows die instantly of grief.

The sidewalk on Derekh Beit Lechem rises up toward you.

Her name is Rachel, but she does not remember you from Café Rosa. She doesn't remember Café Rosa at all, claims to have never set foot inside it, in fact, declares herself a devotee of Café Aroma on the other side of Emek Refaim. She tells this to you in a matter-of-fact way a little while later when you are resting at your apartment, having fainted outside the flower shop and been carried home by two Bulgarian workers whom she tracked down from a nearby construction site that had ceased operation in honor of the approach of Shabbat.

Groggy still from your fainting spell, you shake your head as Rachel speaks. "But I saw you!" you say, perhaps too vehemently, for her eyes narrow. "I saw you that morning!"

"Which morning?" she asks haltingly, tearing off a piece of pita and swiping it over the plate of hummus that you had set down on your coffee table. She is sitting cross-legged on top of a chair, her dirty bare feet resting on her thighs, her sandals kicked carelessly beneath the seat.

"The morning of the blast," you whisper, staring at her. She was there. Why would she deny it? First you must know about Café Rosa. Later you can talk of that other place, a lifetime ago.

"Oh my God!" she says, covering her mouth. "You were *there*? You were inside the café?" Her eyes are dark pools. You nod.

She shakes her head slowly. "It's so weird that you would think I was at Café Rosa because I was supposed to be there to meet a student but at the last minute I had to take care of something with my immigration application," she says, looking directly at you. "He went instead with his sister. She was killed."

The American boy. The girl with the tattoo on her back. You shake your head. You didn't imagine Rachel. She was there.

"Look... are you sure you didn't just stop inside Café Rosa that morning, perhaps to pick something up? I saw you! I know I did!"

Rachel's eyebrows go up. She looks at you closely.

"I believe you," she says finally. "I believe that you saw me at Café Rosa. I wasn't there, I swear it, but I believe that you saw me."

VIII

And why have you come to Jerusalem, extricating yourself from your carefully constructed New York life at the very pinnacle of public achievement, skipping out on the party when you are its guest of honor?

Your actions are counterintuitive, irrational, suspicious, even. What is your business in Jerusalem, the coolly efficient passport agent asked as you arrived at Ben Gurion International last summer, noting your open-ended ticket, absence of wife and children, lightweight carry-on luggage, and the apartment waiting for you in Abu Tor.

Flitting his focus between your documents and your face, he waited for your response, patient, curious, vigilant.

You do not look like the starry-eyed American Jews who arrive in Israel with their worldly possessions in order to fulfill the lifelong dream of *aliyah*—immigration to the state. Nor do you have the mien of the mystic or the purpose-driven egotism of the proselytizer. You have no message to deliver, no business to carry out, no agenda to follow.

What you have is a story but the passport agent has no time to hear it. What you have is a book with accolades from important people but he has no time to read it. What you have are stellar reviews but he doesn't subscribe to *The New Republic*, the *New York Times*, or the *Washington Post*. What you have is a thick file of newspaper clippings announcing readings at the bookshops and universities of major American cities, but these fragments of newsprint would look to him like so much fodder for the recycling bin.

Emanuel. He addresses you by your first name. Do you know what Emanuel means?

He fixes his gaze on you like a stern schoolmaster. You resist rolling your eyes; you are nearly old enough to be his father. Without waiting for you to reply, he supplies the answer:

God is with us.

Rachel becomes your obsession. Your yearning for her is filial, sexual, emotional, and deeply spiritual. Her skin smells like citrus and sweat; you want to dive into the heart of her chaos. You lie awake in the middle of the night, imagining her in her studio apartment on Emek

Refaim at the intersection of Rachel Imenu, Our Matriarch Rachel. Downstairs, there is a small shawarma stand. On the rounded corner, there is a stationer with dusty toy sets from long ago crushed against the inside window. Across the street is Pizza Sababa, a favorite of local families, beloved for their crushed garlic topping, thick Halloumi cheese, and pungent chopped green olives.

The not-unlikely coincidence of someone named Rachel living on Rachel Imenu Street sticks in your brain like a Bible code. You ponder this coincidence until you begin to question your intelligence and your sanity.

But there are other coincidences as well. For instance, there is the coincidence of Elisha Rosensweig, Rachel's husband, the heretic, the great hater of Israel. The realization of your shared connection to Elisha is cataclysmic—terrifying and magical all at once.

It is because of Elisha Rosensweig that you have come to Jerusalem.

Elisha Rosensweig delivered a guest lecture on the Book of Lamentations at St. Joseph's Seminary a lifetime ago, turning your head around, piercing your heart with the language of longing and loss, whispering ancient and erotic poetry into your velvet ear at midnight, leading you to abandon your path to the priesthood and take up residence among that people who dwell alone, who are cast out, exiled, and made a pariah among nations.

Because of Elisha Rosensweig, you became a scholar of ancient Hebrew, a writer, a Jew. Because of him, you fell in love with Jerusalem, the widowed city. Because of him, you changed your name, trading the moniker of that gentle saint of animals, Francis, for a promise.

Emanuel. God is with us.

And now, your name adorns the cover of a memoir. You called it *The Jerusalem Lover* for many reasons—it is a declaration of self, a clandestine act of revenge, a way of naming what took place so long ago. The book is your *cri de couer*, your poem of lamentation. After two decades of unrequited longing, you left everything and rushed into Jerusalem's sheltering arms, sealing the covenant set between God and Abraham, your new father.

And now, in Jerusalem, God fulfilled his ultimate promise to you, providing you with a *yedid nefesh*—a companion for your soul, the lover you have yearned for since the beginning of time.

After lying awake since three in the morning, you can hold out no longer and call Rachel at home. It is barely seven a.m.

I need to talk to you. I haven't been able to stop thinking about you.

I know. Me neither.

There's something I didn't tell you the other day. I was sitting one table over from the boy you were supposed to meet at Café Rosa. I saw him and his sister. Who was he? Why were you supposed to meet him?

You can feel Rachel's agitation, even over the phone.

He's a student from Oakland, California. His name is Jonathan Resnick. His sister's name was Suzanne. Jon took a year to study at Hebrew University before beginning at Yale. He's interested in political science. He'd been research-ing contemporary Jewish anti-Zionists, heard about Elisha from a friend at Columbia and made his way to me.

What was his sister doing in Israel?

She was also taking the year off to study at Hebrew U. They were twins. Inseparable.

You both fall silent. The vastness of this particular tragedy is unspeakable and your shared proximity to it draws you together.

Where is he now? Has he gone back to the States?

No. He's here with his family. They all came over and will stay until the shloshim, *the thirty-day commemoration. The funeral took place in Jerusalem on Sunday. Normally they bury before nightfall in Israel but the family needed to fly over to Israel from California, which is an endless flight. Suzanne was buried in Har Hamenuchot.*

Har Hamenuchot—the beautiful hillside cemetery that greets visitors en route to Jerusalem. During one of your first weeks in Jerusalem you wandered through the Mountain of Resting Souls for hours, winding your way among the white-stoned monuments inscribed in God's sacred tongue, crazed with thirst, courting your own mortality.

The bomber was a girl, you know. An eighteen-year-old Palestinian who was two months pregnant.

You hear the blast in your head. *No, I didn't know.*

Want to hear something unbelievable? My daughter at Penn emailed me a link to an article in The Guardian *written last week by my crazy ex. Evidently, he's supposed to be a scholar-in-residence this summer in London. The article praised the bomber for her heroic and selfless act, calling her a martyr for the cause of freedom. It seems that Elisha believes that Jews sitting in cafes deserve to die. And not just in Jerusalem. Anywhere in the world.*

IX

Suzanne Resnick's death hit Dan especially hard because of his indirect responsibility. It was Dan who brought Elisha Rosensweig to Jon's attention that night in November following the Miller Theatre debacle. Faced with his friend's distress, Jon did what he had always done best—listened. It was only when he got off the phone that he realized that his old friend had just handed him a gift, the perfect subject to comprise the core of his studies that year at Hebrew University.

Thus Jon Resnick became a long-distance scholar of Elisha Rosensweig, researching everything he had written or said publicly. He was immediately captivated by his subject as his rudimentary research revealed two public personae that seemed to have little to do with one another—the refined professor of Hebrew literature and the radical who sounded like the mouthpiece of Al Qaeda. The Jew and the anti-Semite. The Israeli and the Israeli self-divested of his own birthright.

Jon's challenge was to find out how Elisha I morphed into Elisha II.

Until 2002, Rosensweig's primary output had been literary, focusing on the life and work of Eliezer Ben Yehuda, the Lithuanian Jew credited with the revival of modern Hebrew. Throughout the seventies, he wrote a lively weekly column in the Israeli newspaper *Maariv* on innovative uses of Hebrew in contemporary Israeli fiction. Jon tracked down brochures from academic conferences where Rosensweig had presented papers and uncovered articles, mostly in academic journals or the Israeli press, about the influence of Rosensweig's scholarship.

Rosensweig had attended Hebrew University, where he received his bachelor's and master's degrees and then moved to New York in 1970 to undertake his doctoral studies at the Jewish Theological Seminary. He quickly distinguished himself in his field, receiving numerous awards, lecturing widely, and winning fellowships at Oxford University, Harvard, Princeton, and Stanford. He was a faculty member at Brooklyn College and Dartmouth before coming to Columbia in 1976 and receiving tenure there eight years later. In 1983, he married Rachel Sandler, a painter. Rosensweig lived in New York City and was the father of a daughter, who was now nineteen, by Jon's calculation.

Until the winter of 2003, the career of Elisha Rosensweig followed a particular trajectory and then it veered sharply. Though it appeared that he still taught his classes at Columbia at that time, his public speaking on Ben Yehuda and Hebrew fell off abruptly. Invited to serve on a panel at the 92nd Street Y that February dedicated to the role that language plays in capturing catastrophe, Rosensweig catapulted to fame—or infamy—by sidestepping the topic at hand and declaring the United States guilty of wide-scale international terrorism. In the course of his tirade, he belittled the attacks of September 11, which he termed a minor assault on its citizenry compared with America's "long record of human rights violations and atrocities around the world."

The audience at the Y reacted angrily to his pronouncements, but the young metro reporter from the *New York Times* assigned to cover the event knew an opportunity when she saw one. Approaching Rosensweig after the discussion, she spirited him away from the indignant audience, sat him down at the Starbucks on Lexington and 87th Street, extracted his philosophy through careful questioning, then raced down to West 43rd Street to file her article in time for the morning edition of the following day's paper. After a certain amount of late-night editorial consultation, the paper decided to run her article and thus, the media floodgate opened wide, carving out a brand-new career path for him: Elisha Rosensweig, public enemy—or moral watchdog—of the United States...depending on your point of view.

If it was the role of moral watchdog that Rosensweig was playing he gnawed at the bone of the United States for half a year before moving on to a meatier morsel—Israel. If the crimes of America justified the deaths of nearly three thousand of its citizens on September 11, then the plague of Palestinian terrorism against Israel's civilians didn't even begin to amount to the roster of Israel's crimes—the chief of which seemed to be its very existence.

The existence of Israel was, according to Rosensweig, the real impetus for the war in Iraq. Though it concocted the rationale for the war (phantom WMDs) the Bush Administration sought to take out Saddam Hussein in a deal with Israel. In his lectures and articles, Rosensweig portrayed a paranoid, corrupt system of quid pro quo, painting a parallel universe of muffled conversations in undisclosed locations, maps marked in red ink, aliases, assassins, operatives, envelopes of money changing hands, long black cars in the middle of the night, the blood of Christian children baked into matza, hook-nosed bankers and businessmen, a cabal bent upon world domination.

Elisha Rosensweig's newfound views gave him the kind of coveted exposure that no master publicist could have achieved. Half a world away, situated within the epicenter of Rosensweig's rage, Jon Resnick pored through his writings and ramblings, assuming the mantle of madman's biographer.

In January, Jon Resnick uncovered an interview that Rosensweig had given to the NPR reporter based in Israel ten years earlier, in 1995. The subject was Rosensweig's personal and professional passion—the Hebrew language. Jon's efforts paid off. When the NPR tape arrived in the mail, he was rewarded with a rich trove of information about Rosensweig's early life.

Elisha Rosensweig had been born in the cellar of a farmhouse outside of Sarvasz, Hungary, on January 15, 1945, two days before the Russian army captured Budapest. By that time, it was too late to save the nearly 565,000 Hungarian Jews who had already been sent to a variety of Nazi death camps, including Rosensweig's entire extended family, who had fled to Hungary from Germany four years earlier on the advice and invitation of a Hungarian relative.

Rosensweig's teenage parents—second cousins—had survived the German occupation of Hungary by hiding in barns and forests for nearly one year. Both his grandfathers had been shot by the Arrow-Cross operatives of Ferenc Szalasi, their bodies swallowed by the Danube. An uncle and aunt on his father's side were hanged in a public square. The rest of his family perished in Dachau, Bergen-Belsen, or Auschwitz.

In 1947, a two-year-old Elisha Rosensweig and his parents sailed off to Palestine at the invitation of a distant cousin Janusz, now Yosef, who lived on a kibbutz in the Galilee. Elisha's mother, Faige, who was of delicate health and nerves, nearly died during the journey and was ill for most of his childhood. She died two days after Elisha's bar mitzvah. Faige's death plunged his father, Otto, into a depression from which he never emerged, though Jon discovered that the elder Rosensweig was evidently still alive.

Thus Elisha Rosensweig, the child refugee, lost both his parents at once at a tender age. His father became non-communicative and was placed on a limited work schedule in the chicken house. The kibbutz held a special meeting to decide Elisha's care and a foster family was assigned to him—the Rotshilds. The Rotshilds were a kind and caring family with five children of their own, all redheaded and pudgy. They were notable on the kibbutz for their insistence that the children live with them and not in the communal youth house. A bed for Elisha was immediately moved into the children's room, butting up against Adriana's bed, who was one year older than Elisha and the object of his current infatuation.

Though he was instantly absorbed into the Rotshild clan, well-fed and cared for, Elisha was miserable. Mrs. Rotshild, who had enormous breasts and buttocks, could not replace the delicate and soft-spoken Faige and the sight of Otto fumbling around the chicken house, smelling like chicken shit, was a constant source of humiliation for Elisha. Watching his father stumble into meals late, always late, made Elisha's ears burn. His overalls were filthy and his hair was unwashed.

In his clipped, courtly voice, Rosensweig recounted his memories as a grieving teen in the NPR interview: "*I would follow the pitying gazes of the kibbutzniks and wish my father dead.*"

Jon clicked the off button on the audio player and hit rewind.

"*I would follow the pitying gazes of the kibbutzniks and wish my father dead.*"

X

3:00 a.m.

Anya Rosensweig lay awake in her bedroom in the apartment on Claremont Avenue, unable to fall asleep. It was an airless July night and her family's apartment had just one cranky air conditioner. *This sucks*, she thought, sulkily.

Earlier in the day, Anya had come home to retrieve summer clothes for her trip to Israel and now couldn't bring herself to leave. The sight of the apartment bereft of all traces of her mother was unbearable. In the six months since Rachel had left, taking her colorful canvases and clothes with her, the commodious, family-friendly apartment had turned musty and dull, the dwelling of an old man. Now, with her father teaching at some anti-Israel institute in London for the summer, the apartment looked lonelier than ever.

In four days, Anya would be flying to Israel to join her mother in Jerusalem. She had last visited the country four years earlier. When she was younger, the Rosensweig family was there all the time, brought over by Elisha's work. Since her father flipped out, the New York-Jerusalem commute came to an abrupt end.

Anya thought back to a trip she had taken when she was thirteen. Her family was not religious but Rachel had insisted that her daughter receive her religious rite of passage in Israel and together with Anya's Hebrew school teacher, organized an Israel trip for the bar and bat mitzvah children.

While some of the kids on her trip fell madly in love with Israel—seeing it for the first time—Anya held the country at arm's length. It was too familiar, this Jewish nation that had popped up in the middle of nowhere, this unruly blend of humanity from around the world, the hospitality and crankiness, the honeyed guttural language and animated hand gestures, the place where the past met the future, heaven touched the sky. It was the world of her father, the backdrop of her childhood.

And then, there was the matter of the Arabs, or really the Palestinians. Anya's tour group had been given an escort with an Uzi and traveled from site to site on their own protected coach. The kids were warned never to accept a package or gift from someone they did not know, to report suspicious or unattended objects, and to avoid the Arab quarter of the Old City. And then, as if to show that there was yet hope for the future, their teacher facilitated a lunch meeting with a group of Palestinian kids through the offices of a peace organization in Jerusalem.

The lunch was held at the Nature Museum, which sported a dusty model of a Tyrannosaurus Rex in the front yard. While everyone smiled politely, shook hands, and learned how to pronounce each other's names, the entire enterprise felt phony. Anya had learned about the conflict in the bat mitzvah class at her liberal Hebrew school and concluded that these coexistence efforts were a waste of time. The Palestinians hated the Israelis for the same reasons that the black kids from Harlem hated her and her white Morningside Heights friends—their worlds were too far apart. One group had everything; the other, next to nothing.

No amount of friendly field trips or lunches or get-togethers could change that basic fact.

Yet until her father launched his campaign, Anya hadn't thought about Israel in political terms. Her world was close to home, the self-contained Upper West Side of Manhattan. She was a New York teen, consumed by friends, schoolwork, dance lessons, rock concerts, celebrities, standing-room tickets to Broadway shows, IMing, talking for hours on the phone, studying in Starbucks, and trying to sneak into clubs without being carded.

Until recently, Anya would not have even called herself a Zionist. It wasn't that she opposed Israel; she just didn't think that much about it. Her father's recent obsession, however, had placed the country front and center in her mind. His hateful preoccupation broke up her family and not just in the usual way; it crushed its soul and structure. The sad fact was that his politics outweighed his love for them.

But it wasn't only her father who was obsessed with Israel, she knew. The world had become obsessed as well. Even on the heavily Jewish U of P campus, one heard constant accusations lobbed against Israel, deflecting from the crimes of other countries, for instance, the Sudan or North Korea, or Arab countries where girls and women were killed by family members every day.

You didn't have to be a Zionist to notice that when it came to Israel, the world was fucked up.

Shortly after the clock struck four, Anya left the dark prison of her room and padded into the living room, giving a mighty stretch. *This sucks*, she thought, once again. *I'll be jet-lagged before I even arrive in Israel.* Abandoning thoughts of sleep, she pulled out the pile of newspapers and magazines that were stacked several feet high in the corner and settled in for a good, boring read. When this failed to put her to sleep after forty-five minutes, she turned on the television, allowing herself to channel surf the infomercials, music videos and weird late-night offerings before stalling her finger on the remote, staring at the story coming out of London.

XI

Dan Seligman leaned against the statue of Gandhi in Tavistock Square, holding a copy of *Time Out London*, attempting to look casual while craning his head to the left and right, anxiously searching for the man he had arranged to meet—Dr. Elisha Rosensweig. He checked the time on the British cell phone that he rented at Heathrow. It was already

9:45 a.m.—the appointed hour. Rosensweig was reputed to be a stickler for punctuality. He should arrive any second now.

Dan was in London for the first two weeks of July, staying with the family of Ben Cohen, an English friend from Columbia whose family lived in Hampstead Garden. Ben's father, Asher, a diamond dealer, also headed up a group that was tracking the incidence of anti-Semitic attacks in Europe. According to Asher Cohen, these incidents were up dramatically since the beginning of the second Intifada.

"You've probably heard it before, but the Jew is the canary in the coal mine," Mr. Cohen had told his American guest at breakfast the previous morning. "In the past three years, several synagogues have been vandalized and no one dares to wear a yarmulke in public anymore. Just this morning I got a call about a Jewish girl in Cowley, just outside of Oxford. She was beaten up by a group of Muslim boys and forced to swallow her Star of David necklace. Europe ignores the rise of anti-Semitism at its own peril."

Eager to write in his journal, Dan had gotten to Tavistock Square one hour earlier and spent the time writing on his laptop and listening to the mix he had downloaded onto his iPod in preparation for this trip, a brilliant blend of Bowie, Beatles, Mahler, Mozart, Serge Gainsbourg, Talking Heads, Leonard Cohen, The Velvet Underground, and Edith Piaf.

When he had first arrived at 8:30, tourists spilled across the square, walking amiably out of the nearby hotel, clutching guidebooks, freshly fed, adding the finishing touches on the day's itinerary: *Shall we do the Tate Modern first or The National Portrait Gallery? D'you think we can squeeze in Harrods on the way to Victoria and Albert? Kids, how badly do you want to see London Dungeon? Can we catch the matinee performance of Mousetrap?*

Caught up in his journal writing, plugged into the world of his music, he hardly noticed the virtual halt of pedestrian traffic through the square, the tense posture of people as they passed him, the increasing wail of ambulances in the air.

Dan was scheduled to fly to Israel after his stay in London to spend the balance of July and two weeks of August researching, writing, and spending time with Jon. Having taken over Jon's project in April, Dan applied for a modest grant from the Mendelson Institute, a new entity whose mission was to monitor anti-Israel activity on the American college campus. The funds he was subsequently awarded enabled him to catch up with Rosensweig in London where he was presenting a paper at a conference sponsored by the International Centre for Palestinian Return.

If all went according to plan, these funds would also enable him to interview Otto Rosensweig, Elisha Rosensweig's father—now eighty years old and living on Kibbutz Ein Tina in the Upper Galilee.

After Suzanne's death in March, Jon Resnick abandoned his study of Elisha Rosensweig, finding it unbearable to inhabit Rosensweig's universe anymore. Where Jon had been fascinated by Rosensweig, he was now disgusted by him and his crusade. Rosensweig was not worthy of his attention, he decided. Rosensweig would not mourn for his sister.

Waiting for Elisha Rosensweig to arrive, Dan flipped through *Time Out London* in search of the museum listings. What time did the British Museum open, anyway? Somehow, he couldn't see interviewing Rosensweig in a café or any stationary setting, intuited that he needed to be mobile while speaking to the man. Dan had his tiny tape recorder with him and preferred the flow of conversation rather than a volley of answers to scripted questions, the rapid scribble of pen on paper as he strove to capture Rosensweig's exact phrasing.

Instead of breakfast, as they had planned, he would suggest that they conduct their meeting while walking through the British Museum.

Dan was in luck. The Great Court of the museum opened at 9:00 and the galleries at 10:00. This plan might work out if Rosensweig proved amenable. Dan folded the magazine, checking the time on his cell phone: 9:46. He turned off his iPod, interrupting David Byrne in the middle of "Psycho Killer," one of his favorite songs of all time, dating back to his childhood. Dan's parents were obsessed with the Talking Heads when he was growing up; one of his earliest memories was watching the video for "Burning Down the House" on MTV with his mother. Though he never would admit it, that creepy projected image of David Byrne's face on the side of the house gave him nightmares.

Now, Dan folded his earphones around the music player and tucked it into his bag alongside his laptop. Removing his tape recorder, he placed it in his breast pocket, patting it down. He glanced at his cell phone again.

9:47.

Rosensweig was two minutes late.

Suddenly, a huge explosion reverberated through Tavistock Square, making the ground and air vibrate, knocking Dan over, sending his cell phone skating across the pavement. The statue of the seated pacifist wavered for a moment. Tourists screamed and ran or stood paralyzed with panic. There was a burnt smell in the air, a horrible hissing sound. A toddler who had been running in circles around Dan stopped abruptly, dropping her toy.

"Samantha!" cried a young woman, running toward the child, her eyes wild with fear. The sidewalks around the square became dotted with people rushing out of buildings, all staring toward Upper Woburn Place.

Stunned, Dan turned on his side. Before him was a scene from a disaster film—a red double-decker bus stood in the street, caved in from the top, looking as if it had just been hit by a falling meteor. There were people inside. A flurry of physicians came racing out of a nearby building, motorists jumped out of traveling cars, and wails and screams shattered the perfect calm of the London morning.

After a few silent, surreal moments, Dan Seligman stood up. His hands were shaking and his throat was dry. *Be here, now,* he told himself. *You're a reporter. You're on the scene. This is an opportunity. Be brave.*

But he was not brave. Dan knew this about himself. He had brave ideas and brave thoughts, a notebook and a pen and a tape recorder and a cell phone, but he kept getting tripped up by his own cowardice. He found it hard, no, impossible, to be objective about what he was covering. *I'm no journalist,* he thought, bending to retrieve his phone from the ground. *I'm pathetic. I'm a crybaby. I want to go home.*

Tucked inside his breast pocket, his cell phone rang loudly, making his heart jump. Rosensweig! He probably got caught up in the traffic behind the bus or something. Dan checked out the caller ID and was confused to see that it was Jon Resnick, calling from Jerusalem. The time locally was 9:55. Dan did the math. It was nearly noon in Israel.

He flipped the phone open.

"Dan!" shouted Jon, a continent away. "Dan, where are you? I just saw the news. Are you okay?"

The horrible events of the past few months culminated in the present, unbelievable moment. Dan felt woozy. He leaned against the base of the statue. "Jon…I'm right here," he said. "I'm waiting for Rosensweig. A bus just blew up."

Jon closed his eyes, blocking out the images on his computer, broadcasting live from a war-zone version of London. "Where are you?" he asked, again. "I haven't seen anything about a bus explosion, only explosions on the Underground. They say that dozens of people were killed."

"The Underground?" Dan repeated, confused, straightening up, looking toward Upper Woburn Place. People were being taken off the bus. Dan saw immobile bodies on seats. "No, this happened on a bus."

Tentatively, he began walking toward the street. He reached the edge of the square. Not far from him, he saw a human leg lying in the street, still wearing a shoe. It did not look real. Dan stared at it until sheeting was placed over it. Everything felt artificial and remote, as if he were watching from outside his own body.

The London police, stunningly efficient, arrived on the scene and began cordoning off the disaster site. Witnesses were interviewed on the sidewalk by detectives. Reporters and camera crews poured onto sidewalks and streets.

Suddenly Dan remembered Rosensweig. *He's probably trying to reach me; I'd better free up the phone line*, he thought frantically.

"Listen, Jon," said Dan. "Let me call you back in a little while. I think that Rosensweig might be trying to reach me and I don't know how to use the call waiting function on this phone. I might have to arrange to meet him elsewhere."

The image of the burned-out bus now appeared on Jon's computer screen. The London sky was gray, the color of his eyes. Above the bus, a cloud of smoke hovered, a congregation of souls snatched without warning.

A primitive, keening sound filled Jon's head. In his mind's eye, he saw a young girl with auburn hair. She was falling down, wailing. Another auburn-hued voice joined the sorrowful chorus. Newly widowed, it was steeped in ambivalent grief.

Memories of love merged with the sting of betrayal.

"Dan," said Jon carefully. "It's all over. There is no more Elisha Rosensweig."

XII

Anya stretched out on the threadbare living room sofa and fell instantly asleep after talking to her mother. When she had called, she was surprised to find Rachel similarly glued to her television screen in Jerusalem, watching footage of the attacks in London, the highest-profile act of terrorism since 9/11. Her mother's concern for her father's well-being had caught Anya off-guard; she had supposed that the hatred she felt toward him was absolute.

In the middle of the night, alone in her childhood apartment, Anya drew a measure of comfort from this insight into the complexity of the human heart.

Though Anya passed several hours in sleep, it felt to her as if she had just laid her head down on the brocade pillow when she was awakened by an insistent knock on the front door. She arose groggily, stumbling to the front door.

Through the peephole, Anya saw two men in dark, official suits.

"Hello," one repeated loudly, rapping on the door with hard knuckles. Anya's blood froze. Her first thought was that these men were police, came to arrest her father for something heinous, like aiding the London terrorists. That would be exactly like him; what was he doing in London anyway? Heartbeat quickening, she felt a cold rush of panic. *I should refuse the answer the door*, she thought wildly, looking around the apartment for a good hiding spot. *Even though he's a psycho, I still have to protect him. He's my father.*

Despite her fear, Anya opened the door. The men reported that they were with the State Department's Bureau of Consular Affairs.

They were holding a folder with official documents; they showed her their badges. The men looked serious, perhaps even angry. They wanted to know if she was a relative of Elisha Rosensweig.

Trembling, Anya nodded her head.

They asked if they could come in; they inquired as to her mother's whereabouts. The men settled uncomfortably on the couch, sitting opposite the young woman with the auburn hair and the terrified, sleep-lined face. They asked her if she was aware of the London terrorist attacks that took place earlier in the day.

They informed her that they had very bad news.

XIII

Minutes before midnight, an old man in overalls shuffles into the lobby of Kibbutz Ein Tina in the Galilee dragging a chair noisily behind him. Planting himself in the center, he climbs clumsily atop the chair and begins to conduct an invisible orchestra, arms waving wildly in the air.

Tears stream down his deeply lined face. His lips do not stop moving. Guests walk around him gingerly; some giggle in embarrassment. The night manager watches him for a while from behind the reception desk, then rises, sighs, and walks toward him.

"*Bo, abaleh,*" he says kindly, placing his arm around his shoulders, calling him father. The old man is a *vatik*, an ancient member of the kibbutz, having arrived before the establishment of the state. Like many other *vatikim*, he is a survivor of the Holocaust, a Hungarian. The night watchman doesn't know much about him, only that he was widowed young and that his only son—a big-shot professor in America—has not come to see him in over thirty years.

The old man blinks at the sound of the night watchman's voice seems to shrink under the weight of his arm. The smell of the chicken coop clings to his clothes and his skin. There are pieces of hay in his hair. His sadness is as vast as the universe.

XIV

How does the city sit desolate
That was full of people?
How has she become as a widow
She who was great among the nations?

Do you believe in the covenant, you asked Rachel this evening as she lay in your arms, spent with sorrow. Sweeping the hair off your face with her hands, she looked at you with the eyes of her namesake, the matriarch Rachel, loving and eternal.

Yes, said Rachel, your Jerusalem lover, your Jerusalem sister, your Jerusalem mother. *Yes*, she whispered, kissing you on your open, waiting mouth.

Jerusalem seduced you both, beckoned with sly gestures and whispered promises. She said she was your city of refuge, your promised land. She called to you from across mighty oceans and wide continents, spirited you away, claimed you as her children, her beloved.

She offered you comfort in the midst of your wandering, your lamentation. She murmured ancient spells and incantations into your velvet ear at midnight.

Nothing that has happened makes any sense. A lifetime ago, a lover of Zion recited the poignant poetry of Jerusalem's destruction and his people became your people, his God became your God. Where he went, you followed even as it led you straight into the heart of *tohu va'vohu*.

Jerusalem remembers
In the days of her affliction and
Of her anguish

All the treasures that she had
In the days of old.

Within the heart of Rachel's chaos, there is a scent of citrus groves. Within the lamentation of her new widowhood, there is the remembrance of the fragrant promise of Eden.

How does the poet of Jerusalem become Nebuchadnezzar? His couplets turned into daggers. He falls by his own sword.

There is a mystery woven into your journey. Elisha woke you then broke you. He led you through heartbreak and *tohu va'vohu* to Rachel. You saw her bathed in sadness and fell captive to her spell. With her practiced hand, she makes you gasp in delight. She is your *yedid nefesh*, your soul's companion, widowed like the beautiful Bathsheba, whose husband was sent to die on the battlefield.

Leaving you as horrified and besotted as that ancient Jerusalem lover—David, King of Israel.

Everything that has happened will make sense as time unfolds. History will judge Elisha Rosensweig, branding him a madman or martyr.

We will be judged as well.

Unseen forces operate daily in our lives.

In Jerusalem, time unfolds according to its own plan.

God is with us.

AFTERWORD AND ACKNOWLEDGMENTS

THE STORIES CONTAINED IN THIS book, while works of fiction, draw heavily on numerous aspects of my own life. Though I had long ago realized that I had a uniquely rich—if imperfect—childhood, it was not until recently that I understood what a golden era I was born into. New York City in the Sixties and Seventies was alive, vital, and electric with protests, ideas, art, and happenings. We who were kids during this time enjoyed the kind of benign parental neglect that spawned true adventure and occasionally led to memorable trouble. The additional fact that I lived with my family in the young State of Israel from 1968 to 1969, in that glorious aftermath of the Six-Day War, added color, dimension, and depth to my formative years.

As this book heads into production, we are six weeks past October 7th, the horrific Simchat Torah massacre and terrorist attack by Hamas on Israel. The cocoon of Jewish security has dissolved, not just in Israel but globally. Outside my Morningside Heights apartment, the Columbia University campus roils with hateful slogans. Our lives are enveloped in anxiety: for the hostages, for the survival of Israel, for our brothers and sisters around the world. For ourselves.

Editing my stories during this time has been a welcome retreat from the terrible present moment to the magical bubble of post-war America.

Growing up as a rabbi's kid in the leafy Queens community of Douglaston—a suburban-like bastion of New York City on the Nassau County border—shaped me in so many ways and provided me with a safety net that I carry with me through life. Rather than having felt hounded by expectation, I felt myself surrounded by benevolent adults. Protected. When necessary, I took my rebellion underground.

Every adopted child arrives on Earth in a space capsule from Krypton and lives a dual identity as a mortal being and superhero. I had a soft landing, arriving from foster care into the home of my loving parents, Rochelle and Henry Dicker, who surrounded me with love and security within a home whose walls breathed the best of Yiddishkeit: Jewish practice, texts, music, liturgy, beliefs, and traditions.

Like Rebecca, the protagonist of the title story, my immersive though liberal Jewish upbringing shaped me in a holistic way:

"Wow," I said, trying to imagine not understanding what it meant to be Jewish. I was so Jewish that there was not a day that I didn't think about it, about God, about praying, about Israel, about doing mitzvahs, which are good deeds and talking to God when I said Shema every night before I go to sleep. From Lolita at Leonard's of Great Neck.

This description of my childhood identity was ripped from the pages of my own life.

Counterbalancing my spiritual foundation was psychological awareness. My father, a congregational rabbi for twenty-one years, pursued his doctorate in clinical psychology when I was a young teen and transitioned out of the rabbinate into a full-time and successful private practice as I was graduating high school. Following suit, my artistic mother received her MSW and began working in the NYC school system, counseling kids at the mostly minority John Bowne High School in Flushing, one of the city's toughest schools. She loved her kids and was their staunch advocate, seeing them as victims of cynical leaders and an unfair social system.

My siblings and I were raised with psychological awareness, with our bookshelves groaning under the weight of the works of Sigmund

Freud, Alfred Adler, William James, B. F. Skinner, Erik Erikson, Carl Jung, Carl Rogers, Rollo May, Viktor Frankl, and so many others. *Psychology Today* was delivered to our home for years and I read every single issue. As a result, I often practiced psychology without a degree or license in my peer group, interpreting puzzling behavior, and handing out diagnoses for friends.

And speaking of books, we were raised with permission to read everything. And I mean everything. My Queensboro Public Library card was my portal to the world of ideas, to the adult world, to great fiction, to sex, to travel, to disrupt existing systems and change the world. I read *The Godfather* with my best friend of the time, Eileen Lobelson, in her bathroom on a series of Shabbat afternoons. I read a dog-eared paperback copy of *Portnoy's Complaint* in my maternal grandparents' home in Boro Park, Brooklyn, on a family weekend when I was stricken with the flu. I read *Rosemary's Baby* in the stairwell of my high school with my friends Lisa and Shelley. I read *Candy* and *Blue Movie* in my Douglaston bedroom. I read books that are now banned. I lingered over copies of *Esquire* magazine in the periodicals section. I encountered the world at the Queensboro Public Library.

During my Israel year (the first of many) when we lived in the Jerusalem apartment of the philosopher Pinchas Peli, I read my way from one end of the bookcase to the next. Television was primitive, broadcasting only the news, it seemed, and Mighty Mouse cartoons. In that modest apartment, I made the acquaintance of Tom and Huck, Charlotte, Wilbur, Oliver Twist, Sydney Carton, Pip, Alice, Robinson Crusoe, Pinocchio and friends, while yet in the third grade.

Back in New York, I also encountered the passion of the great Russian composers as my mother, a classically-trained pianist, would periodically tear herself away from her duties as the rabbi's wife and our mother and sit down at our baby grand piano to pour out her soul.

She specialized in Rachmaninoff and Tchaikovsky, but Beethoven's "Moonlight Sonata" was a favorite of hers. I still get chills whenever I hear it. It is the melodic interpretation of heartbreak and deep loss. Chopin also made a variety of appearances, especially his "Prelude in C Minor," which I was thrilled to discover as the introduction to Barry Manilow's "Could it be Magic." Leaning into the keyboard, playing sometimes without sheet music, another facet of my carefully coiffed, well-mannered mother came into view.

Everything I was given by my parents influenced my mothering and nothing else has shaped me on par with my upbringing than the experience of birthing and raising my remarkable children: Adam, Emma, and Judah.

I fell into motherhood at a relatively young age and was dazzled and delighted to discover that there was nothing more fun than hanging out with your own child, perhaps because I was still in touch with my own childhood. The most creative undertaking of all is raising up a child, inviting them to reveal themselves, to surprise you, to challenge you, to break you, to make you whole. Even as they are now adults, I will always and forever be Adam's mom, Emma's mom, and Judah's mom.

I am marked and shaped by the moment of their births, by the long days and fast-moving years, by their infant selves, the toddlers they became, their childhood beings, and the adolescence each traversed along the path to adulthood. Whether I did them a favor by shunning rigid bedtime is up to them to decide but our favorite time was always story time. I simply wanted it to go on forever.

Every parent is honored with the privilege of observing their children's lives, watching them be and become. What unfolds is both in your hands and entirely out of your hands. It is magical. It is mysterious.

I treasure it all: the illness, the Sunday excursions as a solo parent, the parent-teacher conferences, the sticky hands, the laughter, tears, backyard adventures, misadventures, travel, bills, my deferred personal dreams. Everything. No matter what I accomplish in life, my children will be my proudest creations.

And now, through some kind of grace, I have been gifted with grandchildren. Neil, Arlo, and Ruby, you are the extra scoops of ice cream on the cone of life, yummy and treasured treats. Our hangouts return me to the native joy of being with small humans. Cuddling to read books is a rocket ship back to the most wonderful moments in my life. I love your little selves and cannot wait to watch your future selves emerge.

To my parents, my children, and my grandchildren, I extend the deepest thanks, the greatest gratitude. Here is the circle of life.

And to Ari, I salute our perfectly imperfect marriage, which has provided me with sustenance and shpilkes, with access and adventure, with space to grow independently and together, with a useful amount of convergence, conflict, and coming together. This work is being published as we mark forty years together, a biblical amount of years, wandering in the desert, heading toward the Promised Land.

Deepest thanks to my sister Adina and brother Mordi. We shared a unique childhood, rich with love. We were raised with the solid values of hard work, loyalty to family, the importance of being charitable, American patriotism, and Jewish pride. Together, we cared for and buried our magnificent father, the axis of our shared life. We grieved together. Nearly daily, I seek signs of his lingering presence, his wise counsel, his love, his no-nonsense way of calling out BS. A tight sibling group, we come together in joy and celebration as well as sorrow. Emerging from a shared home, we have forged our own unique Jewish paths. We support one another, challenge one another, and look after one another. Adina, you are my soul, my first roommate, my other self. Our childhood collaborations and fights form some of my fondest memories. I'm sorry for being mean in the manner of all big sisters. Mordi, you were too small for me to fight with and you were that alien object: a boy. For decades, you have been a rock in our family, the doctor on call, always available. We will always be The Rabbi's Kids wherever we go in life.

To my Other Family: cousins Rena and Mordy and my wonderful aunt Irene, who showed me that it is never too late to publish a book. Our childhoods were wrapped up with one another's. As I search for my dad's presence in my daily life, I know you do the same with your dad, my gentle uncle Normy. Somewhere in the Great Beyond, the Dicker brothers are together, watching a celestial football game, shouting and cursing from the couch, two boys from Bensonhurst.

And to all my in-laws and outlaws: son-in-law Michael (Gerg); daughters-in-law Anna and Rafi; sisters-in-law Nicole, Laurie, and Miriam; brothers-in-law Yorai, Shalom, and Dovie; cousins-in-law Wendy and Jerry...to name but a few. Aunts Mimi and Debby. My loving, late Uncle Oscar and distinguished Uncle Sol. Cousins Lisa and Earl, Steven and Karen and David.

To Gabrielle, Scott, Griffin, Corey and baby Maya and Lindsey: treasures I have recovered in my adulthood, vestiges of my journey from Krypton. And to Adam and Aaron, found more recently.

So I guess that with the publication of this, my first work of fiction, the lion's share of thanks goes to my family. There are also so many friends to name, with special thanks to those who served as readers or cheerleaders along the way. I am afraid of leaving people out so I will refrain from naming names but you know who you are. I'll see you at one of my book launch events!

A special thanks to Marshall Messer who reminded me of my own work at a music club in Harlem back in February 2023 at a gig where Judah and his band, Dr. Ted and the Stone, performed. Caught up in the flow of my work as a publicist, I had neglected to champion my own writing. Eternal thanks, Mr. Messer, for serving as the spark for the publication of this work, reminding me of its worthiness.

Finally to my publisher, Adam Bellow. One of the most joyful moments of my recent life was getting your enthusiastic email after I submitted my manuscript. Morphing from a publicist of other people's books to my own has been a dream. I have greatly enjoyed our collaboration. Thank you for breathing life into the stories of Rebecca, Anna, Claire, Sarah, and Rachel. Thank you for honoring the right of writers to tell stories that disturb, disrupt, and tell messy truths.

ABOUT THE AUTHOR

Author photo credit: Melanie Einzig

SHIRA DICKER IS A RESTLESS writer-at-large, activist and publicist, who is captivated by contemporary culture. She has written for newspapers, magazines, and news sites that are local, national, and global. She was an early blogger, launched a podcast during the pandemic, and offers real-time commentary on various social media platforms.

Educated in the US and abroad, Ms. Dicker's sensibility is global, though her lens is stubbornly American. The mother of three adult children and grandmother of three little ones, she lives with her husband, the writer Ari L. Goldman, and her Pomeranian Luke Wilson on Manhattan's Upper West Side.